The Publishing Unwins

By the same author

Book Publishing as a Career
Hamish Hamilton

From Manuscript to Bookshop
Cambridge University Press

The Publishing Unwins

by
Philip Unwin

HEINEMANN : LONDON

William Heinemann Ltd
15 Queen Street, Mayfair, London W1X 8BE
LONDON MELBOURNE TORONTO
JOHANNESBURG AUCKLAND

First published 1972
© Philip Unwin 1972

Printed in Great Britain by
Western Printing Services Ltd, Bristol

Contents

Illustrations

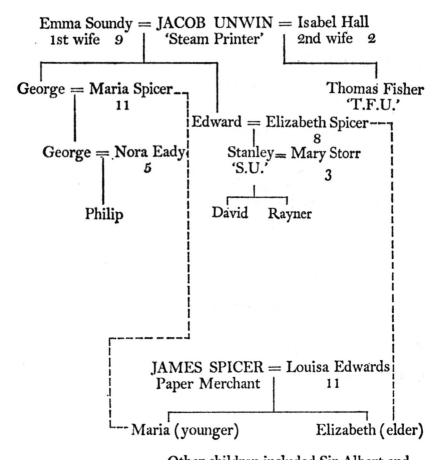

Emma Soundy = JACOB UNWIN = Isabel Hall
1st wife 9   'Steam Printer'   2nd wife 2

George = Maria Spicer   Thomas Fisher
         11   'T.F.U.'

         Edward = Elizabeth Spicer
                      8

George = Nora Eady   Stanley = Mary Storr
         5   'S.U.'   3

Philip   David   Rayner

JAMES SPICER = Louisa Edwards
Paper Merchant   11

Maria (younger)   Elizabeth (elder)

Other children included Sir Albert and
Sir Evan Spicer—'Forsytean Uncles'

Simplified Family Tree to show the Unwin–Spicer relationship.

The figure after the wife's name indicates the number
of her children.

Introduction

As one who had known the late Sir Stanley Unwin almost daily for over forty years, I had often thought of attempting some close-up personal record of him, but in view of his own autobiography, there seemed scarcely a case for a formal life. Mr. Dwye Evans, however, the Chairman of Heinemann, on hearing of my forthcoming retirement urged me to write a book about my uncle. Upon the advice of one or two friends I have cast it mainly in the form of personal reminiscence of my years in publishing.

In this, naturally, my two publishing uncles, T. Fisher and Stanley, take the most prominent part: each was a character in his own right and each made his impression on the book world of his day. As well as the creation and building up of two publishing firms, with their different books and authors, my aim has been to fill in also the family background of both men and into this, naturally, come a good many of my own curious recollections—at times entertaining, I hope—of family life half a century ago.

Whatever else it may be, publishing is a sociable occupation bringing one into touch with a large number of interesting men and women, authors, agents, booksellers and other publishers. The emphasis in a book about publishing is inevitably on the books and their authors, but in trying to avoid a catalogue of names and titles I have had to omit many whom I should wish to have included. One in particular is Sir Robert Lusty, who remains one of my staunchest friends in publishing. For over forty years, beginning in teashops we have lunched at intervals to groan or exult—sometimes I must admit, quietly to boast—about our progress in this hazardous but always absorbing business in which so many of us manage to remain in friendly competition. One could fill another book with the 'People I Have Known in Publishing' and Storer Lunt for America and Adam Helms for Sweden would take leading places.

I would tender my warm thanks to Sir Stanley's sons David and Rayner for having checked the many personal references to their father, and to my cousin George Unwin for his careful editing of my first draft. Others to whom I owe much for their help are Lancelot Spicer (son of Sir Albert), my brother Rolf, Miss Doris Davis, Sir Stanley's secretary, and my own secretary of the war years Mrs. Jean Riley who successfully deciphered my original manuscript.

To her sympathy and encouragement and her readiness to listen to evening 'readings' I owe to my wife, Evelyn, more than I can say.

HASLEMERE
November 1970

1 I 'Go into Publishing'

One sunny September morning in 1923 I walked to my first day's work across Hungerford Bridge, alongside the old South Eastern & Chatham Railway. The line had just become part of the newly created 'Southern', but the initials S E & C R still decorated the sides of the smoky little tank engines and four-wheeled carriages as they bumped along beside me into Charing Cross Station. Rennie's lovely stone-built Waterloo Bridge, exactly matching Somerset House, stretched across to the east, its middle piers beginning to subside into the river bed. My destination, the old Adam-built Adelphi Terrace, lay, low and elegant, just to the west of the Hotel Cecil, showy and bulbous, and soon to make way for the austere lines of the Shell building.

My first publishing uncle, T. Fisher Unwin, had his offices at No. 1 Adelphi Terrace. He was the most prominent member of our family— he was even in *Who's Who*—and he was thought, mistakenly, to be the richest. His business, though then in decline, still had world-wide fame and he had been in many ways a remarkable publisher, with Joseph Conrad, John Oliver Hobbes, W. B. Yeats and H. G. Wells among the authors on his list, not forgetting Ethel M. Dell as the prime money-maker. 'Great-Uncle Fisher'—half-brother of my grandfather George Unwin—was very friendly with my father and he had generously paid for part of my education at Mill Hill School. He had married late in life and was childless, so the slightly vague suggestion that if I wished, I could make a start in his business, was attractive, though of course there were 'no promises—it all depends entirely upon you'.

So there was I unbearably innocent, plump of face, a thick mat of dark hair growing down almost to the eyebrows, gloved and hatted, and clad in my school 'second-best suit' with a starched linen collar. The *best* suit was the Sunday outfit of black coat and striped trousers. Though I had passed such examinations as were put before me at a basically Edwardian school, and had done well in English, I was ridiculously ill-equipped for the world, grossly ignorant of the ways of business, yet thrilled to imagine that I was 'going into publishing', and that I should soon start earning. The canny Fisher had stipulated no pay for the first three months, but he gave me ten guineas at the end of the year, before putting me on the pay roll at 30s. a week. Well, many a young man has paid a premium for the privilege of being a publisher's dog's-body.

As I descended the steps at the end of the bridge, I found that under the general tension of the situation my breakfast cups of tea were pressing upon me. It would never do to *begin* my publishing career by asking the way to the lavatory, so I sprinted to the end of the Strand to find manly accommodation in Trafalgar Square. Thus eased, I nipped back to Villiers Street, my adolescence impressed by the peculiarly frank appliances displayed in some of its shop windows, and so by way of John Street into Adelphi Terrace.

I walked through the door of No. 1 just over eleven years after my second publishing uncle, Stanley Unwin, had walked out of it for the last time. The family gossip, as it reached my youthful ears, had been no more than that 'after doing very well in Uncle Fisher's business Uncle Stanley had decided to set up on his own'. I was blissfully unaware that the younger had found the elder uncle temperamentally impossible to work with, and that two other nephews before me, one of them Richard Cobden Sanderson, had reached the same conclusion and had taken their departure.

It was known that Fisher Unwin had had one or two bad years and that the astronomically best-selling Ethel M. Dell had moved off to another publisher, but one imagined that his luck would soon turn. With my great respect for his name and reputation, it did not occur to me that at the age of 75 the autocratic head of the firm was unlikely to revitalize it successfully. That discovery was to come.

On that gentle autumn morning I was received in the stone-flagged hall by the commissionaire, an ex-sergeant of Marines. That gave authors a good impression; few publishers had commissionaires. He led me up the graceful, easy, eighteenth-century flying staircase, at one end of which the stone steps seemed to rest on air, and up to the door of my uncle's office. On the landing wall outside hung two boldly coloured posters depicting what seemed to me strangely misshapen females. They were Aubrey Beardsley originals, commissioned with some enterprise, to advertise Fisher Unwin's *Pseudonym Library* in the 1890s.

So just before nine o'clock I entered my first publisher's office. Architecturally it was probably one of the most beautiful in London. It lay on the first floor and had been the drawing-room of the original private house. From the full-length french windows one looked over the Embankment gardens and onto the river, the thunder and thud of the L.C.C.'s chocolate-coloured trams partially muted by the trees. The original Adam ceiling and marble fireplace were still there and T.F.U. worked at an imposing, mahogany partners' desk, which had belonged to his father-in-law, Richard Cobden, whose bust looked on gravely from a side table. To complete the picture of an ideal publisher's office, one wall was lined with books, mainly his own publications, many of them specially bound in white buckram; even the ordinary pre-1914 bindings, with their lavish gold blocking, looked more sumptuous than is the case today.

Promptly at nine o'clock Uncle Fisher entered from his flat at No. 3 Adelphi Terrace, where he always breakfasted in bed. He was an imposing figure of fair height, substantial build and remarkably erect carriage, rather like a horse with a bearing rein; he held his back very stiff. His piercing blue eyes, long, well-trimmed wavy beard and the invariable morning coat, with which he always wore a floppy, yellow bow-tie, gave him an undoubted if curious air of distinction.

He handled and sorted all the incoming mail and it became my morning job to sit on the opposite side of the great desk slitting the envelopes on three sides and passing them over to him, while he sang to himself over and over again, 'yes—yes', mostly in octaves and sometimes quavering. Occasionally he would interpolate a run of 'I don't think so', repeated several times, and he would take a delight in shooting some odd question at me, literary or geographical (he was good on both). If I was floored, there would come a slow wink and then, 'Say you don't know'—a procedure he used on everybody.

That first morning I had the somewhat embarrassing ordeal of standing beside him while he summoned the heads of departments one by one, to whom I was duly presented, half feeling a fool and half warmed by the handshakes and the good wishes expressed; conscious of the fact that I was supposed to be boss material, but that initially I had everything to learn about publishing routines from these men of supposedly lesser standing than myself. There were odd and colourful characters among them, who broadened my suburban mind, and I soon began to know the satisfaction of friendly working relationships with people for whom one has respect.

For the rest of that first day my place was upon a high stool at a vintage Victorian office desk in a corner of the large room directly above the office of the chief. Here again was a superb view over the Thames above Cleopatra's Needle—the whole sweep of the river from Westminster to Waterloo Bridge. My immediate concern, however, was the time-honoured chore for a junior in any publishing house; dealing with the Press cuttings. In 1923 it was done far more ponderously and expensively than necessary. Each review was pasted into a vast leather-backed guard book and duly indexed with elaborate 'continued on page x' directions where the review cuttings overflowed the number of pages originally allowed for the book in question. Today, one just files the cuttings for each book in a large envelope, which is much simpler and easier to handle. However, it was no bad thing for the embryonic publisher to spend some time going through those journals of the day that reviewed books. How many there were which are now, alas, extinct, such as the *Morning Post, Westminster Gazette, Daily News, Daily Chronicle, Daily Graphic* and *Star*, among the London dailies, and good literary reviews like the *Nation, Truth, Saturday Review* and *London Mercury*.

In that large south room, warmed on cold days—with unbelievable extravagance—by a coal fire as well as central heating, there were six of us, five men and a typist, who together covered the work of production, advertising, and authors' accounts. Into each of these mysteries I was initiated in turn.

In those days there was more variety and individuality in a group of office workers. The Production Manager was an easygoing man of about fifty, of respectable enough appearance except that his bushy moustache failed to conceal the fact that he possessed no front teeth, and that he apparently used only the bluntest of razors. He bore a three-day growth of beard on his chin at all times. It never varied and I thought he perhaps just took the scissors to it. He always gave himself an hour and a half for lunch and sometimes enjoyed a nap at his desk in the afternoon. His knowledge of printing was limited and he did little to keep down costs.

The elderly royalty accountant was the embodiment of Victorian clerical skill. A rather good-looking man in a doleful, hen-pecked fashion, he had a well-trained dark moustache and always wore the high, starched 'drain pipe' pattern of collar, about three inches deep and so close fitting that, as one of his irreverent Cockney colleagues said to me, 'one day 'e'll drop through that collar and it'll cut 'is ears clean orf'. In some mysterious way he seemed to be sustained and retained by that great and always immaculate collar. One could not conceive him without it. He covered it carefully with a white scarf when he left the office to bicycle back to his home in Purley. His handsome, but disdainful daughter also worked in the firm (and for a few weeks I conceived a most ill-advised and undeclared passion for her)—but she ignored her father and made the journey from home by tram—not even leaving it on the day when she saw the unfortunate royalty expert knocked off his bike alongside.

The era of the loose-leaf ledger had not reached Adelphi Terrace and the accounting machine was far ahead, so this most conscientious man made every calculation in his head and wrote out every figure in his spidery copperplate. Forty years later I was able to turn up some of his old royalty ledgers in the offices of Ernest Benn Ltd., and my eye lit upon the historic entry: '*Almayer's Folly* by Joseph Conrad, £25 paid for entire copyright.'

Perched on his stool at the long, high mahogany desk with its brass rails in front and the battery of ledgers behind him, this little man was the unquestioned king of royalty accounts, though his methods were desperately cumbersome. Even T.F.U. told me that his work was 'most intricate', and for this he earned about £300 a year.

The third character in that room was a remarkable man with the sharpest flow of Cockney wit I have ever known. Then Advertising Manager, he had formerly been a ledger clerk in the 'Counting House' of a famous store and bore a life-long grudge against the founder, who once borrowed half-a-crown from him, one evening as they were both leaving, and never repaid it. I can still see the look of fiendish delight on his face when he learned that his old employers had been called upon quite heavily as guarantors for the Wembley Exhibition of 1924. 'Yah! serve 'em bloody well right', he burst out across the department.

His father had been a jockey and the son was an enthusiastic punter. Blessed with a copious flow of saliva, he seemed literally to spit his words out between the gaps in the prominent ruins of his teeth. A savage attacker of the capitalist system, he revelled in fiery argument over Stanley Baldwin and the coal-owners. Yet he regarded the pre-1914 world as far superior to the 1920s, when money was being spent on the wrong things. One day he said to me, of a newish office boy: 'What d'ya think?—this godless little bugger is going to Aberystwyth for his fortnight's holiday. When I was his age a day at Margate was all we could afford.' But he was essentially a warm-hearted man, possessed of a quickness of brain which could have carried him far had he been born in other circumstances.

To return to my first day, I do not think T.F.U. ever came up to that second floor in my time; he had to climb to its equivalent to reach his own flat in No. 3, where there was also no lift, and he doubtless considered that was enough exercise for one day. Unlike other members of the family, my 'Uncle Stan' in particular, Fisher had no obsession about violent exercise—or indeed any exercise at all after middle age; yet he lived to eighty-seven. In earlier years he had been a quite considerable mountaineer, had climbed the Matterhorn and was a member of the Alpine Club.

He hated the telephone, regarding it as an infernal instrument, and kept it as far away from his desk as possible. So he never used the office 'intercom', but communicated through a nest of push buttons beside him. In a room shared by several people, one had to listen carefully for the signals, one, two or three rings. His aim was not unerring and sometimes an unlooked-for face turned up in his room, whereupon he would look a little pained, give a charming, blue-eyed wink and admit: 'I made a mistake, please ask Mr. X to come and see me.'

Another respect in which his aim was not unerring, and one in which his personal habits would not have accorded with present-day standards of hygiene, was his habit of spitting. I suppose, in his old age, he had a form of chronic catarrh, which meant that three or four times in the morning, sometimes later in the day, he would have a hearty cough and hawk up a load of mucus which he would either spit into an envelope and drop into his waste-paper basket or, in winter-time, shoot with a fat sizzle into his open coal fire. But sometimes he forgot that the fire was not alight—and sometimes he missed the fireplace. Another form of disposal in summer-time would be a rush to the french windows, to send his offering whizzing over the heads of pedestrians into the roadway of Adelphi Terrace. I am not aware that there were ever any complaints, though members of his staff did think his personal habits were 'a bit much'. It is fair to say, however, that such behaviour would have been by no means exceptional to men of his generation. The many notices in public vehicles, 'DO NOT SPIT penalty 40s.', were well warranted.

There were enough press cuttings to keep me going for that first morning, as the regular operator had been away sick and there was quite an accumulation. Being the junior in the office I was naturally given the off-course lunch time, 12–1. So at midday I set off into the Strand, along Adam Street, a section of which still survives, though at that time the swanky new Tivoli cinema had bitten a chunk off the west corner, where the street led into the Strand.

It was still largely a horse-drawn and gas-lit world, in which Mrs. Pat Campbell would say, not so very long before, that she 'didn't mind what people did, so long as they didn't do it in the streets, and frighten the horses'. Apart from the buses, traffic was more horse-drawn than motor at that time. Magnificent pairs of cart horses pulled big drays, taking two tons or so of goods, and almost shook the street with the thunder of their hooves. The iron-tyred wheels made a good old row as they rattled along, and in the midst of the city streets one was always conscious of the needs of animals: the explosive cascades of splendid manure which fell from them—a valuable deposit to be quickly scooped up by the street sweepers—and the occasional pause, holding up all the traffic behind, during which the noble animal emptied its bladder, only to refill it soon after with a copious draught from one of the available horse-troughs. It was always interesting to see how readily these were patronized in snowy weather. It cost the horses far more effort to pull their loads and keep their feet in slippery streets; one saw them plastered with sweat in a way which did not occur normally, so naturally they needed to drink more. In such conditions one could see a little queue of vans drawn up by the big trough which in those days stood close to St. Clement Danes Church. All the buses were still clumping along on solid tyres, driven by fairly crude four-cylinder petrol engines (which continually boiled over in warm weather), and of course they were all open-topped, with hard wooden seats on the upper deck—spartan in winter but a real delight in summer.

It would probably seem extraordinary to any eighteen-year-old today that he could possibly feel embarrassed at the prospect of going into a Lyons tea-shop to order a simple meal, but forty years ago I was not alone in this, I even remember my father remarking at the time that it was strange how shy one could feel on first 'giving an order to the waitress'. It was no doubt due to the cloistered upbringing of a middle-class youth, away at boarding school, entirely deprived of feminine company, for about nine months in the year. At the time I began work I had had scarcely any social contact with girls, other than my sisters and the occasional visiting cousin. In this was a great danger, of course. The first mildly intimate contact was liable to sweep a young man off his feet, into thinking he had met the love of his life, when he was merely being attracted, quite naturally and properly, for the first time by sex. It was apt to have excruciating, if repressed, effects upon mere schoolboys as they began to meet typists and other young ladies in an office; but that is another story.

I squared my shoulders, screwed my courage to the sticking point and plunged into the faintly onion-laden breath of the nearest Lyons. With a supreme effort, I managed to stammer out my request for curried beef, a bit watery and gristly in those days, but still not a bad meal for about 10d. It was probably followed by fruit pie and coffee, and the whole thing was done for not more than 1s. 6d. The tables were all of the solid, brown marble variety on cast-iron legs, standard in the tea-shops at that time, and there was no nonsense about self-service. One sat on the bentwood chair with its unupholstered seat and a wait-ress, looking like a sort of parlourmaid, in neat black dress with patterned white apron and cap, came up and took one's order. I had suppressed my initial terrors that she would (a) not deign to notice me, (b) notice me and just laugh, (c) go off and never bring the order; and extraordinary as it seemed at the time—to her I was doubtless just one of a hundred customers that day—the food came quickly and that was that.

Outside the day had developed into the most perfect, still, warm specimen of late September, one on which I just yearned to be pedalling through the Surrey lanes on my cherished bicycle, or at least strolling round the grounds of Mill Hill on the first day back. I was suddenly struck by the awful thought that for the rest of my life, apart from holidays and weekends, I would have to go back into a humanity-smelling office every day, however beautiful the world outside might be. And how humanity could smell in those days! I am not thinking of the very poor, who lacked decent facilities for washing bodies and clothes, but of middle-class people, who were quite capable of spreading a good pong around them, because of grossly neglected teeth, coupled perhaps with heavy smoking, and the fact that the blessed secrets of deodorants were not yet generally known.

Back to my high stool and a further batch of papers and cuttings from Durrants, the famous press-cuttings agency. This was another early wonder. It never occurred to me that there were people who made a living out of snipping from the paper everything which had the name of T. Fisher Unwin upon it. Having been brought up in a strictly teetotal home, I was vaguely shocked to smell beer on the breath of the advertising manager, though the poor chap had probably had no more than half a pint after his tea-shop lunch. An afternoon lasting from one p.m. to six with no tea break and no variety, in the shape of interviews, telephone calls, or visits from colleagues, seemed interminable, particularly for me, as my work ran out by about four o'clock. For the first week or two, though never again, I experienced the terrible boredom and embarrassment of not having enough to do, without knowing sufficient about the job to dig out something that needed to be done.

One external delight, however, was the sight of the steamer *Wandle*, of the then famous Gas Light and Coke Co., making its way down the river after having discharged a load of coal at the Wandsworth gas-works. Being steam driven, she had an enormous funnel, which had to be lowered for each one of the bridges. It was impressive to see how precisely she was navigated, plumb through the middle of the narrow central arch of the old Waterloo Bridge, when the funnel was hauled down and the smoke belched all over the deck. About a week later, she would return up stream loaded full of coal and low in the water.

Around five o'clock I was summoned to T.F.U.'s office and presented with two of his books, the *Literary History of the Adelphi* by Austen Brererton, a book that had just achieved a second small impression in 1908, and a much more obscure one on *The Millers of Haddington, Dunbar and Dunfermiline*, who had been connected with bookselling and were the forebears of Fisher's mother (see family tree, p. viii). I have them still, and was not to be discouraged when my father, on being shown them that evening, remarked that he believed they were both now on the firm's remainder list.

So, back across Hungerford Bridge, with a different and more mysterious view of the river now, the odd hugger-mugger of the South Bank dominated by the once-famous Shot Tower, which was swept away to make room for the Queen Elizabeth Hall, along the slummy street at the end of the bridge, beside what is now the Festival Hall, across York Road and up into Waterloo Station, where I was thoroughly at home—and nicely in time for the 6.20 train back to

Surbiton. An interesting 'working' this, from the standpoint of the railway enthusiast. The eleven-coach train had worked up from Portsmouth as an express during the afternoon behind a massive 4–6–0 engine, which stood simmering quietly at the buffer stops. The train now became a dawdling 'all stations' after Surbiton and was drawn by nothing more than a little tank engine, which with such a load could do little more than forty miles an hour. Some of the carriages would be gas-lit; many would have that Edwardian luxury of a separate 'loo' for individual compartments. So, five a side on rather bony upholstery, I jogged home, a little disappointed that the day had not brought forth more of a challenge, relieved that I had made no bloomer, and longing for a chance to have a go at something; what, I did not yet know. At least I had 'gone into publishing', though the door had opened only a small crack so far.

2 Of Unwins and Spicers

The 'father' of all the printing and publishing Unwins was my great-grandfather Jacob Unwin (1802–1855). From him have descended no fewer than eight of us who have engaged in printing and four in publishing, His branch of the family lived at Black Notley Hall, a moderate-sized, eighteenth-century house in Essex, and his father Fisher Unwin (1776–1819) was a brewer.

Jacob's portrait, which hangs on a wall in my home, shows a firm mouth, a good head of hair and a slightly anxious expression, with an eyeline very like that of my youngest sister. I had often wondered what sort of man he was and by a great stroke of luck, as I was planning this book, my nephew Michael (Jacob's great-great-grandson and the eldest of my brother Rolf's four sons) told me that a mysterious typescript had come to light in an old safe at the works of Unwin Bros at Woking. 'Would you like to see it—it might be something to do with Jacob Unwin?' Would I not! The outside folder just bore the words in my father's handwriting 'from May 15 1817 to June 11, 1828'—though in fact there are a few entries up to 1831. Jacob's name does not appear on it, but there can be no doubt whatever that it is a copy of his original diary, prepared in 1926, the year of Unwin Brothers' centenary.

Just what took him away from the prospect of a pleasant country occupation in brewing is not known, but certainly printing could have been seen as a growing business at that time. His diary shows that in 1817 he was apprenticed for seven years to a small printer in the city of London, a Mr. Kelly. The first entry reads: 'While I was making this book Mrs. Kelly said that I should be taught to bind in a proper manner when I was about half through my time.' He had evidently improvised the binding in some unorthodox fashion of his own. He would have to wait another three years before binding properly.

The next entry records that 'My Mother was put to bed with a little girl' (late arrival, five years after the previous child). A fortnight later, 'was sorry to hear that my Mother has been so ill, but now is getting better.' Next day, 'Had a walk to Charlotte Street, Portland Place, for tops and bottoms for my Mother.* Set off at five and got back at 7.30

* These 'tops and bottoms' are mysterious. Neither Alison Adburgham nor Phyllis Cunnington has been able to identify these for me as items of clothing.

rather tired.' As well he might be, having walked from the city to the West End and back along the narrow unevenly paved streets, either dusty or muddy and reeking of horse droppings. Less than three weeks later comes a sudden entry on June 18, 'Received a letter that my Dear Mother was much worse . . . in the course of the afternoon was informed that she was no more; that her spirit had fled from her to worlds on high at $\frac{1}{4}$ to nine on the preceding morning. How wonderful are the ways of Providence. . . .'

So Jacob lost his mother when he was only fifteen, and barely two years later his father. The parents had produced nine children during the seventeen years of their married life and all but three survived to a ripe old age.

He by no means had an iron constitution and makes many references to headaches, colds and stomach upsets. On one occasion, 'Very unwell . . . had some rhubarb which operated very powerfully. Mrs. Kelly took particular care of me.' But a few days later, 'great pain in my bowels', and alas, 'the relaxation in my bowels continued'—he gets medicine from a Doctor Buxton and then 'I mended daily. . . . Mr. Kelly was very anxious I should be well taken care of but he did not offer to pay the Doctor's bill.' Poor young man, he must sometimes have suffered acute discomfort from the primitive sanitation of the times.

He had the deep religious sense of the typical nonconformist of those days and there was punctilious chapel-going. The Unwins were Congregationalists—descendants of the fearless Independents of Puritan England. 'Heard twice at Broad Street and attended School' are regular Sunday occupations. And this earnest, hard-working youth is burdened by an appalling sense of guilt if he finds himself thinking too much about the girls, or is even too deeply engrossed in his work.

On a March day in 1819, 'Through another week of great bustle and fatigue in business I have been upheld . . . how oft have my sinful passions rose to an unexampled height and lusted after evil, but His restraining grace has kept me from open violation.'

There is a rather touching account of a little adventure one fine August evening which reflects the confusion of mind on religion and sex that has troubled so many others before and since. 'Sunday. Went to Camberwell (to see some relatives). All quite well. Went to hear Dr. Collyer in the evening; returned home by the fields. When in Cobourg Road, I accosted a very genteel young female; after walking some time and talking upon various topics, I offered my arm, which she declined. After walking some distance further, we went into the road

A modern dictionary suggests they could be part of the equipment for hand weaving. An older one defines them as strips of dough baked then split and baked again 'for infants' (but not surely at a fortnight old?). Again, they could be just the Regency equivalent of bras and panties.

and I took her arm in mine—she did not refuse. I then said my reason for accosting her was I thought she was among the number of those who were going the road to destruction. She confessed she did not like to go to Church or Chapel; it was so confining. I told her of her sinful state in the best manner I was able, and intreated her to seek pardon thro' the blood of the Lamb. Her sentiment was she thought she should be as well off as those who went to Church, and it was no use to try to serve God unless she could do it properly in every degree. I was rather taken with her person; my passions strove within me, and I bless God that I was prevented from offering any liberties to her which I am sure she would have accepted. God grant unto her repentance unto life.'

Continually he calls upon his maker to lead him more firmly into the paths of righteousness. On his nineteenth birthday, 'Numerous mercies have I received from the hand of God yet how unmindful have I been. I have fell into snares. . . . O God grant that this next year may be spent more to Thy glory.'

It fascinates me to think that this man Jacob, in whom I find many resemblances to my father and to myself, was learning his 'craft' or trade in the days of the Regency, the time of 'Prinny', who laid out Regent Street and built the Pavilion at Brighton. He knew no railways until middle-aged. Everywhere he went in London as a young man, he walked—from the City to Islington, to Highgate and to Mill Hill. No mention of a horse-bus as yet—and of course his longer journeys were done by coach. One Sunday he walks 12 miles before chapel and another time does 40 miles on horseback. Once, on his way home to Essex, he walks as far as Ingatestone, where he 'happens' upon a returning post-chaise and has a lift on to Braintree. The theatre, of which as a non-conformist he doubtless disapproved, is only mentioned once. On the invitation of a friend 'we entered the Royalty Theatre past nine o'clock. This was my first attempt and the scene I then saw would not induce me to go again.'

But he attends meetings of the local literary and philosophical society and there are frequent references to music in the homes he visits. There was no shortage of aunts and uncles upon whom he called regularly, 'tead and dined (or supped)', and they were always hospitable to their young nephew. He enjoyed company, but his face in middle-age suggests anxiety and probably too little relaxation.

He records in July 1821, 'This day King George the Fourth was crowned in Westminster Abbey. It was expected there would be great disturbance as the Queen insisted on going and she was refused as Queen.'

Steam power at this time was not used for the printing of books in London, though it had been adopted by *The Times*. Thus in all of Jacob's early years in the trade it was simply the hand press upon which

the work depended, and of course all the type was set by hand. Up to
1800, as Mr. Ellic Howe has written, 'the technical equipment of the
craft hardly differed from that in use throughout the preceding cen-
turies'. It was the simplicity and cheapness of the plant which made it
possible for a man who could save or borrow £200 to set up on his
own.

After he had served the seven years of his apprenticeship (admitting
to his diary one day that working at the press he 'spoiled 80 sheets;
letter left out'), he left Mr. Kelly, who proposed his health at a fare-
well supper, and Jacob as a journeyman 'out of his time' took a job
with another printer for three years. Then in 1826 came the bold
plunge. He bought the small printing business of a Mr. Robins for
about £200. He had probably saved during those three years, he
might have inherited a little money and the purchase price was in any
case to be paid off by instalments. So his diary could record: 'June 26,
1826. I rose this morning in a new character—Master of an establishment.' And on June 30, 'Worked off first job this morning at my own
office. Bathed in evening at Peerless Pool (City Road). Returned home
very tired; went to sleep. At 2.0 a.m. awoke and wrote to Mr. —.'
Just the sort of thing his great-grandson is liable to do after over-
exertion.

Eighteen months later he is hard at it: 'Jan 30. 1828. Very busy;
took on extra hands; worked all night. . . .' (Plenty of labour to be had
—no Union restrictions in those days.) 'April 3. Still very busy . . . in
B's absence obliged to work myself.' How they must have sweated
away, one man applying the roller to ink the type, another to pull on
the bar which turned the great screw and pressed the paper on to the
type—all this to produce a single sheet. 250 sheets an hour was good
going.

After 1800 the traditional wooden press was replaced by the iron
Stanhope press, firmer and stronger and able to print a larger sheet,
but still hand-operated. It was not until the middle of the century,
according to Ellic Howe, that printing machines began to be installed
in other than newspaper offices; so my great-grandfather did well to
have steam power by 1847. A little later the business, known for a time
rather splendidly as 'Jacob Unwin Steam Printer', was re-christened
'The Gresham Steam Press'.

It is strange to recall that this industrial activity was going on in
the heart of the City, around Cornhill; first in White Lion Court, then
St. Peter's Alley, where my grandfather George was born, later in
Bucklersbury, near the Bank of England.

Stanley Unwin did not, I think, have much sense of family history
beyond his father's generation, and I never heard him refer to Jacob,
but I am sure that some of his genius for taking endless pains in the

building up of a small publishing business must have been inherited from his grandfather. Jacob combined appreciation of the small with ambition for the great, and he was good at handling difficult work and knowing how to obtain it. At first he was not beneath buying such little publications as *The Youth's Magazine* for 3d. in Paternoster Row and selling copies for 4d., to friends and others who could not at that time buy them locally. Then he produced several books, mostly of an uplifting nature, under a joint imprint with one or other of the bookseller-publishers in 'The Row'.

He got on well with the great P. & O. Steamship line and did handbooks and stationery for them, as well as labels in many different colours for their Overland Mail (across Egypt to the Red Sea before the building of the Suez Canal). Gas, Water, Railway and Insurance companies were all among his customers, and so of course were members of the New Broad Street Congregational Church, where he was a member—and this led on to the Congregational Union of England and Wales, for whom Jacob did their first Year Book in 1846. There was a useful clannishness in nonconformity.

In addition to solid commercial sense he was a good printer, of craftsmanship, high standards and real feeling for typography, with a proper enthusiasm for one of the greatest types, Caslon Old Face.

In 1828, Jacob married Emma Soundy, after an initial rebuff from his future father-in-law, William Mattingly Soundy, who survived to the age of 96 and was famed for attending his local Congregational Church twice a Sunday, almost without a break for 74 years. The Soundys lived near Henley, and he had met Emma in 1823, when visiting Unwin relatives there.

At 21 he had confided to his diary that she was 'a very pleasant and agreeable young person: affable and mild in her manners. . . . When asleep dreamed that the knot was tied between Emma and myself—so powerful were my thoughts fixed on her when retiring to bed.' The next day, 'the object of my present attachment was by my side'. He had to persevere for five years, and build up his own business for two, before William Soundy gave his consent; yet curiously enough, one of Jacob's uncles had earlier disapproved of Emma, because there was little money in that direction.

While the printing and publishing Unwins have not done too badly in the long run, none of them ever had much to offer in cash at the time of their marriages. Forty years later both of Jacob's sons, George and Edward, had to overcome fierce opposition from *their* prospective father-in-law, the formidable James Spicer, before he would consent to their marrying his daughters, Maria and Elizabeth.

Jacob had seven children from his first marriage; the two elder boys were tragically lost in a fire at his house in Bucklersbury (adjoining the

'Steam' printing works), and so it was my grandfather George, the third son, who inherited the business. When Emma died at the early age of 36, having married at 19, Jacob married Isabel Hall, by whom he had two sons. The younger of these was to make his name in late Victorian publishing as T. Fisher Unwin.

My great-grandfather continued to build up the Gresham Steam Press until his sudden death at 53. What had cost him £240 at the outset was valued when his son took it over at a conservative £4,200—the equivalent of at least £40,000 today. Not a bad effort for 30 years in print, long before universal education and in days when a majority of the population was illiterate. He left his sons George and Edward a wonderful base from which to advance into the second half of the century, with the tremendous potential to be offered by the first Education Act of 1870.

Almost exactly contemporary with Jacob Unwin was another 'father' of the clan, James Spicer—for me always a name to conjure with, the source of my grandma's money. To go back one generation, his father John Edward, who early lost his parents, had trained for the Congregational ministry but being apparently slow of speech, he was told he could not be a successful preacher.

Greatly distressed he then turned to an uncle who owned a small paper mill and he secured a training in that trade. John Edward Spicer, with a small inheritance from his father, bought a little mill at Alton in Hampshire in 1796 where he produced good hand-made paper. This he took to London by horse-drawn wagon and after selling it in the market he would shovel the gold coins into his saddle-bags and ride back to Alton, suitably armed against the highwaymen whom he more than once beat off successfully. Throughout his life, however, he remained an earnest evangelical and still preached occasionally in the Hampshire villages.

About 1815, in the depression after the Napoleonic wars, finding himself overstocked with paper at Alton, John Edward conceived the idea of bringing it all up to a London warehouse and then giving printers and publishers the chance to buy it in small quantities as required. In this way, his great-grandson, Lancelot Spicer (formerly Chairman of Spicers Ltd.), believes that he became the pioneer wholesale paper merchant buying from the mills and selling the paper for them.

After a few more years and then with the help of his sons he developed a prosperous business, to be known later as Spicer Bros. James, the third son, was the driving force, I believe, but at some stage he had a bitter row with his brothers and cut off to establish a rival firm. As he had produced four able sons of his own, this business, too, James

Spicer & Sons, prospered exceedingly and in time outstripped the original Spicer Bros. After the First World War, the two amalgamated to form Spicers Ltd., which ran on very well mainly under the direction of James's descendants.

James was a real Forsyte. In her book, *From One Generation to Another*, Hilda Martindale, a granddaughter, describes him as 'a lovable man in many ways, but dominating . . . and inclined to be tyrannical in his own home'. According to one of his grandsons, James could produce a hot temper at times and was inclined to vent his wrath on the family when things had not gone well at the office. Tales were told of his wife and daughters being driven to their rooms in tears.

My own mother's view, culled from the opinions of her in-laws, was that 'he was a jolly autocratic old boy', furious when any of his daughters failed to 'love where money is' and fiercely discouraging to any suitors who fell short of his financial standards.

James was another keen Congregationalist; but while being a devout chapel-goer, he also enjoyed the good things of life, like some other nonconformists of his day He contrived to marry Louisa Edwards (C. of E., and by no means penniless!), one for four beautiful sisters who lived in some style at Denmark Hill in South London, where they knew the Ruskins. All these young ladies had good, clear-cut features and pink and white complexions, and were much admired. The best looks in the Spicer family subsequently came from Louisa and found expression in the pretty colouring, bright eyes and high cheekbones of my grandmother and various aunts and cousins. Several, mainly the men, produced the flattened, drop-away, pale cheeks and fierce-eyed, shaggy-browed look of old James. At family gatherings I used to enjoy trying to spot a 'James' or a 'Louisa' among the assembled uncles, aunts and cousins.

By comparison with Jacob Unwin, James Spicer had the advantage of a running start in a business already begun by his father, and he must have had a tougher and more ruthless side to him in business dealings. There can be no doubt whatever of his shrewdness and financial acumen, which was passed on to his descendants for at least two generations. Both at home and in business, when a crisis arose, family or partners were at once called together to pray over it—and who shall say this was not effective?

He combined genuine piety, and hard work for his church, with worldly success. His great capacity for seeing things through himself made him a tough fighter for the various public causes which he took up, including Liberalism. Here one can see two clear strands inherited by Stanley—the keen commercial sense, with a touch of ruthlessness, and the ability and will vigorously to apply his time and energy to things outside his immediate financial interest.

The Equitable Life Assurance Society might be regarded as one of these. James was proud to be invited on to its board in 1867, and to the end of his life he rarely missed a meeting. His younger son Evan, and subsequently Evan's son Ernest Spicer, followed in James's footsteps; and it was one of the memorable days in Stanley's life when he was asked to serve on the board of the Equitable. In the view of at least one section of the City he was seen as comparable with those rich and successful Spicers.

The great house and estate of Harts—now a hospital—on Woodford Green, Essex, ten miles from London, is still intact. It was there that James took his beautiful Louisa to live in 1858, having started married life at Brixton. Built in 1816 on the site of an Elizabethan house, it strikes one as an imposing mansion, with classical columns flanking the main entrance, an exterior of cream-painted stucco and a 200-yard drive from the lodge gates. In the lodge, in the black lace and net cap of those days, dwelt a Mrs. Ferret, whose duty it was to open the great gates at the sound of a whistle from the homecoming carriage. The situation of the house in 30 acres of park-like grounds sloping gently to the south, is magnificent, and in Spicer times everything was kept up superbly, including a vast walled garden with peaches and nectarines (grandchildren permitted to eat any that had 'dropped').

The level of personal service which a wealthy man could command in those days was impressive; there must have been at least a dozen of staff in the house alone. The main corridor on each of the three floors measured thirty yards, with about six large rooms on each; the mind boggles at the task of keeping clean all that heavy Victorian furnishing and hangings without a vacuum cleaner, at the daily trimming and filling of all the oil lamps, and the carting of endless jugs of hot water upstairs for the ablutions of a family of ten, plus frequent guests.

To ensure that no unwanted smell of cooking reached the house, the kitchens were in a separate block connected by a covered corridor. I have paced this out and found that the distance agrees exactly with my father's boyhood recollection of 'fifty yards from dining-room to kitchen'; along it the great joints of meat—set on a vast hot-water dish—would be conveyed—slightly uphill!—by a couple of stalwart footmen. The butler who presided over all this was a handsome, friendly Irishman named Wallace, from Donegal. He was so devoted to his master that after James's death he bought a strip of land behind his grave. He had always stood behind his master's chair, he said, so he wanted to lie behind him in death.

James's six daughters and four sons made up a splendid battery of aunts and uncles for the next generation. My father had vivid recollections of Christmas holidays spent at his mother's old home, and particularly the kindness of the younger aunts, one of whom spent the whole of a frosty afternoon teaching him to skate on the lake in the grounds. After that there was tea served before a log fire in the ruined chapel nearby.

But before there could be grandchildren, there had to be suitors persistent enough to brave the Master of Harts. He demanded in any prospective son-in-law both nonconformity and wealth, or good 'expectations'. George Unwin had taken over Jacob's steam printing firm when he was only 20, but although he was making steady progress after a few years, he could scarcely be called rich. This failed to prevent him from falling in love with Maria, James's third daughter and a member of the same Congregational church. They were also fellow labourers in the same Sunday school, so my grandfather George could not be disqualified on religious grounds. His financial means, however, were not up to standard and all James's tyrannical quality came out. At first he forbade the engagement, but my little five-foot grandmother stood her ground, stoutly defended by her eldest sister, Louisa, for whom James had great respect; their father-daughter relationship resembled that of the Prince Consort to his eldest daughter Vicky.

In the end he gave way, but showed his displeasure by allowing my grandfather to invite only twelve guests to the huge wedding, which was laid on in February 1866; and the first child was born punctually in November.

There was worse to come for poor old James. Edward Unwin, George's younger brother, who was to become the father of Stanley, now fell in love with Elizabeth Spicer, Maria's elder sister, so that the younger suitor sought the hand of the older bride. Edward, five years junior to his brother George, was naturally drawing less from the business, and all the resourcefulness of Louisa had to be marshalled before her father's consent was given—and then it was subject to an important condition.

So that Elizabeth should not be worse off than her younger sister Maria, James insisted that both George and Edward must have the same income. To this they officially agreed, but according to Stanley there was a secret agreement under which Edward (his father) handed over 'the difference' to George (my grandfather) until the end of his life—some forty years later. How much it was I do not know and I have never heard the story from any other source, but it is unlikely that S.U. was misinformed. Having some clue as to the relative contribution which the two partners made to Unwin Bros, and considering George's seniority, I cannot see the secret agreement as altogether unreasonable; but for years it rankled and Stanley would say to me, 'In my youth, your side of the family was always better off than mine.'

In the end there was the unusual situation of two brothers married to two sisters, and thus a double relationship between eleven 'George Unwins' and nine 'Edward Unwins'. The two marriages, so strongly opposed, proved very happy and most of the twenty offspring lived to over eighty. It is curious that of the Spicer-daughter marriages which *were* approved, one was childless, and the other ended with the early death of the husband.

There was, however, a Parthian shot in James's will, to mark his final disapproval. In 1880, when Unwin Bros, as the printing firm was then known, built new London premises in Pilgrim Street, off Ludgate Hill, they had to raise a loan of about £8,000. To do so, they turned to their father-in-law, who found them the money, but deducted it from what Elizabeth and Maria would inherit, so that each received about £4,000 less than her sisters. As Unwin Bros. duly repaid the loan in time, it could be said that in effect the partners, with their wives, paid it twice over.

James Spicer naturally left all his large family well provided for; daughters who had not offended were left about £20,000 each. The last to survive were my great-Aunt Harriet and her unmarried sister, Charlotte, who lived together for about forty years. Both were full of good works and made a point throughout their lives of giving generous help to their many nieces. Charlotte died first and left her money to Harriet. After Harriet died, there was a headline in an evening paper: 'Miss Spicer leaves £48,000 to her nieces—but there are 24 of them!'

All of James is there—the successful paper merchant who made the money, the prolific family man who left so many descendants, and the over-proud father who had turned away the men who should have married Harriet and Charlotte nearly half a century before.

All of his ten children, men and women alike, had character—my Forsytean great-aunts and uncles. The four sons, James, Albert, Evan and George, all engaged in public work, and all pursued highly successful careers in the paper business, each earning about £10,000 a year when income tax was a shilling in the pound (and no surtax). I remember particularly Sir Albert Spicer, Bart., M.P., who lived at Lancaster Gate, neat-bearded—at one time wax-moustached and frock-coated—on his regular visits to Mill Hill School as Chairman of the Court of Governors when I was there. As a Liberal member, respected by all parties, he was given the unenviable job of Chairman to the Marconi Committee in 1912, for which he was later made a Privy Counsellor. A genuine 'Swithin' touch was his habit of driving his own phaeton and pair most mornings from Lancaster Gate to his Thames Street office; whereupon his coachman would trot the horses home again, often accompanied by one of the master's eleven children.

Albert and his wife Jessie (always to me a surprising Christian name for 'Lady Spicer') entertained generously, and gave gorgeous children's parties and dinner parties at their very fine and well-staffed house. I can still hear my mother's woeful description of an evening when in response to a Lancaster Gate invitation, she and father attempted to travel up from Surbiton in a thick fog. The train was hopelessly delayed—as often happened in the days of steam and no electric signalling—and by the time they at length got to Waterloo, it was far too late to reach their hosts in time for dinner. 'And so,' said Mother, 'instead of dining at Uncle Albert's we had to go, in full evening dress, to a little restaurant in the Waterloo Road.'

The words 'dining at Uncle Albert's' represented for years the pinnacle of distant family splendour, and Mother always enjoyed the Spicer hospitality to the full. At their house she could still find a coal fire in the bedroom, a maid would come to offer help with the final stages of her dressing, and there would be entertaining company and a jolly good dinner.

A younger son of James's, Sir Evan, was first Chairman of the L.C.C., and another well-turned-out figure, frock-coated and with white slips to the waistcoat. An Orpen portrait at County Hall in London shows him shrewd, keen-eyed and bearded, with a few 'gooseberry' hairs down the bridge of his nose. I can still hear his slightly yapping voice, pronouncing all his 'r's as 'w's. He was a tough nut in business, but a devoted husband (married at 21; 'Nonsense—a boy and girl affair', said old James) with a large family, and most generous to his relations, including ten-bob tips to great-nephews.

Another Forsyte characteristic came out in the sharp differences in the domestic details between Albert and Evan. The former was amazingly modern in outlook: though unquestioned master in his own house, his rule was never arduous or oppressive. He had electric light and a passenger lift in his home in 1893, telephone in 1906 as well as central heating. By contrast, his younger brother Evan, despite his outward geniality, was a martinet and very strict with his family (front door locked by himself every night at 10 o'clock—high-spirited sons regularly climbing in late through a window!). Well into the present century his home was still lit only by lamps and candles and by the 1930s when I last visited him it was no more than gas-lit.

We may chuckle at these men of Victorian-evangelical background, but with their exuberant vitality and serious outlook, their devoted and complaisant wives, they lived extraordinarily full and happy, well-regulated lives. Doubtless some of their children had problems, but one never heard of scandal or nervous breakdowns among them, and their money seems always to have been wisely spent.

Uncle Evan was also a fine host and specialized in magnificent garden parties at his great early-nineteenth-century, cream-stucco house, Belair, in old Dulwich. I was taken to one in about 1912, decked out in my Sunday summer-rig of white sailor-suit and straw hat. The ices and the band were my special memories, coupled with the childish puzzle as to how my *Uncle* Evan could be a grandfather—to certain of my Spicer cousins. The only true grandfather in the world was my mother's father, Joseph Eady of Market Harborough, who could be reached only after eighty miles in a smart crimson-lake Midland Railway corridor express—not this pottering little dusty suburban train which had brought me to Dulwich. For all his fine big house and beautiful garden and peacocks, Evan was, to me at seven, slightly suspect as a 'grandpa'.

After his retirement from Spicers, when he adroitly managed to sell out at the height of the post-war boom in about 1920, Evan travelled, widely, enthusiastically and luxuriously. It became a tradition for members of the family to gather at the boat train to see him off, and I recall one early morning at Waterloo when I too joined the admiring circle of relatives, on my way to the Fisher Unwin office. It was winter and there was this perky, spruce old boy holding court on the platform in his fur-lined coat, about to sail off to South America, and looking forward to warm weather in three days' time. His wife, our Aunt Annie, sat back quietly in the compartment and when asked once whether she liked all this travelling, she just replied, 'Where Evan goes, I go.'

In his business life, we left my paternal grandfather George Unwin as having just taken over the Gresham Steam Press. It is one of my regrets that I never knew him: he died when I was one year old, but I have always believed that such taste as I possess in printing matters and feel for books has been inherited from him. Moreover, unlike his own sons, I could in time have shared his interest in wines, if not in the formidably strong cigars he used to enjoy, and which sometimes knocked out the unsuspecting guest. Stanley was critical of his financial judgement, but described him to me once as 'an artist to his finger tips'; and T. Fisher Unwin (George's half-brother) had great regard for him as a printer.

He quickly gained the confidence of Jacob's customers and within a few years the firm could advertise the names of nine magazines they were printing regularly—not only *Christian Penny Magazine* and *Christian Witness*, but such journals as *Produce Market Review*. George also established a solid reputation as a quality printer by producing in 1862 a magnificent type-specimen book, *George Unwin Specimens*, which demonstrated that the firm had more regard for good typography than most of its competitors.

In his first seven years on his own (1855–1862), while only in his twenties, my grandfather survived the commercial upheavals caused by the Crimean War, the Indian Mutiny, various bank failures and the American Civil War. It was said of him that his 'efficiency and reliability were all the while telling'. Though perhaps not the most pushful of men, he got what he wanted out of his workmen, he knew his job, and above all his customers liked and trusted him.

By 1862 he had to rent extra space in Oxford Court, Cannon Street. Next, the City Corporation drove the new Queen Victoria Street through Bucklersbury, and all the plant of the Gresham Steam Press was then concentrated at Oxford Court. The noise and vibration of the machinery there upset the adjoining Salters' Company, who threatened legal action; and that brought about the firm's final London move to Pilgrim Street, the building of their own premises and the need for that £8,000 loan from James Spicer. On May 12, 1881, Grandfather George topped off the new building by laying the coping stone of the chimney which carried off the smoke from the steam engine which drove the machines.

My father told me that when the famous engineer Professor Cawthorne Unwin, a relative, was consulted about the type of engine to be installed, he recommended, to the partners' horror, a Cornish Beam Engine—economical probably, but bulky and fearfully slow in action. It was a case where practical men had to set aside the opinion of the expert.

The Pilgrim Street building on five floors would have seemed small and inconvenient by industrial standards today. Yet in the next ten years it brought Unwin Bros. to their peak of Victorian prosperity, with the flat-bed presses pounding away night and day on 350,000 copies a month of the famous *Strand Magazine* (with its original Sherlock Holmes stories). They also printed the *Royal Magazine* and the *Sunday Strand*, and enjoyed that golden condition of a printing plant full to capacity, and therefore pretty certain to make money.

George and Edward coined it during the early '90s, each of them drawing between £3,000 and £4,000 a year—incomes neither of them was ever to see again. My father used to complain that in those years, whatever the profits, the partners 'took the lot', making no provision for reserves within the business. They believed that after years in the wilderness, they had reached the promised land for all time. There was a rude awakening when one by one they lost the magazines. As circulations grew, the proprietors, Sir George Newnes and Sir Arthur Pearson respectively, decided to have their own printing plants, and around 1895 it became increasingly difficult for the London works to show a profit. I suspect also that the decline in George's health, which began about then, and his partial retirement had their effect on the business.

In 1871, however, he had made an enterprising move, which ulti-
mately was to become their salvation. He became one of the first
London printers to establish works in the country, taking a nucleus of
London men, and recruiting others locally, to a disused paper-mill at
Chilworth in Surrey, on the river Tillingbourne. The great John
Ruskin wrote to congratulate the firm on their wisdom in taking their
work-people from the foul smoke of London. The idea was thoroughly
sound economically, for it took advantage of lower costs outside
London. The competition from country printers was already being felt,
and this tendency grew. By 1914 few, if any, book printers remained in
London; and it was mainly book work that was done at Chilworth.
Less than half a century after the move to Chilworth, the heavy losses
of their London business forced Unwin Bros. to sell up the Pilgrim
Street works. Thereafter, their major operations were in the country—
by that time at Woking.

At Chilworth they were tenants of the Duke of Northumberland,
who refused to allow them to make any real extension to the buildings
of the old mill, or to put up new houses for their workmen; it is surprising, in fact, that he allowed printing, or any sort of 'trade', on his
land at all. Many of the staff had to walk several miles to their work,
but apparently did so cheerfully. Steam power, with its smoke, was
out of the question, but a waterfall in the river supplied the power for
turbines and that was sufficient to drive the few small printing
machines of the time. Oddly enough, Unwin Bros. achieved a certain
fame in that steam age for being the first printers to use water power.

The works were separated from a very pleasant, part-eighteenth-
century house by a stretch of lawn, which grandfather had only to
stroll across to reach his office. Behind the house the beech woods of
the North Downs rose steeply to the Pilgrim's Way and St. Martha's
Chapel; and this was a full half-century before the hill and the adjoining Newlands Corner were to swarm at holiday times with walkers,
and later motorists.

In this rather lovely countryside most of George and Maria's
eleven children were born, and there my father, George Soundy
Unwin, the eldest son, spent his childhood, growing up as a true
country boy with country tastes and instincts. For forty years he was
to live a suburban life at Surbiton, but he never lost his love for the
country, his delight in trees and in discovering bird's nests or an
unusual wild flower. And though *his* children grew up in bricks-and-
mortar surroundings, we had the matchless blessing of a father who
revelled in every chance to take us out into the nearby country—
walking or cycling—and so give to all five of us something of his
feeling for nature.

To this day one can still pick up an old book—perhaps a Fisher

Unwin publication of the 1890s—and find on the last page the words

'Printed by Unwin Brothers
Chilworth and London'

the first word 'Chilworth' showing that the book had been printed in the country. (And I would bet that the page will have been well designed, and the machining of the hand-set type sharp and clear.) My dapper, well-turned-out grandfather, with his Trollopean beard, oval spectacles and diamond ring, kept a close eye on all the typography and was often his own proof-reader in the early Chilworth days. He was also adept at the organ for the nearby Congregational chapel at Tangley.

The only communication with the outside world was the South Eastern Railway cross-country line from Redhill to Reading, and it took about two hours to lumber along the forty miles to London (via Redhill). The journey to Guildford and up by the London and South Western route to Waterloo would have been shorter in mileage, but the fiercely competitive attitudes of railways in Victorian days ensured that there was never a satisfactory connection to be made between the trains of the two companies at Guildford.

Still, the supplies of type and ink and paper came down by goods train to Chilworth station, were manhandled on to a donkey cart, trundled the half-mile to the works, and turned into print 'by water power'. Then, by the same simple means, the printed sheets went back to London to be bound. The railway might be nicknamed by some the Slow and Easy (except for its boat trains to Dover), but it served Unwin Bros. well; the stationmaster at Chilworth even had an understanding with the guard that the early morning train must be held until 'the old gent'—my grandfather—was safely aboard. While the engine stood blowing off steam, a porter would run out into the road to see if the pony trap containing the bushy white beard was on its way.

Thus George Unwin, between the ages of forty to sixty, would travel two or three times a week in the rough-riding little railway carriages of the day, unplumbed and unheated in winter, except for a tin-can foot warmer, if he were lucky, and lit only by a feeble oil lamp at night. Yet his grandson has dared to complain a hundred years later because the Southern's electric train, warm and well-lit, sometimes lurched about too much at 80 m.p.h.!

At Chilworth, where George and Maria Unwin always took a lively —if feudal—personal interest in their work-people, Unwin Bros. celebrated their jubilee in 1876 with a magnificent 'wayzgoose'—the printers' name for an annual outing—with all the London staff in attendance; and in 1889, the twenty-first birthday of the boss's son, my father. Then in 1895, that happy country venture came to a sudden end. On a Saturday night in November the all-wooden buildings of the works were burnt to the ground.

In the days before automatic sprinkler systems all printers, with their vast stocks of paper, were a prey to fire. As it was three miles from the nearest steam fire engine, summoned only by a man on foot, the Unwin plant was doomed.

My father organized heroic fire-fighting, first with a hand pump and then, with his brothers and sisters, a human chain of buckets from a nearby pond; but a strong north-east wind settled the matter. On the following Sunday morning Grandfather could only survey heat-twisted, broken machinery and sodden masses of paper, where twelve hours before there had been a thriving factory.

A smart piece of improvisation brought many of the Chilworth staff to London the next Monday, to work in a building temporarily obtained near Pilgrim Street; but there must have been a big drop in production for many months. As Stanley has described in his autobiography, Unwin Bros. were shabbily treated by their insurance company. 'I am quite sure the results would have been very different if I had handled that claim', he once said to me. I do not doubt it; he was particularly adroit and skilful over insurance matters.

The Duke of Northumberland still refused to allow any improvement to the works, if they were rebuilt, so a move was imperative.

With an exaggerated faith in water power still, the firm took on another old paper mill, this time on the river Wey at Old Woking in Surrey. Though the bigger stream and two modern turbines produced a larger horsepower, this had soon to be supplemented by gas engines, as the business grew. The significance of the river situation thus diminished—except for some bad floods in wet winters.

Over the next forty years Woking became virtually the whole of Unwin Bros., and the development and growth of the plant was the life-work of my father, George Soundy Unwin.

3 A Printing Childhood

I first met the august T.F.U. when I was ten, and strangely enough it was our roly-poly little cook, Mary, who handled the encounter. Mary had been one of my mother's greatest coups in the selection of maids. A robust little figure, blessed with enormously powerful arms, she had had some row in a previous place, twelve years earlier, and been dismissed 'without a character'. Mother had been impressed by her capabilities, Father noted the level gaze of her honest brown eyes, and they took a chance. She became a devoted friend of the family, the best cook we ever had, and only left us—in tears and for a better-paid job—when we had a fierce economy drive in 1916 (because by then the London works of Unwin Bros. were losing heavily).

One Saturday in 1915, when Father and Mother were away for the weekend, my twin sisters, Nora and Nancy, and I were enjoying a peaceful tea with Mary in the kitchen of our Surbiton home—slabs of good, thick bread and butter, home-made jam and a plainish fruit cake, which she would have baked 'for the children'. Suddenly came a clang on the old wire-hauled bell which announced a call at the front door. Hastily putting on the official starched cap above her black dress and apron, Mary went to answer it. She brought back the alarming news that it was 'Mr. and Mrs. Fisher Unwin', and that she had showed them into the shut-up and, for that weekend, rather airless drawing-room. We must tidy ourselves and go in to see them at once.

The twins' hair took longer to brush than my bullet crop, so I was spruced up sooner and was first man in. Mrs. Fisher Unwin, our kindly but formidable Aunt Jane, had popped up to the lav on the landing, known locally as 'the half-way house', so Fisher, then in his late sixties, stood alone before the marble mantelpiece, a stately, upright figure, with tummy well set off even on a Saturday afternoon by the usual morning coat, his longish, pointed beard partly covering his yellow bow-tie, the emblem of the Reformers' Club, not the hostelry in Pall Mall but an odd little Liberal group which he supported.

With the piercing blue eyes which had intimidated Stanley in his youth, to say nothing of countless authors, he gazed down at me and said:

'D'you know who I am?'

'Mister Fisher Unwin,' I replied, hesitantly.

'Well, shall we say *Uncle* Fisher?'

And thereby hangs this tale.

The subsequent conversation I do not recall. The entry of the twins, looking dead alike in childhood, though they were not identical, was always a good diversion on a sticky occasion. They each had an engaging lisp at that stage and if a visitor asked how to tell the difference between them, the elder, Nora (who for the past twenty-five years has been a successful artist and author of children's books in America), was apt to say gravely, 'I am Norwah—becauth I've got a thpot!'—displaying proudly the large mole on her wrist.

Though Fisher had always been friendly with my father, and had been very fond of my grandfather, who was his half-brother, that impromptu visit of Uncle Fisher and Aunt Jane seemed to spark off a closer relationship between them and my parents. Mary served them tea. Jane—like my father—was taken with her warm brown eyes ('such a nice maid you have', she said later to Mother). They took to dropping in more often, possibly when visiting a Fisher Unwin author, McLure Hamilton, a portraitist, who lived in Kingston.

T.F.U. asked Father to serve on the board of his firm when it became a limited company. At one time he pressed him to forsake printing, and make publishing his full-time career—finally he appointed Father his executor. Later, he offered to pay my fees at Mill Hill School, which was not unusual among the wealthier members of a family, and eventually he gave me some sort of foothold for a time in publishing. Who knows how much I may not owe indirectly to our Mary, the sensible, well-trained cook-general who did not muff her lines that Saturday afternoon in 1915?

I had begun this life, in a thunderstorm, on Sunday, July 9th, 1905. Born under the sign of Cancer, I am supposed, according to astrologers, to be well adapted to publishing, journalism or hotel management, and to be sensitive and thin-skinned. The latter qualities can be a curse in many ways, but in so far as I may have them, they have perhaps been useful sometimes in helping me to feel my way with difficult authors. I had a heritage of printing through three previous generations, and this had already spilled over into publishing.

At the time of my birth, my bearded father, George Soundy Unwin, was Joint Managing Director of Unwin Brothers with his cousin Edward (eldest brother of Stanley), Father being responsible for the Woking works. As we have seen, he was a countryman at heart and left to himself might well have migrated to New Zealand or Australia, as did some of his brothers and cousins. A stern sense of duty and the wish to help his father settled him for a printing career, and he made a success of it: though in some ways it was not his true *métier*. Short in stature, he had a well-knit, sturdy, athletic body, a deep chest and impressive muscular development. Forswearing the pleasures of pipe and glass, he imbibed deeply the Victorian version of 'a healthy mind in a healthy body'.

When he was a young man living alone in London, he joined the Honourable Artillery Company for their gym., drill and shooting practice. All through the summer there were regular visits to the swimming baths in Westminster, and on winter evenings dumb-bells were heaved and Indian clubs swung in the bedroom. 'In those days I worshipped muscle', he once confessed to me. Late in life he amused Mother by continuing an attenuated form of 'press-ups' for the not-so-young against the bed rail. At all events, it gave him a fine physique and his children the security of a manly, all-powerful 'Daddy', who never knew defeat in the practical details of living and who gave zest to every kind of outdoor expedition.

Throughout his working life he was a great reader. There was always a book in his attaché case to read on the homeward journey (evening papers were a waste of time), and he was a steady book buyer, largely Everyman Library editions. So, with a home full of books and being read to regularly on Saturday evenings—*Black Beauty*, Henty, Ballantyne, Jerome K. Jerome—one had an early feeling for them.

My mother was the eldest daughter of Joseph Eady, J.P., in the Leicestershire hunting country. A rubicund brewer who rode to hounds, enjoyed his glass and was also a keen Congregationalist, he was to me the pattern of all that a jolly 'grandpa' should be, and I was very fond of him. A treasured memory still is the brisk trot of his horse as I sat beside him in the high dog-cart when he went to visit one of his tied houses (an inn owned by his brewery) on a Saturday morning. He sent his daughters to a boarding school run by a 'good' Congregational woman at Isleworth (of all odd places), and grandfather Unwin did the same with *his* daughters. Father's favourite sister, Edyth, brought Nora Eady home to stay in the holidays, and though he found her first handshake too limp, and she disliked young men with beards, the association thus begun was to last for over fifty years.

They married on £400 a year in September of the Diamond Jubilee year, 1897. One of Father's engagement treats for his girl had been to get expensive seats in Parliament Square to view the royal Jubilee procession, and years later Mother's account of that day brought home to me delicious evidence of her unsuspected frailties. A bastion of perfect health—like one of Arnold Bennett's characters, 'her digestion was glorious'—she was unaccountably taken short on this occasion. She had to leave her expensive place and in her considerable finery seek sanctuary in unspeakably primitive accommodation below the stands. Then, when Queen Victoria came by in her open carriage, *she* was looking cross and turned away from my mother-to-be to address some remark to 'Bertie', Prince of Wales, as he rode beside her on horse-back. 'In the end,' said Mother, 'we came away early. Daddy took me out in a boat on the river and we sat and spooned in the back seat just like any other couple, and that really was the part that I enjoyed most.'

Bless her heart, until that confession I never thought that my well-corseted mama would have had such ideas, but remembering the affectionate way my father used always to kiss her, I think perhaps my parents knew more physical happiness together than many married couples of their generation.

It was to a new, red-brick villa on the edge of Surbiton in Surrey, and midway between the London and Woking establishments of Unwin Bros., that my father brought his bride. Soundly built, semi-detached and gas-lit, though without any 'constant hot water', it was a good house and it had up-to-date sanitation, decorated I remember with chrysanthemums in the glazed ware of its vital parts.

Though not as prolific as either of their parents, my father and mother did not do so badly. After a year or so of hope deferred, my eldest sister Joyce squeezed into the Victorian era in 1899 and brother Rolf saluted the new century in 1901; there I know my mother would gladly have settled for a family of two. Splendid Mum as she was in so many respects, and happily sharing the double bed all her married life, she did not really care for the business of reproduction. Birth control was far more chancy sixty years ago, and Father, more-over, did not altogether 'believe' in it. Anyhow, there was that second son four years after Rolf, and I was only eighteen months old when Mother was again blessed, this time with twin daughters.

Antenatal care for healthy women was almost non-existent in 1907, and though Mother had had her suspicions, when a doctor sister of Father's, our Aunt Ethel, had made an examination towards the end of the pregnancy, she had firmly pronounced 'only one head'! All the same, twenty minutes after the arrival of my younger sister Nora, her twin Nancy emerged—and with one of the best heads in the family.

In the middle of that February night Father had to get out his bike, light its oil lamp and dash off in search of another nurse—good drains he might have, but no telephone for another seven years. At first Mother was in despair as to how such a brood was to be raised and educated. Printing was not doing well then and I doubt if Father's income was above £600 a year. Mother was apt to say in gloomy moments that she had brought bad luck on Unwin Bros: soon after she met Father they lost the profitable *Strand Magazine* and had the Chilworth fire, and these disasters heralded a long spell of lean years. She had a good contralto, drawing-room voice and when she sang *Three Fishers* she imparted great feeling to the line: 'There's little to earn and many to keep.'

However, Father loved the idea of a large family; he firmly assured Mother that all would be well, and indeed the richer relations, especially the Spicers, rallied magnificently, popping nice cheques into their kind letters of inquiry.

Before the Liberal government of 1906 had really got going with its social legislation, income tax was still very light, prices were low and even my Father's modest salary could support two full-time maids, plus a nurse. Not until the 1914 war was well advanced did he ever have to tackle so much as washing-up or shoe-cleaning himself. The wholesome, kindly young women who cooked and did all the chores for a family of seven did not expect much more than £12 or £15 a year, including keep of course, and probably uniforms and aprons: print dress for the morning's work, after which the housemaid would get into a black dress and apron to serve lunch, while the cook would probably not change until afternoon.

Mother was a good mistress of the household, just and fair, expecting good work and adept at picking young girls who would respond to training.

Of course, to us today it looks like penal servitude: no hot water from the tap until the coal-fired kitchen range had been alight for an hour, two open fires to be cleared, re-laid and lit in dining-room and nursery before the family breakfasted; no detergents to help the washing up—only soda, which was rough on the hands; brass taps to be polished daily, because chromium plate was twenty-five years away, and no vacuum cleaner.

Besides all this, it is so true, as Osbert Lancaster has said, that one supreme value of maids was that they provided someone for the children to talk to. Good maids in a well-run house could be an unfailing source of interest, of horse-sense education and of comfort in trouble. Mother might be out or busy, and elder brother and sister at school, but there was always someone in the kitchen.

I had become an old man of eight by 1913, but found myself heavy with grief on the chilly September afternoon when my big, all-capable brother Rolf was being dispatched for his first term to Taunton School —the first sign of family break-up! Had I but known it, my level-headed mama standing at that moment on Paddington Station was horrified to realize how little and vulnerable he looked among the other boys in the reserved saloon-coach as the train pulled out ('a master in charge', said the prospectus). At all events our dear Mary looked by chance into the schoolroom where I was grizzling against the window pane.

'Oh, Mary, I'm so miserable,' I groaned. 'Rolf's gone and I don't know when I shall see him again!' There was no other bosom into which I could cry unashamedly at that moment, and Mary's was both ample and understanding.

'Oh, poor old Phil,' she said, 'but you mustn't cry, it won't be long before he's home again. Here, you come on down to the kitchen. There's a nice fire, we'll make some dripping toast.' A friendly buck-up and soon all was well. Another of Mary's virtues was the way in which her total loyalty to my parents, and her respect for them, carried over to us boys, in the shape of remarks like: 'You'll have to work hard when you grow up, if you're going to be as good a man as your father.'

I was born just at the time the tram lines were laid, so I literally grew up with trams—and when I married and left home they were replaced by trolley-buses. This may be the reason for my lifelong interest in railed transport. Trams meant much more to my generation than buses do to children now. Originally, the tram was the fastest thing on the road, over 20 m.p.h., and the quick 'dun-di-di-dun' of its short wheelbase on the rails made it sound even faster. Ours, of the London United Tramways, were painted blue and cream and lettered in gold, later red and gold, with an experimental go at yellow. The lower-deck saloon had soft plush seats and veneered panels in its roof. Above, the trams were open-topped and picked up their power from an overhead wire. Their trolley-booms had a small wheel at the end which raced round against the wire and made a grand hissing, whistling noise. On the open top deck one could watch this little wheel whizzing along with the boom, bobbing and swaying round the curves and occasionally ducking down low, almost level with the passengers, if the tram went under a railway bridge. Sometimes the trams themselves would provide first-class entertainment, when their trolley-booms bobbed off the wire and they came to an involuntary standstill. Best of all was when a tram ran off the rails. Sometimes at a junction, if the points were not properly set, the front set of bogie wheels went one way while the rear ones took the other line, so that the whole tram slewed round almost at right angles to the track. Occasionally it would part company with the rails altogether, and then it was quite powerless, until another one came and shoved it into position; but generally trams behaved well and were good, kindly vehicles. They were rather noisy, but they made no smell and scarcely ever caused injury. For one penny they would take a child a couple of miles from the centre of the town, to the fields which bordered the terminus. It was only when one learned to ride a bicycle that one realized their great disadvantage: the tram-lines, with their nasty little grooves set into the surface of the road, were just made to trap one's bicycle wheel if one crossed them at too fine an angle.

Bicycles were a great part of our family life, right up to the middle 1920s; Father's hopes for a car had to be deferred during the years of his heaviest family expenditure. Although the Woking works made money, the ailing London end of the printing business held back profits until after the 1914 war. There was a resurgence in the post-war boom of about 1920, but then the slump and a disastrous printing strike pushed the firm back into the red for two or three years more. But in spite of this, my Father's love of outdoor pursuits saw to it that as children we never lacked interesting outings of one kind or another.

Father himself was a keen cyclist and had been since about 1885: he just missed the 'penny farthing', but had plenty of experience with clumsy great tricycles (including a tandem type on which the two riders did well if they could surpass the speed of a horse and cart over several miles). At the turn of the century the 'free-wheel' machine had come in, a great luxury—he had done over 3,000 miles one year on his old fixed-wheel, on which you had to take your feet right off the pedals if you wanted to coast down a hill.

Warning Mother before marriage that they would not be able to afford to keep a carriage—at first—he bought her a nice new bike and bade her learn to ride it. She had wheeled the beautiful gleaming thing—lined out in green and gold—into the drawing-room at Market Harborough, to show it proudly to her invalid mother. Mama was no athlete and it is enormously to her credit as a devoted wife that she clocked up some thousands of miles with her husband on that faithful Premier machine, before it went to the scrap heap twenty-five years later.

Runs of 25 or 30 miles into the Surrey hills were a frequent Saturday exploit for them; but their greatest epic was to cycle the 60 miles from Surbiton to Portsmouth in the day against a vicious south-westerly gale, in order to spend the weekend with friends in the Isle of Wight. The last ten miles had to be run 'in tandem'—Father as the leading horse, with his machine harnessed to Mother's by a piece of rope. Still, they made it, and the strong wind held to bowl them home easily on the Monday. So often if one rides out against the wind, it has a nasty habit of changing, to hit one in the face on the way back. All this cycling was done, of course, before main roads were tarred, and there were mud and dust and punctures to add to the hazards.

Father's finest hour of enterprise in family outings was at the stage when we all had bicycles except the twins. At about ten years old they could not always be left at home or planted out on friends, so they were taught to ride on the 'step'—a little fixed projection of less than two inches which stuck out from the frame at the centre of the rear wheel. The passenger had to support most of her weight on the left leg while a little was taken by the right knee resting on the carrier just behind the saddle. To this hazardous practice, Father liked to add his patent method of carrying a can of milk. He stuck a springy hazel stick about four feet long under the saddle of his bicycle and on the whippy end of it tied the milk-can by its handle. So behind the small child clutching the ample shoulder was the dangling milk—only occasionally did it slop through the lid, if the cyclist swerved suddenly.

Because I had been a rather tiresome baby at night, and owing to a tendency towards a hernia was not supposed to be left to cry too much, my father frequently had to walk the floor with me in the classic Edwardian manner. Apparently I was always quiet the moment I was in his arms, but would sometimes think otherwise when put back in the cot. Whether because of this, or my nauseating tendency to develop into what female relations called 'a dear little boy', I seemed to have a close tie with him, and in my mental processes I was possibly nearer to him than was the case with my brother and sisters. We must have walked and cycled hundreds of miles together through Surrey and Sussex, and in the course of these exploits—including one of 95 miles in the day when he was 55 and I was 18—he was more forthcoming on family matters, printing and life in general than he was when all of us were together.

Before the 48-hour working week was established in printing, just after the 1914 war, Father always went to the Woking works on Saturday mornings, and I must have been no more than six when he took me with him, along with Rolf, for my first visit. As an easement for Saturday, he had on his tweed Norfolk jacket and knee-breeches, instead of the regulation morning coat he wore for London, so the whole outing had a sniff of the country about it. At Woking Station we were hoisted up into a dog-cart, and clip-clopped the two miles behind the chestnut mare which regularly conveyed Father to the works.

The approach to the factory was, and still is, delightful. From Old Woking village one turned off on to the private, tree-lined road, which led along the bank of the River Wey; and there, if one were lucky, the driver might suddenly point with his whip to a kingfisher flashing out from the trees. Then one heard the sharp cough of the gas engine exhaust, 'chah-bong, chah-bong' it echoed across the fields; next, as one pulled up at the main entrance, there was the deep, bass rumble of the turbines and the swoosh of the torrent of water—a veritable mill-race—pouring out under the bridge from the seven-foot fall which drove the turbines.

None of these exciting features concerned printing as such, but they all spoke to me, as a boy, of Father's work being done and the family money being earned; though as it turned out I was to become a publisher, not a printer. I must confess that on my earliest visits it was the sight of the 50 h.p. gas engine and the huge gleaming fist of its crank, punching round hour after hour, which gave me the greatest thrill. That was the power that drove nearly all of the plant, via shafts and belts and pulleys. Later, there were 90 and 150 h.p. engines, to keep pace with the growth of the works.

The turbines were coupled to the main shaft and also made their contribution. The water power on its own could generate enough electricity to light the whole place. Fifty years ago there was no main electricity in Woking village. Even after Unwins had become an all-electric plant, the turbines still played a vital part during the power cuts after the last war.

On later visits as a schoolboy, and when Rolf was serving his apprenticeship in the works, I began to understand something of the skill and fiendish intricacy of the printers' craft, the labour of patiently interpreting an inconsistent manuscript, or a difficult author's corrections, and then the 'make ready' of the formes of type, so that sheets could be printed immaculately at 1,200 an hour on the great Miehle 'Perfector'. That particular machine was Father's pride and joy before 1914, not only because it printed both sides of the sheet in one operation, hence the name 'Perfector', but because it was driven by its own electric motor. It thus heralded the day, many years ahead, when the vast length of shafting with its dangerous belt drives to the different machines, could be scrapped, and when the bark of the gas engine was no longer to be heard across the fields. Today printing is a more scientific, white-coated job, and the amount of skilled handwork of the past would now be hopelessly uneconomic; but some aspects of workmanship seemed far better forty years ago.

Nosing round the Woking plant as a boy, I inevitably came across vast piles of printed sheets of Fisher Unwin's famous best-seller, *The Way of an Eagle* by Ethel M. Dell, which Mother and her friends seemed to have enjoyed so much. The authoress was fabulously successful, it was said—Uncle Fisher had made a lot of money out of her—and he too was rich and successful, by all accounts.

Our family might have riches of its own in the fun we had together —we were seldom bored and we never lacked security; Mother and Father, it seemed in our childhood, constituted a firm rock of all that was Right and Sensible and Orderly—but we never seemed to have cash to spare. Very early, I suppose, I became attracted by the reputedly rich Uncle, who in addition practised the mysterious and deeply interesting craft of publishing.

There was, too, I discovered later on, that remarkable fact, another Unwin firm. What was this Allen & Unwin, I asked my sister Joyce one day. 'Oh, that's Uncle Stanley,' she said. 'At Drummonds Bank they call him Jesus. It's very naughty, but he does look rather like Him—youngish man with a brown beard.' (Such beards were then a rarity; and she had a friend who knew someone in Drummonds.) 'They say he's very clever.'

Thus my publishing uncles began to cast their shadows before—but it would be many years before I caught up with them.

Sometimes Father would remark in the evening that T.F.U. had given them a big manuscript that day. 'Something to keep Woking busy for two or three weeks.' Then, later, that 'Stanley is turning out a rare lot of stuff—where he sells it all I can't imagine.' But the printing of it was all precious grist to the Woking mill.

Behind his workaday attitude of seeing books as the raw material of a factory, Father was, as I have said, a keen reader. Gradually he built up a collection of Dickens, Hardy, Kipling, Trollope, books on flowers and birds, and an invaluable set of *Chambers' Encyclopaedia*, so that at home we were always surrounded by books. It was obvious and natural to turn to them for reference or pleasure. He would never pick up any new book without giving it his critical scrutiny, the page of type, margins, texture of paper; then, 'Who's the printer?' Finally, off came the jacket for a look at the binding, to see if he could detect any fault. To read a well-made book gave him a double pleasure, and plenty of this rubbed off on me.

Neither Rolf nor I showed any streaks of brilliance, and until we were both well into our 'teens there was no real plan as to what we were going to do with our lives. Only by degrees did it emerge that he had better go into his father's business, and that it would be nice if I could get into one of the family publishing firms. There was not the slightest guarantee that I should have the chance to, but it is only fair to remember that fifty years ago the name was a great help in a family concern; and also that vast numbers of young men—at least in England—took up a business career without any initial vocational training, and learnt the job as they went along. In 1920 one had to be exceptional to get a university education without cost to one's parents, and the state of Unwin Brothers at the time made it impossible for Father—even with partial help from Uncle Fisher—to do more than see us through our minor public schools, Taunton and Mill Hill.

The realistic policy for Unwin Brothers would have been to phase out the London works as soon as the Woking end had been firmly established. I write this inevitably as a Woking partisan, but the facts speak for themselves: almost from the start Woking was profitable, whereas after the loss of the big-circulation magazines the London end began to lose money. No other comparable magazines were found to take their place, and at that time Unwins failed to get in sufficiently well with the city banks and other wealthy institutions, whose endless reports and prospectuses can offer profitable work for London printers.

The natural gifts of those members of the family who were responsible for the Pilgrim Street plant—Grandfather's brother Edward and the latter's son Ted, Stanley's eldest brother—lay in directions other than those of works management. Edward, well into his sixties at the time of my birth, was primarily concerned with his innumerable philanthropic and religious interests, while his son Ted, my father's cousin and joint managing director, was essentially the 'good mixer'. A popular Rotarian and Freemason, he was a good talker and in his day secured some very fine customers for the firm; but he seemed to be less successful in continuing to service them, in finding efficient managers for the London works, and in attending to all the prosaic day-to-day details which are inevitable in business. I was fond of Uncle Ted. He was a kindly man and his sociable and extrovert qualities should have complemented my father's natural caution and painstaking capacities; but it did not really work out that way.

Meanwhile, to the Edward Unwins, as Londoners, the Pilgrim Street works were all that really mattered; Woking was seen—at first —as just a little country appendage. For them, there must have been a sense of envy and irritation as the cheaper 'country rates' for printing made it essential for more and more work to be done at Woking, and as those works, achieving a high standard of quality, became increasingly profitable. A sentimental attachment to the idea of a London headquarters by two of the partners caused the firm to hang on to the Pilgrim Street works far too long after the writing was plainly on the wall. Up to 1914, Woking profits largely cancelled out London losses, and it was not until 1917 that the losses became so catastrophic as to swamp Woking, and so necessitate the closing down of the London end. After this the firm's position began to improve.

But for the nationwide slump of 1921 and the printing strike, my later school days might have found Father at his most prosperous. As it was, however, much of our early family life was dogged financially by 'London'. It was not until the year 1930, when despite the possession of a car, Father and I were enjoying one of our last bicycle rides together, and were contentedly munching our sandwiches on a grassy bank somewhere in Bucks, that he could remark, 'Well, there's waiting for me at home the biggest dividend cheque I've ever had from Unwin Bros.' From then on, he enjoyed comparative affluence for the remaining twenty years of his life.

He might not have been the most brilliant of business men, but for over forty years he was the unflagging mainstay of the Woking end of Unwin Bros. From what he built up there, often under difficulty and discouragement, the next generation evolved a plant technically far ahead of most competitors, and the £1 deferred ordinary shares, which for much of Father's life had yielded him nothing, were then valued at £40 apiece.

4 *T. Fisher Unwin*

My great-uncle Fisher is given a hard time in Stanley Unwin's autobiography, *The Truth About a Publisher*; but even there, he is summed up as 'in some ways a great and most certainly a remarkable publisher'. Certain of the authors who owed their start to T.F.U. might accuse him of meanness, but he made no great fortune, although he undoubtedly left his mark in the 'nineties and the early nineteen hundreds. The fourth edition of Mumby's *Publishing and Bookselling*, issued thirty years after Fisher Unwin had retired from business, still devoted a page and a half to him—a space exceeded in that chapter only by what was given to William Heinemann.

Fisher was the younger son of Jacob Unwin by his second wife Isobel Hall, whom he married within a year or so of the death of his first wife Emma. The name Fisher was borne by Jacob's father, but how far back in the family it goes, I do not know. As Jacob himself died when Fisher was seven years old, this younger son grew up fatherless, but his mother probably exercised considerable influence on his choice of career.

She was descended from the Miller family whose annals were set forth in *The Millers of Haddington, Dunbar and Dunfermline: a Record of Scottish Bookselling*, which her son published in 1914 (it was a surplus copy of this book that he gave me in 1923). The Millers were also printers and publishers, producing the so-called *Cheap Magazine*, which achieved a monthly circulation of 20,000 copies in Scotland. As Jacob himself had done a certain amount of publishing, Fisher had it in the blood, and it was doubtless with his mother's encouragement that he entered the book trade.

Much of his youth was spent with his family at Hackney, and like his brother Edward, eight years his senior, he went to the City of London School. Unlike Edward, however, he did not have to walk the three and a half miles there and back to school, six days a week, because by Fisher's boyhood the North London Railway had been built. All that open-air exercise was supposed to have been responsible for Edward's exceptional vigour in his eighties, but Fisher did almost as well, surviving cheerfully to the ripe age of 87. Latterly, however, he did not continue to dash about in the quick, fussy manner of his elder step-brother.

It is interesting to speculate why Edward, Stanley's father, imbibed the spirit and outward forms of nonconformity so deeply, while in the same family Fisher remained unaffected—preferring in later life to imbibe, moderately, quite other spirits which were anathema to Edward. The eldest brother, too, my grandfather George, was no tee-totaller, as we have seen; and Fisher's brother Buxton (another family name) was to become, like Ruskin's father, an importer of sherry.

Fisher was apprenticed to Jackson Walford & Hodder, predecessors of Hodder & Stoughton. Whether formal indentures were signed to cover a seven-year period is not known, but probably some premium was paid and an undertaking given to teach him the business. At all events, he certainly got a full training in every side of publishing, and he appears to have finished off as one of the firm's leading travellers. He enjoyed travelling, and he was good at it, both commercially and in the physical sense. He always possessed one of those prerequisites of the good publisher, an excellent memory; and he would have known his firm's catalogue inside out. He was fairly gregarious, enjoyed his contacts with booksellers and without doubt had an iron constitution. I never heard of his being ill, beyond heavy colds in old age. He retained most of his teeth throughout his life, and twitted me as a youth for having to go to the dentist: 'A young man doesn't need to go to the dentist!'

In the course of travelling for Hodder's he often went to the Continent, and was particularly fond of Paris. He had some knowledge of French and liked to air a phrase or two in conversation. He also had the foresight to purchase one or two of the French impressionists at an early stage, and was able to sell them at a useful—though not astronomical—profit around 1930. When well over seventy he made a selling trip to Paris, taking orders for over £200 worth of his books and paying himself a ten per cent commission! Altogether he acquired, in our somewhat parochial family, a certain reputation for Continental sophistication and an international outlook.

Another well-known publisher who set up his own business after some years 'on the road' was Jonathan Cape; and there is no doubt that it can be a wonderful training for certain publishing requirements. It teaches one to become a good book *trade* man, with a sense of what is practical and what booksellers can sell. It shows one, too, what other publishers are doing, and it gives one an exceptional feel for books in the commercial sense.

Though I remember being told by my grandmother that Uncle Fisher had an exceptionally 'long apprenticeship', this presumably referred merely to the whole length of time in which he worked for another firm—and I have no doubt that he worked hard and for long hours. Fisher had no holidays from business in his youth, and this accounted for his grudging attitude to holidays where his own staff were concerned.

He was no more than thirty-four years of age when he took the plunge and bought the little publishing business of Marshall Japp, then in Holborn Viaduct. Fisher soon moved to Paternoster Square, and to Adelphi Terrace in about 1905. Whatever might be said later in disparagement of some of T.F.U.'s business methods, no one could fault that purchase of Marshall Japp. The price of £1,000 was paid over a period of months, and during that time the business produced enough profit to meet the instalments, so that the new owner was able to keep his savings intact to serve as working capital.

Fisher got off the mark pretty smartly, pouring out his ideas for books and pamphlets, chasing up the booksellers he had known and probably acting very largely as his own traveller. His first agreement book, containing the actual contracts made with authors from 1882–1895, includes the names of Annie Besant, Augustine Birrel, Conrad, Crockett, Mark Rutherford, Olive Schreiner and W. B. Yeats—not bad names for a newish publisher.

In pre-war days at Allen & Unwin, some of us, in a lust for self-improvement, persuaded various people to give lunchtime talks to the more earnest members of the staff. The best one we ever had was from Stanley on 'Starting a Publishing Business', and I well remember his point that in the search for authors the new publisher must at the outset follow up and exploit every conceivable personal connection he possesses—family, relations, friends, school and club contacts, etc.—making it known as widely as possible that he has become a publisher, and that he wants manuscripts.

Fisher undoubtedly followed this policy vigorously, and indeed, S.U. may well have learned it from him. Mountaineering, liberalism, free trade, international affairs and anything to do with persecution of minorities were some of T.F.U.'s personal interests early represented on his list.

T.F.U. was an imposing figure to the end of his days. Taller than other Unwins of his generation, he always held himself rigidly upright, as if his neck and torso were encased in plaster. His nose looked as if it had started out as a typical Unwin beak and had then been accidentally squashed and flattened at the tip; but with those fine blue eyes, strong colour, full beard and general demeanour of solidity, he undoubtedly had *dignity*, as Mr. Frank Swinnerton has written in *The Bookman's London*—though he goes on to say, 'He [Fisher Unwin] needed this dignity, for his costume was unusual. He wore a grey, tailed morning suit: and upon his large, imposing head he carried an elderly straw boater.' It is fair to point out, however, that this was only his hot-weather garb, as I saw for myself in the summer of 1925.

For most days it was black morning-coat and top hat (elderly), which towards the end became a trilby.

The drawing done by his one-time manager (later director), A. D. Marks, is a lifelike impression of T.F.U. as he trotted four times a day between No. 3 Adelphi Terrace, where he had a beautiful flat over-looking the river, and the office at No. 1. Always in winter there was the coat thrown over his shoulders, the hat cocked to the back of his head, and under his arm the inevitable publisher's bundle of papers, with probably a set of proofs and part of a manuscript.

His fine living quarters were not achieved, however, until after his marriage to Jane, daughter of Richard Cobden the great 19th-century MP and Free Trade advocate. Just how they met is uncertain, but according to the family story, 'Uncle Fisher came back from a holiday in Italy with his beard trimmed down to half its former size—then everyone knew there was a woman in the case.' Beyond the fact that he had dared to be keen on one of the Spicer girls, my grandmother's younger sister, I do not know what earlier feminine companionship he enjoyed, if any.

He married in 1892 at the age of 44—I still possess the massive silver salver presented to him by his staff, touchingly inscribed, after the custom of the period, 'as a token of respect and esteem'—and at one stroke he acquired a wife, with a charming house in the depths of Sussex, near Midhurst, plus £1,000 a year of her own. As I knew her, she was a handsome old lady, broad in the beam like Queen Victoria, with warm eyes and beautiful white hair—in middle life, with her great vitality, she must have been very attractive.

At the time of her marriage, Jane would have been close on forty herself, and not surprisingly they had no children. Whether the marriage was ever consummated I should doubt; certainly in my time they had separate rooms in Adelphi Terrace. But there was real affection on both sides. He always called her 'Janie', and her appellation was invariably 'Fisher dear'. During the general strike of 1926, and on one or two other occasions, they put me up for the night in their London flat, and to me at the age of twenty they seemed, though formidable, a charming, widely-informed and in many ways sophisticated couple. They knew how to live: they had *savoir faire*.

At the lunches in his flat Fisher's favourite dishes were shoulder of lamb, carved stiffly and at arm's length, with apple charlotte to follow, washed down with Graves (I was unfortunately a teetotaller then). Any liquid he always swallowed with a curious, extra glottal squeeze, producing a noise rather like a goat feeding. He resolutely refused to play cards for money and thus avoided bridge, but he was fond of a game of whist and almost invariably this was how our evenings ended. 'Aunt Janie' took the dummy, as there were only the three of us, and he liked to rumble out between puffs on his pipe, with a wink at me, that 'Janie makes a very good dummy.' So to bed on the top floor, with the late trams rumbling along the Embankment and the chimes of Big Ben almost at one's ear.

Tiresome, obstinate and capricious he could be in his office, and Jane could suddenly lash herself into embarrassing furies over the Bread Tax of the 1840s, birth control, or the Bolsheviks; but they were a great couple, with wide interests, and they were good to me. I treasure their memory.

In 1887, after he had been running his own business for five years, T.F.U. added to his modest pay roll—at ten shillings a week to begin with—the man who was to become over the next forty years the most famous publisher's reader in England. This was Edward Garnett, son of Richard Garnett, Superintendent of the Reading Room at the British Museum, who brought T.F.U. some of his most famous fiction discoveries of the 1890s. It came about by one of those strange chances of literary history.

Carolyn Heilbrunn, in her book *The Garnett Family*, describes how Edward, at the age of twenty, was at a loose end, with no profession in view. After leaving the City of London School, he had spent two years lying on the hearthrug doing what mattered most to him, reading books. The idea of his learning shorthand and taking a position on *The Manchester Guardian* had come to nothing. Two years earlier, as 'a very tall, thin boy who looked as if he had outgrown his clothes and his strength', and yet was very charming, with his 'bright eyes, curly head, dimples and roguish expression'—like a 'kitten on top of a maypole'—this attractive youth had fallen in love with Constance Black, who was six years older than he. She was a politically-minded young woman, who took him along to Fabian and Socialist meetings, which he did not view very seriously, and her resolute action on one important occasion may have decided the course of his life.

It had been arranged eventually that Edward should enter the office of T. Fisher Unwin 'as a wrapper of parcels'; and at that time he was staying in the flat of Constance and her sister Clementine. On the morning he was due to begin at Paternoster Square he was so slow to get up that Constance 'fetched a hansom . . . in those days a terrible extravagance, and with a sinking heart, sent him off. It is quite possible, however, that this reckless unpunctuality was more diplomatic than a humble eagerness to please would have been. It possibly gave Unwin the impression that Edward, though so young, was a person of consequence, and this idea must have been confirmed by his studious inability to pack books, etc. He quite soon slipped into the position of "publisher's reader", which was of all callings the one he was fitted for by character, tastes and habits.'

Later, he married Constance, and together they made their distinguished contribution to the world of English letters—he by his discovery and encouragement of new authors, and she by her translations from the Russian.

Garnett's greatest discovery for T.F.U. was Joseph Conrad, and Garnett's friendship and encouragement was crucial to the continuance of Conrad's career as a writer. Conrad had been disappointed by the sales of his first book, *Almayer's Folly,* and at a somewhat awkward meeting with Garnett and T.F.U. in the Smoking Room of the National Liberal Club, when his publisher made a pointed reference to his next book, Conrad replied: 'I don't expect to write again. It is likely that I shall soon be going to sea.' T.F.U. then made some excuse, so the story goes, and went to greet some friends on the other side of the room. Left to themselves, Conrad and Garnett talked together more freely. This I can well imagine: though he was never tongue-tied Fisher was not an easy conversationalist. As Carolyn Heilbrunn has written, 'Edward said that Conrad's life on land and sea would utterly vanish unless Conrad himself recorded it in literature. *Almayer's Folly* showed that he had the power. Conrad listened attentively. It seemed to Edward Garnett later that Conrad . . . deeply desired to be encouraged to write.'

It had all begun with an interesting idea of Garnett's, a series known as *The Pseudonym Library,* paper-bound, but stiff-covered, little volumes at eighteen pence which introduced to the world a number of brilliant new writers, each of whom appeared under an assumed name, John Oliver Hobbes, Ouida, Olive Schreiner and W. B. Yeats among them. Conrad submitted the manuscript of his first book to Fisher Unwin thinking it would be suitable for this collection. As a full-length novel it was far too long for publication—as a new book—at 1s. 6d., but it was the fame of the *Pseudonym Library,* the books of which were fashionable upon the occasional tables of the 'nineties, that brought Conrad to the firm, and Garnett immediately recognized the quality of his work.

Then had come the not unusual publisher's offer of that period, for a first book—£25 for the entire copyright. However many copies the book might sell subsequently, the author was legally entitled to nothing more whatever. Of course, with hindsight it looks extremely mean when we know that the book has sold for seventy years; but I suggest that £25 for a novel by an *unknown* author was a considerable risk to T.F.U. in the book market of 1894. The book might well have sold no more than 500 copies. The £250 sometimes paid *for all rights* today to an acknowledged authority on his subject (where the book in question can be one of an established series sold in America and foreign language editions) represents quite arguably a lesser risk. The present-day publisher can be much more certain of recouping his £250 than T.F.U. his £25 seventy-five years ago, yet the modern author of a book published on such terms still gets nothing beyond the once and only £250.

I am not trying to defend the system of outright payments, and I cannot recall ever making such an agreement myself. If sales are problematical, and the publisher's risk seems particularly heavy, an initial payment can be made on an assumed sale of a given number of copies, until costs have been covered; but thereafter it is more reasonable for some further payment to be made according to the numbers sold. My point is simply that in the terms T.F.U. offered to Conrad on his *first* book, he was not quite the avaricious villain that some writers on the period would lead one to suppose. Moreover, it is not as if T.F.U. were making a fortune for himself at that time.

Stanley has described in his autobiography how slim were the profits of his uncle's business at the turn of the century: 'It is doubtful whether during at any rate the first five years following their first publication, T. Fisher Unwin made any money out of a tithe of his more important discoveries. He certainly made none out of the publication of the early work of Joseph Conrad, George Moore, John Galsworthy (under the pseudonym John Sinjohn), H. G. Wells, H. de Vere Stacpoole, W. B. Yeats and many others, and up to the time I joined him his profits, when he made any, averaged about £600 or £700 a year.' This, however, did not prevent some authors, who owed everything to T.F.U. for their start, from criticizing him because, in cases where the risk of loss was considerable, he did not feel justified in paying royalty until he had recovered part of his outlay.

I make no apology for this dissertation upon the economics of publishing first novels, because it is relevant to the relationship between T.F.U. and his gifted young reader. Edward Garnett appeared to regard publishers with some contempt because, it was said, they posed as patrons of literature while in fact they honoured most those authors who sold most. They employed readers, he thought, only because they had no standards by which to judge literary value. Well, undoubtedly Fisher Unwin, and other publishers after him, recognized a first-rate reader, and acted upon his advice; but it is a fact that a great many of Garnett's recommendations lost money initially. It was not until the early nineteen-twenties, when he worked for Jonathan Cape, that public taste caught up with him sufficiently for more of the authors he was sponsoring to succeed more quickly.

Evidently dissatisfied with T.F.U.'s conditions, Edward Garnett left him after about ten years to go to Heinemann. After a few years there, he was in trouble with the peppery Willy Heinemann, which resulted in his dismissal; and for a whole summer he was unemployed, he and his wife and son living mainly on mushrooms. Then he went to Duckworth's, where he remained until the outbreak of the 1914 war. Subsequently he was with John Lane, where Mrs. Heilbrunn tells us 'he did badly', and it was only in the atmosphere of the late 1920s and early 1930s that he came into his own. 'He was', she relates, 'a study in contradictions. Incredibly clumsy in appearance, he was in fact agile and quick, able for example to juggle three or four eggs successfully. He had a life-long disability to keep his fly-buttons done up, to the great distress of his wife.'

One way and another, therefore, T.F.U. did not do too badly to have supported Garnett's choices and to have retained his services for ten years; and there is no doubt that Edward Garnett greatly enhanced the distinction of the Fisher Unwin imprint at that time. The same *Pseudonym Library* also attracted the youthful Somerset Maugham, and provided the introduction which led to his writing his first novel, *Liza of Lambeth*, for T.F.U. Maugham's subsequent attack upon the terms offered for this book (which *did* provide full royalties after the first edition) has been fully answered in Stanley's autobiography and I will not repeat it here.

What plainly emerges is that by a willingness to back manuscripts of genuine literary quality—and he always believed that such books would make their way in the end, even if the author were unknown—T.F.U. was building up a list which attracted the attention of critics and promising authors. From this policy stemmed his *First Novel Library*, which he started in about 1910, curiously enough with a book by his sister-in-law. There is no evidence, however, that the indomitable Janie had any hand in its acceptance; probably quite the contrary, because she and her two sisters were rather jealous of each other.

All three of the Cobden girls had married men of some distinction, the other two being the artist Sickert and Cobden Sanderson, the printer who produced beautiful editions de luxe at The Doves Press, Chiswick. The three sisters each insisted upon adding their maiden name to their married style, so that they were known as Mrs. Cobden Unwin, or Mrs. Cobden Sickert; but only one persuaded her husband to tack the name on to his own and thus become for the rest of his life Cobden Sanderson. The name was perpetuated further by the latter's son Richard, who ran a small but distinguished publishing house of his own in the nineteen-twenties and 'thirties.

In the year 1912 the *First Novel Library* attracted Ethel M. Dell, whose books ensured bumper profits for the firm for the next seven or eight years, and in my time it brought in Susan Ertz and no less a find than Dorothy Sayers's first book *Whose Body?*

T.F.U. was always a great one for series of books, and many of them did well in their day, though he clung on to some long after their sales had declined to an uneconomic level. His catalogue of 1917 shows no fewer than twenty-eight different series, ranging from the important and authoritative *Story of the Nations*, *The Mermaid Series* (Restoration Plays) and *Literary History Series* down to literary byways such as *The Welsh Library* or *The Idle Hour Series* (paper covers 1s., cloth 2s.); and he also had an excellent line in children's books with the work of E. Nesbit, whose *Railway Children* has become a successful film. An amusing oddity was *How to be Happy Though Married* by the Rev. E. J. Hardy (not a word about sex), done in six different styles from a Presentation edition in white vellum 7s. 6d., down to a 6d. edition. It sold for years. Their range of subject reveals many of his personal interests, and he did not hesitate to do a book of propaganda for one of his favourite causes even though it was unlikely ever to show a profit.

One of these must have been *The Hungry Forties: An Account of Life under the Bread Tax from the Letters of Living Witnesses*, 'Large Cr. 8vo, cloth 6s.' It is, in its old-fashioned way, an effective polemic for free trade and a typical T.F.U. operation, since over the years he squeezed every ounce of possible sales out of it. After the original edition there was the Reformers Bookshelf at 3s. 6d. (still in cloth) and then the People's Edition in paper at 6d., followed at last by a (surprisingly) 'Complete Edition', again in paper, at 1d.! The second and the last of these manifestations were probably disguised remainders of the immediately previous edition. It was all a splendid tribute to the principles of Richard Cobden and Janie loved it. The book remained in the firm's catalogue to the very end, but what the economics of that penny edition could have been I shudder to think.

Alongside his theory that a book of quality would always make its way in the end was Fisher's reluctance to believe that a book which he cared about could ever die. In a personally-owned business—and until it became a company in about 1920 its style was always 'Mr. T. Fisher Unwin'—it must have been very satisfying to be able to indulge one's own tastes and interests without too much regard for the financial results. Salaries were so low in those days—office workers married and started a family on 30s. a week—that a smallish firm on slender profits could survive without undue difficulties.

Stanley joined T.F.U. in the year 1904, and the next chapter describes his part in the development of the firm. On the surface, his commercial genius complemented admirably his step-uncle's publishing flair, yet mutual antipathies were to destroy the relationship and ruin the chances of any long-term partnership.

Among T.F.U.'s many pioneer activities was his publication of one of the first Freud books to appear in an English translation, *The Psychopathology of Everyday Life*, in the translation by A. A. Brill—

and there was the one author who could probably have probed the cause of Fisher's personality difficulty. Though seemingly of an imperturbable disposition, and not lacking physical courage, he had a highly nervous and irrational streak.

I remember his giving strict instructions to a taxi-driver to take him to Waterloo Station via Westminster, solely to avoid the old Waterloo Bridge, which was then showing signs of weakness and was subject to a 5 m.p.h. speed restriction. Yet at the same time, he did not hesitate to travel on the French railways, which in the early 1920s had an exceptionally bad accident record. On another occasion he went to embarrassing lengths, clad in full evening dress at some Royal Academy soirée, to try to avoid meeting Stanley, though this was over ten years after they had parted in business. In the end they met head on. Stanley was ready for an exchange of courtesies and all passed off without incident, but Fisher, who could show astonishing timidity in some situations, had apparently worked himself up into a state of anxiety over the whole matter.

This basic anxiety was probably responsible for his unfortunate pose, adopted as a protection of some sort, which irritated so many people. He had to be seen as the great and omniscient publisher, the patron of authors, who were exceptionally fortunate to be published by him. If there were some dispute over the terms of an agreement, he would have been reluctant to discuss and explain: his line would have been 'take it or leave it', probably followed by 'Good-bye, good-bye, good-bye', with an airy wave of his hand; his method of terminating an interview which had not gone as he wished.

As A. D. Marks has written, 'My impression of T.F.U. was that he was a lonely man who did not like loneliness. His sense of humour was only slightly developed. He could never understand how he antagonised people yet he was doing it all the time.' He also developed irrational jealousies of members of his staff. There is no firm evidence, but I suspect that he had no close friends, either male or female, of the sort who would have been able to utter the late-Victorian equivalent of 'Fisher, come off it!' I doubt if there had ever been a woman in whose arms he knew total release and that stripping away of pose and pretension which can help a man to find himself. Though Janie was well able to criticize him on some points ('You Unwins are all so placid'— as he peacefully drew on his pipe while she ranted on about cruelty to animals or votes for women), they each had such regard for the importance of the other that she would never have attacked his unfortunate office manner.

When he grew into his seventies and his profits slumped, as the Ethel M. Dell books declined after the 1914 war, poor Fisher found it increasingly hard to make up his mind. As Marks has written, 'In business his ability to avoid a decision was considerable. I have been with him when people have just got up and walked out.'

How the late J. B. Pinker contrived to bring him and Conrad together for the publication of *The Rover* remains a tribute to the skill of a good literary agent. It was in the course of discussion with Pinker, as Fisher wriggled and strove to evade a precise undertaking, that Conrad threatened to chuck his publisher out of his own window on to Adelphi Terrace.

Yet T.F.U. went on to achieve a deserved and resounding success with that book. Its publication on December 3, 1923, was the great event of my three years in his office. Months earlier, before I had started work, my father has spoken with satisfaction of this great book which Unwin Bros. were to print. Two or three times the printing number of the first edition was increased, eventually to 40,000 copies.

'How can Uncle Fisher *know* that he will sell so many?' I asked my father.

'He already has the advance orders from booksellers,' he explained, imparting to me one of my first great truths about publishing.

Conrad had less than a year to live; it was like the publication of a classic in the author's lifetime. The press was tremendous and the book's speed of sale exceeded that of Arnold Bennett's *Riceyman's Steps*, which came out simultaneously. When I ventured to compliment T.F.U. upon his success, which included press interviews with the publisher of this best-seller, he remarked a little grimly, 'we need more *Rovers*'. By then the firm was losing money and one best-seller, particularly when it claimed a 20 per cent royalty, was not enough to retrieve the situation.

His difficulty in personal relations was the tragedy of Fisher's business life. As a publisher he had genuine flair, a sense of the market place, and he knew where to turn to for advice. Even Somerset Maugham wrote that 'he knew how to push his wares and he sent my novel (*Liza of Lambeth*) to a number of influential persons'—not perhaps a very generous reference to a publisher's efforts in the difficult task of securing attention for the work of an unknown author. I have many letters from celebrities of the past thanking T.F.U. for advance copies of his books: in his time he could certainly have given a few tips to many a present-day publicity manager.

He had unfortunately none of Stanley's inbred financial sense, but if he had been prepared sometimes to accept the advice of an accountant with some understanding of publishing he could probably have been saved many losses. After Stanley had taken his departure in 1912, however, I doubt whether Fisher ever listened seriously to, or acted upon, the advice of anyone on the likely profit or loss of the books which he accepted. Even after the formation of the limited Company, the board contained only one man with experience of publishing, A. D. Marks, who had joined the firm as an office boy; Fisher became Governing Director, with power to outvote the rest of the board.

He badly needed a good business partner to keep a tight hold on finances, leaving him to develop the publishing opportunities. Being childless himself, he made great efforts to get some member of the family into the business, but two other nephews, besides Stanley, who had a shot at it both pulled out after a few years. How far I was seen as any sort of successor to them I will never know. He obviously liked to have a young nephew about the place, but it may have been just that he wanted someone to patronize.

Personally, I was always fond of him, as indeed were many of his staff; and probably something of my father's mantle had descended upon me, since he and Janie and Fisher got on well together. After two years in the firm even my inexperienced eye had seen a number of points where economies were possible, and the Governing Director seemed prepared to listen to me. A few changes were made, but they came far too late.

The book-trade strike of 1925 and the General Strike of 1926 dealt body-blows at a business already reeling and facing a serious cash shortage. Moreover, its style was essentially Edwardian, with its emphasis on fiction, memoirs, travel and adventure—much of it excellent in its day, but now no longer in the forefront of public taste. Most serious was the scarcity of textbooks of any sort on the T.F.U. list, those splendid bread-and-butter items which have ever been essential bulwarks to a sound publishing business. Thus the firm became particularly vulnerable to the changing state of the book market, the decline in the purchasing power of the more cultured middle class, who could no longer afford to buy its seven-and-sixpenny novels or half-guinea biographies.

So it was that in the September of 1926, when he was 78, Uncle Fisher, then regarded as the wealthiest and most prominent member of the family, shocked us all, as well as his own staff, by suddenly announcing that he had decided to 'federate' his business with that of Ernest Benn. It was actually a complete take-over, in consideration of a quite good annuity for himself, and with about a third of it to continue for Jane after his death. No one could have believed at that time that he would live on—without his beloved publishing—for nearly nine years more, and that his widow would survive him by over ten years.

They led a comfortable retired existence at their Sussex home Oatscroft, near Heyshott village; and at Dunford House, Cobden's old home nearby, they valiantly organized meetings and conferences to keep alive the Free Trade interest. Right into old age there was no stopping our Aunt Janie.

When T.F.U. died in 1935, the press paid good tribute to the 'doyen' of publishers and recalled his earlier triumphs. But Janie was broken by his death, and for her remaining ten years she lived the life of a total recluse, turning away from the lovely front view of the Downs and retreating into a sunless back bedroom. At over ninety she became increasingly irascible—the parlous state of the world was due to neglect of the principles of Richard Cobden—and she would emphasize her points alarmingly by brandishing at her visitors the stick kept at her bedside to summon her attendant from the floor below. For my father, then well over seventy, the burden of his trusteeship became almost insupportable.

As for me, I reported for duty at Benn's with the rest of the staff on the first Monday in October 1926, and experienced a very different atmosphere there.

5 Background to Stanley Unwin

Stanley always spoke of his parents with affection and often referred to the happiness of his life in the family, but he continually stressed the financial hardship of his youth. In a press interview late in life he spoke of his father as 'practically ruined' after the Chilworth printing works were burnt out in 1895, and to me he once referred to himself and his brothers as 'penniless'.

The word was used in comparison with the more affluent Spicer relatives, but it was rather an exaggeration for a family which, in Stanley's boyhood, must always have had well over £1,000 a year, a quite substantial figure at the price and taxation level of the 1890s. His mother, Elizabeth, received about £800 per annum from the estate of her father James Spicer, and Edward Unwin must have had a like amount from Unwin Bros., even in their lean years. However, his rigid determination never to give less than one-eighth of his income to good causes, plus the heavy mortgage and upkeep of his vast Victorian home near Bromley, in Kent, doubtless made him seem permanently hard up until his old age. Then at last—with Stanley's help—he was able to clear the mortgage and sell the house which had been such an incubus.

Without the gullibility of the father over that unfortunate matter of the house, known as The Mount, his youngest son might never have known that spur of 'poverty' in youth which was certainly a factor in developing his capacity for money-making. All the same, it made a marvellous home for a large Victorian family—six boys and two girls—and for all Edward's grandchildren, who flocked there until he was over eighty. It has now been cut up into five separate dwellings.

Set on the top of Mays Hill, leading up from Shortlands Station, the house had a tennis court, a paddock and stables, as well as the seven greenhouses (requiring constant painting and a full-time gardener to tend the orchids and grapes), which were such a drain on the family's resources. There were no fewer than nine bedrooms—not excessive, allowing for eight children, at least two living-in maids, plus regular visitors—and a huge billiard room on the top floor, which was converted into a children's dormitory at Christmas time. Then twenty-five or more would sit down together for dinner.

Edward was a champion carver, but he never gave anyone enough. He was an artist on the job, cleaned up between every portion and never left a loose crumb of meat on the dish. As he became older he grew slower, so that the senior guests, waiting politely for their host, would have a stone-cold portion by the time they began. If they yielded to the temptation 'not to wait' they were liable to have finished, and be ready for a second helping, before the carver had a chance to eat. But second helpings *were* certainly given. Only when he reached extreme old age did he finally abdicate and leave one of his sons to operate on the joint.

When I knew him he was very much the grand old man of the family. He was in many ways a *dear* old man, and generous to a fault. He was a Past Master of the Worshipful Company of Stationers, and he paid my dues for me to enter the Company when I was only twenty-five and thus young enough to have a chance to achieve worthwhile seniority. His first idea had been to put Stanley in—something he had been unable to afford earlier—but his son, then in his mid-forties, pointed out that he would be too old to enjoy possible Mastership in the Company, if indeed he survived long enough. He therefore urged his father to put me in, if he wanted to continue the family association for as long as possible. That was at a time when Edward had just received a particularly good dividend from Unwin Brothers. Stanley's tart observation to me was that 'Money always burns a hole in his pocket'—though he wholly approved of my becoming a liveryman of the Company.

Edward was not tall, but he was a remarkable figure in old age, with his great, snowy, untrimmed beard, reaching well down on his chest. At the bottom it became a little forked and in earlier photographs, when it was darker in colour, it gave him a slightly Rasputin-like appearance, because his eyes had then a somewhat fanatical look. Later, they seemed merely to twinkle benignly, and with his astonishingly clear pink-and-white complexion he looked the picture of healthy innocence and uprightness. 'Pure and fresh and sinless' was my Mother's description of him, from the famous Baring-Gould hymn *Now the day is over*. Actually this whole verse was probably in the old boy's head every time he went to bed:

> 'When the morning wakens,
> Then may I arise
> Pure and fresh and sinless
> In Thy holy eyes.'

Allied to the terrific beard was a bushy moustache, which hung down over his mouth, concealing a very full lower lip. After eating or drinking he had to resort to the fascinating technique—not unfamiliar in those days—of sucking in the lower part of the moustache to clean off the fragments of the meal adhering to it.

A narrow and rigid form of the Congregational faith was the mainspring of Edward Unwin's life, and his devoted work in that Woodford Sunday School had brought about the introduction to Elizabeth Spicer. No doubt his firm faith helped him to stand his ground against the irate objections of her father, and later it must have sustained him through the years of financial problems. The sure confidence of his faith that all things worked together for good to them that loved the Lord, even if it were in the *very* long run, was plainly his shield and buckler and a complete guard against the acute anxiety and depression which might have struck others in similar circumstances.

In one sense, too, I think that in business matters many high-minded Victorians adopted a somewhat fatalistic attitude towards profits. A 'good' year or a 'bad' year was by no means all their doing— the Almighty took a hand. Thus while they could attribute to His favour a bountiful flow of orders and good profits in one year they did not by any means blame themselves for neglect or misjudgement when business slumped. I am sure Edward lost no sleep over the things he might have done better, or more profitably, for Unwin Brothers and his transparent honesty and good-heartedness brought him the respect of his competitors. For twenty years he was Treasurer of the British Federation of Master Printers.

Within his home the genuine religious faith was buttressed with an appalling amount of outward observance. Where most members of any church today feel they have done well if they attend a Sunday morning service, Edward Unwin's day of rest began with his own Bible reading, followed by his private devotions, probably in the bedroom. Next came the family prayers—originally before breakfast, but altered later to *after* the meal, as unaccountably the older sons increasingly came down just too late for the ritual. Into the drawing-room they trooped, including the maids in their clean print dresses and aprons, freshly washed and ironed for Sunday. A hymn would be sung, accompanied on the piano (books would have been laid out on each of the dozen or so chairs; seventy years ago any 'Non-con' household always had plenty of hymn books), and then there was a Bible reading. After it came that curious movement when all except Father turned about, shuffled reverently on to their knees and buried faces in hands, elbows supported on the recently vacated and nicely warmed chair seat.

Then, as Stanley has written: '. . . my father prayed. His capacity for extempore prayer was unrivalled. There seemed no reason why he should ever stop, and there were times when I irreligiously wondered whether he ever would.' It was mainly a wide-ranging schedule of the manifold blessings of the Almighty and, in the view of at least one of his grandchildren, it had little bearing upon the daily lives of the assembled family. One of them remembers incessantly tracing with her finger the patterned velvet on the back of her chair, another anxiously watched a boy cousin picking a hole through his rush-bottomed chair—but still the unfaltering prayers flowed on. It usually lasted twelve to fifteen minutes—rather more than the average sermon today. Whether the phrases actually included that alleged classic, 'O Lord, as Thou hast doubtless seen in yesterday's *Daily News*', I do not know. (That predecessor of the old *News Chronicle* was standard reading for most Nonconformists.)

The full-dress Chapel service followed, with plenty of hymns and probably a forty-five-minute sermon, and Sunday School in the afternoon. Chapel once more in the evening, and after supper—a final twist of the pious screw—yet again into the drawing-room for another hymn, a reading of the twenty-third psalm and still more prayers. It is not surprising that Stanley, though by no means irreligious, was no churchgoer in adult life. 'I had such a dose of it in my youth', he would say: and once, when I asked him the origin of some unusual quotation in one of his letters, he replied with a benign smile, 'You must remember, the only Sunday reading I was allowed as a boy was the Bible, and you can safely assume that almost any quotation I make is a Biblical one.'

Besides this overladen side of Edward's life, there was the extraordinary amount of his philanthropic activity, which resulted finally in his membership of no fewer than 47 different committees and trusteeships. It is impossible that anyone could make any worthwhile contribution to such a variety of causes, but he left his mark on some of them, such as the Congregational Union and the School for the Sons of Missionaries. To the end of his life, it was a point of honour for him to turn up at all meetings, even though latterly he could hear little of the proceedings. He loved to be seen and to greet people with a busy little wave of the hand, a waggle of the beard and a smile which plainly said, 'Nice to see you, but I'm too busy to stop now.'

Naturally this over-generous devotion of his time to others had to be at the expense of his business life. He reigned as Chairman of Unwin Brothers for close on thirty years, but the evidence of my father's diaries does not suggest that Edward achieved much beyond presiding with unfailing regularity at board meetings, which he kept up until close on ninety. And until the age of 88, he regularly caught the 8.25 train to Holborn every morning.

So, from his father, Stanley derived, apart from a good constitution, a horror of financial mismanagement and a determination not to be short of money in his own life. There was also a strong sense of social obligation and a readiness to lend a hand to the unfortunate, yet a resolute refusal to be drawn into some well-meaning organization if he did not believe he could cut any ice for the cause thereby.

I will not attempt to add much to the moving account of his mother which Stanley wrote in his autobiography. The second eldest child of James Spicer, she was small in stature, but of 'deep underlying power'; as he wrote of her, 'in quietness and confidence was her strength'. She was genuinely religious and one of her favourite maxims was 'Be sure your sins will find you out'—repeated in later life by her youngest son as a warning to anyone in A. & U. that if he—or she—cut some corner in office routine or concealed a mistake, it would not escape the eagle eye of the boss.

Elizabeth Spicer—our 'Aunt Lizzie'—had much of her father's acumen, which obviously ran straight on to S.U. In any sort of business situation he trusted her judgement more than his father's. Understandably, when he grew up, she trusted him with the management of her financial affairs. After her husband's doubtful competence in money matters, it must have been a satisfaction to find a member of her own family possessed of great shrewdness. I often think this was largely responsible for the fact that Stanley's perpetual readiness to hold forth upon his achievements seems never to have come in for a maternal rebuke. Though 'modest' was a favourite word of his, especially in relation to salary increases or royalty rates to authors, personal modesty was not one of the virtues inculcated in his youth.

Lizzie's devotion to the welfare of others less well-off than herself meant that the only visitors to the home, apart from numerous relatives, were largely missionaries and their families, connected with the school which Edward supported so ardently. In effect, the Edward Unwins had no social life in their neighbourhood; they remained apart and 'different', but this increased their independence and firm belief in their own point of view. If one adds to this Stanley's position as the youngest among six argumentative and outspoken brothers—all but one of them bearded—one can readily see how he came to stick up for himself, to develop the combative side of his nature and become, as more than one observer has remarked to me, 'a good chap to have on your side in a scrap', especially if it were against officialdom.

The other great influence in Stanley's youth was Abbotsholme School and its fiery headmaster, Dr. Cecil Reddie, whom he described as 'both a genius and a crank'. The doctor's highly unconventional methods and hypnotic influence were disastrous for some of his pupils, but they undoubtedly succeeded with 'Unwin 6'. Stanley was preceded at the school by three of his brothers and two cousins: one of them would say that Reddie had transformed his whole outlook on life; another, that his education had been 'completely mucked up' at Abbotsholme. Certainly there was no guarantee that an average Abbotsholme pupil would be ready to matriculate at seventeen, and since S.U. left at fourteen, he had no chance to distinguish himself scholastically. His reputation as a law-abiding little boy plus his quickness of thought earned him the nickname of 'The Holy Ghost on Wheels'.

C.R., as the headmaster was known, was an undoubted pioneer, and many of his ideas, considered as outlandish at the time, have been adopted today by public schools. Stanley wrote that C.R. 'had the greatest contempt for the mere memorizing of facts for examination purposes'. 'Facts', he used to thunder, 'can be got by any fool from works of reference: what matters is that you should learn to *think*.' As early as 1898 he would warn them of the growing competition of the Germans, who came to England to work as volunteers in our factories, 'sucked our brains' and then returned to their own country, to improve on English methods and do the job better than we did.

'I determined', said Stanley, 'that when I left school I would go to Germany and do some of the sucking.' And this he insisted upon doing, after about three years in a city shipping office, before he started with T. Fisher Unwin. Throughout his life he never neglected that dictum to think for himself. The simplest action or situation was rarely settled purely by routine; every pro and con was weighed up briskly before the decision was taken. No opportunity to save money was ever missed.

On an early visit to Germany he learned that excellent system by which one can buy, on the trams, a form of season ticket which entitles one to about ten journeys at a slightly reduced price. The ticket is punched for each journey one makes. Some sixty years later I was with him at Frankfurt one morning, at a time when he could, if he had wished, have put his hands on a six-figure sum. Disdaining the bunch of publishers waiting for taxis to take them from the Frankfurter Hof Hotel to the Book Exhibition, we scooted off to the nearby tram stop.

'Don't forget,' he said, as we stepped aboard the tram, 'you can save ten per cent by getting the season ticket.' I duly saved it. The system had been familiar to me about thirty years earlier, but I had not troubled with it since—there was always the risk of losing the damn ticket. Four days later, on the Sunday morning when I was packing up to return to London on an early flight, he looked into my room. He was clad in his dressing-gown and had come, very decently I thought, to say good-bye, as he was staying on for a few days. 'By the way,' he said, 'have you got any journeys left on your tram ticket?—if so, I'll have it!'

To some it might appear as meanness, but it was also characteristic of his unflagging capacity to 'use his loaf' under all circumstances. To think independently and to have the courage of his convictions were undoubted legacies of his Abbotsholme days, and the tough roots in

Nonconformity ensured that he never cared tuppence for the opposing views of others. There was no need to 'if', as he would say a trifle piously, 'you have thought out the situation and you are convinced that what you are doing is right'.

It is interesting that Stanley's start in publishing did not come about through any premeditation on his part; indeed *I* could claim to have had a more definite eye on it from an early age than he. In his own writing he makes no reference to the possibilities of publishing as a career until his father's younger step-brother, T. Fisher Unwin, invited S.U. and his elder brother for a weekend to the Cobden-Unwin home near Midhurst. It became clear that he had been sent for 'on sale or return', as Stanley put it. He was duly inspected and approved, and on the Sunday evening T.F.U. asked if he would like to enter his business. Even at the age of about eighteen, Stanley had a searching look at and into the mouth of the gift horse, and much to the annoyance of his step-uncle, who wanted him to begin at once, insisted on a visit to Germany before starting his publishing career.

S.U. was a born entrepreneur. I have often wondered whether his natural ability to handle money might not have led him further into the City. Once, when speaking of the career of an enormously success-ful financier who had just died, Stanley remarked to me (a shade wist-fully?), 'It's the sort of thing I could have done on my head.' But he added, 'Only I should have been ashamed to have spent my life that way.' It was true, and there lay the influence of home and school. Certainly he had far more interest out of life as a publisher.

S.U. has described at some length his hardships and privations during those nine months in Germany, when he lived with rigid economy upon a very small allowance from his father, buttressed by a few very carefully nurtured Christmas boxes from the Spicer uncles. It was a considerable feat to have covered the distances he did in Ger-many and to have sustained life, while travelling, on a diet of bread, cheese and sausage bought, as he quaintly put it, 'by weight' and eaten in his bedroom.

Again, it was a masterpiece of youthful ingenuity and sheer guts to have contrived to travel from Leipzig to Berlin and back (about 100 miles each way), and to live in the capital for a fortnight, on a total sum of £3, at the same time cajoling *German* booksellers to place firm orders to the value of £150 for Fisher Unwin books in *English*, when they normally took their books on sale or return. It was an achievement which he delighted to recount to any willing listener in years to come, but one cannot help feeling that at the time he was a glutton for punishment. Still, he was agog to prove himself and he succeeded to the hilt: it was a far cry from the travelling scholarships and lush expense accounts of today.

Years later, he would say to would-be book trade recruits—myself included—'If you are to make good in publishing you must have German experience'; but in fact he had little or no *publishing* experience during his months there apart from acting as traveller for Fisher Unwin. After a term's intensive study of German in a school, he spent three and a half months working twelve hours a day as a 'volunteer' (without pay) in a Leipzig bookshop, whence he derived his life-long admiration of German book trade organization. His time in Germany, moreover, turned him to some extent into a European; it began to give him an international outlook, shared at that time by few other English publishers besides William Heinemann and T.F.U. himself. It was partly responsible for the strongly German flavour in the Allen & Unwin list fifteen years later, and above all, it inspired Stanley's intensely professional attitude towards every detail of publishing.

His early encounter with Fisher Unwin set the pattern for their eight years together. The older and the younger, their different qualities complementary to each other, were able together to achieve so much in a publishing business. At the same time there was arrogance and jealousy (at first meanness) on one side and a degree of confidence and a maddening tendency to be right every time on the other—coupled with a difficulty of communication—which must have made frank discussion impossible.

One must, of course, accept the statement that T.F.U.'s profits rose tenfold, from about £700 to £7,000 a year, during Stanley's time with him; but these results were not the work of a single man. (I could claim with equally doubtful relevance, that Allen & Unwin's profits went up well over forty times during the forty years I was there.) It seems likely that the Fisher Unwin business was ripe for a breakthrough around 1904. His literary discoveries of the 'nineties, such as Conrad, were beginning to sell more. Helped by the establishment of the Net Book Agreement, booksellers were in a less precarious situation. Possibly, too, State education was having its effect, with a growing public for books: Frank Swinnerton has described the Edwardian era as a time when the book trade was no longer in a 'parlous' condition.

I am not suggesting for one moment that Stanley's intensive work and his commercial genius did not have a considerable effect on his uncle's business, but it is interesting to assess how much of it was shrewd handling of business detail and how much was 'publishing' as it is generally understood. With one important exception, he never spoke of having personally secured any new author for the firm, apart from the Canadian Robert W. Service. A volume of his poems, *The Songs of a Sourdough*, had been offered by the Canadian publishers, and against a general feeling in the editorial committee, S.U. had very sensibly pressed for a trial importation of 250 copies. The eventual sale of Service's books ran up to many thousands and they were a staple item in the firm's list a good ten years later—in my time.

The other exception was H. G. Wells's *Ann Veronica*, which resulted from S.U.'s having suggested to Fisher Unwin that he write to Wells saying that he would welcome the opportunity to publish 'some further work from his pen' (what earlier book he had published for Wells I cannot now trace). As Stanley described in his autobiography, he persuaded his uncle to gamble on the £1,500 outright payment which Wells demanded. It was a big amount for those days, and I have seen the old T.F.U. ledger which records the rapid sale of the serial rights for £400 and the American rights for the lump sum of £525, by which Stanley quickly began to justify the original expenditure.

I suspect that it still took quite a long time before the remaining £675, out of the £1,500, was earned on the published price of 6s. (usual for a pre-1914 novel). However, the book sold for years: it unquestionably proved profitable, after a year or two, and the whole transaction was a considerable feather in Stanley's cap. Not many in publishing land so big a fish at the age of twenty-three, and it all demonstrated to the full his remarkable capacity to see the financial bearings of any situation. Even at that tender age, as he coolly remarked years later, T.F.U. 'on financial matters . . . invariably followed my advice'.

Two other coups that he pulled off, getting the agencies for the sale of the Baedeker Guides and of the Ordnance Survey Maps, were both highly profitable in those far-off days of low wages. Nowadays such agencies are not so attractive, as they offer less than the normal margin of profit, while thanks to much higher wages, the costs to a publisher of merely handling any books are so much greater. These outstanding examples of good business deals, it will be seen, were essentially at the commercial (including the sale of American, foreign and serial rights) rather than the 'literary' end of publishing, and the state of T.F.U.'s business was ideal for development by Stanley's talents.

The firm had the books and some famous authors, many of them Garnett's discoveries; now they had another good reader in Will Dircks. They had a fine trade manager in A. D. Marks, and one of the best-known London travellers in 'Jack' Crane. An Irishman, with his full share of blarney, he was a real bookman and one who could coax a good order out of the most stony-hearted buyer. He was a great admirer of Stanley, and he recalled to me once the shock he felt on hearing that Stanley had resigned—and still worse that the resignation had been accepted.

'I said to the Governor,' were Crane's words to me, ' "You are not going to let that young man go?"—"Yes," he said, and just left it at that. Oh, Mr. Stanley [went on Crane, with a catch in his voice], he was wonderful—he knew just how to exaggerate the truth!'

Crane was the highest paid member of the staff, earning, with his commission, over £1,000 a year before 1914, and I know that Stanley regarded him at times as an expensive luxury. But he was a super-salesman, and he played a crucial part in putting over the first Ethel M. Dell novel. The whole business of that book showed the qualities of T.F.U., S.U. and Crane all in a perfect combination. Fisher had the ideas originally, for his *First Novel Library*, then for the prize competition for first novels which brought in *The Way of an Eagle*. It had been declined by eight other publishers, but the firm's reader patiently coached the author through extensive revision and Stanley tied her up with a contract to cover four novels. The royalty terms were fair and the advances reasonable, if not extravagant.

Jack Crane then performed one of his most passionate selling operations in building up the advance orders from London booksellers. Guessing rightly that Ethel M. Dell could be a huge success with women readers, he insisted that the chief buyer of W. H. Smith's head office should get his *wife* to read the advance copy. She sat up all night, so the story goes, entranced by 'the novel with the ugly hero'—then insisted that her husband should support it well. What number the buyer originally offered to take is not known, but Crane said, 'If you take a thousand copies I'll arrange for you to have another thousand on sale or return.' It was agreed; so Smith's gave the book full distribution right from the start, and it was a resounding success.

Within three years, from 1912 to 1915, there were twenty-seven printings, 'each larger than the previous one' it was said. Ten years later, when I was in the Adelphi Terrace office, I came upon printing order books which recorded cheap reprints of 250,000 at a time, done during the 1914 war.

A fifth novel, *Greatheart*, was taken later on; but much stiffer terms were demanded, since Stanley's four-novel contract had then been fulfilled.

The break between Fisher and the highly-profitable Ethel, who by that time was a wealthy woman, came over such a trivial matter as the number of free copies she should have of her books. I can imagine his irritation that an author whom he had made so successful should squeeze the firm in this way, but he paid dearly for his refusal to pander to her whim. At their peak, her books accounted for half the total sales of the business.

I have outlined these strengths of the Fisher Unwin firm not to denigrate Stanley, whose qualities of salesmanship and financial acumen were second to none, and far beyond anything that I could ever claim, but to show that he did have particularly good material to work with and associates of exceptional capacity and enthusiasm.

That he worked hard, skilfully and conscientiously for his 'step-uncle' there can be no doubt, and the pay, for the first five years, was modest, to say the least. Stanley joined him in 1904, and as late as 1908—after the nephew had made his first and highly successful trip to the States, had acted as the principal witness for the firm in a libel action, and held a power of attorney for the Principal—he was still being paid only £150 a year. That may well have been above average for a young man of only twenty-three, but it was scarcely adequate to his responsibilities and his contribution to the success of the business. On pressure from Stanley, T.F.U. raised him to £200 and promised another £50 at the end of 1908, and similar increases for the next two years.

By the time he reached £300 in 1910, he had found 'the constant pin-pricks unbearable' (petty ways in which T.F.U. often treated him like the merest junior), and he resigned; whereupon there was an immediate doubling of his salary to £600. The same thing happened in 1911, when he reached £1,200—quite princely for pre-1914 days (the equivalent of at least £10,000 today), and coming from Fisher Unwin a crystal clear indication of Stanley's value to him. The younger man was then willing to remain only if he could be Managing Director of a newly formed company under the chairmanship of his senior. But the onerous terms laid down in the draft articles of association proved quite unacceptable to Stanley, and they parted company for ever on April 1, 1912—a date I always associate with the sinking of the *Titanic*, a fortnight later.

Family dovecots fluttered. Naturally enough, S.U. was thought by many to have been a fool to give up so good a job with nothing else immediately in prospect. Indeed, it was about another seven years before his income again reached £1,200 per annum. The T.F.U. profits burgeoned, largely on Ethel M. Dell, until the end of the war, but then declined sharply.

With characteristic independence of mind, coupled still with the determination to master every detail of his profession, Stanley promptly invested part of his savings in the world tour he made in 1913 of all the overseas markets for British books, apart from Europe and North America, which he already knew. In those days, it was a pioneering effort, which gained him great good will among Dominion booksellers and a small number of valuable contacts with authors. It was his proud and justifiable boast that on one deal he made later with an Australian bookseller, whose special requirements he had studied, he recouped the entire cost of the tour.

When I first met Stanley, nothing impressed me more than the sublime confidence which had led him (a) to throw up an excellent job because he did not like his chief, (b) to spend much of his money going round the world to improve his knowledge—also, it must be admitted, for the fun of it, then (c) to buy his way into a bankrupt publishing house, and at the same time (d) to get married.

Once, when asked whether he had any serious qualms over the outcome of (c), his reply was characteristic, if a little hard on Fisher: 'I had built up one derelict concern and I didn't doubt my ability to do it again.'

Having known both of them, I can imagine the point of view of each; but plainly it was that inordinate jealousy of Fisher's, referred to in the previous chapter, which made Stanley feel his position to be impossible. Yet even without that, since T.F.U. remained active in the business for another fourteen years, it would have been difficult for S.U. to have developed it, during the whole of that time, along the radical and left-wing lines which appealed to him.

It remains a tribute to his courage and clear-sightedness that he was prepared to take the decision when he did.

6 The Start of Allen & Unwin

Of the many difficult and complex tasks which my Uncle Stanley tackled in the course of his long life the resuscitation of the old firm of George Allen was surely the most involved, and it was the one upon which, in 1914, he risked all of his capital and his reputation.

After Ruskin's death in 1900 the sales of his books declined, and this had a serious effect on the profits of his publisher. Allen's, by 1911, were an amalgamation of two firms, each of which had begun in the 'seventies of the last century, 'each in its way representing and furthering all that was most serious, forward-looking and responsible in Victorian thinking and writing'. This quotation is from a booklet produced in 1964 to mark the Jubilee of Allen & Unwin. It continued: 'The first of these two houses, George Allen, originated in 1871, when John Ruskin appointed his pupil, Allen, a skilled engraver and joiner, and later a teacher of art, to act as publisher of the sage's books. The other was Swan Sonnenschein & Co., founded in 1878 by the English-born son of a Moravian immigrant who had made a substantial contribution to the educational life of his adopted land.' Ruskin, who had started Allen on his way, and Adolf Sonnenschein, father of the founder of the other firm, were both linked through their work for adult education, and especially the Working Men's College. It is not surprising, therefore, that the books published by these two houses should have shown a strong social consciousness and a leaning towards education and social reform. There was no other publishing house in London at that moment whose general character was better suited to Stanley's whole outlook; as he has written, it was 'an ideal firm from my point of view' and—a favourite phrase—'it looked as if providence was very much on my side'.

The more technical aspects of an insolvent publisher's accounts and stock valuation can mislead many a chartered accountant unfamiliar with the book trade, but by the time he was 29, Stanley was well versed in such matters, and he knew the pitfalls.

The probing search for the reality behind the figures, the long, patient analysis of stock schedules, in order to arrive at a realistic valuation, and then the presentation of his case, and the ensuing arguments, were meat and drink to him. All this, followed by the unresting drive to build up the newly created firm, brought his exceptional business talents into full play. I believe there was nothing else in the world which gave him greater satisfaction, and certainly for nearly thirty years, long after A. & U. was firmly established, he never lost his appetite for the buying up of small publishing houses which came on to the market.

It was his nature to master every fact of any situation which confronted him. In his later years, it might be said that he devoted too much of his time to minor details (and the maddening presentation of them late in the afternoon to colleagues fully occupied with what they thought were more important matters), but always he 'knew his stuff' and he had the imagination and elasticity of mind to seek solutions to the problem by a side, or even a back door, if the front one was barred.

His total grasp of liens and their implication was a key factor in the success of his offer for the assets of George Allen & Co. A 'lien' is defined as the 'right to hold another's property until a debt is paid', and a bankrupt publisher's stock usually contains some thousands of books held by printers and binders whose bills have not been paid. As he wrote in his autobiography, 'An offer for the assets [of a business] free of lien—the usual method—means that the receiver has to pay off all the liens, which reduces the value of the offer by that amount.' S.U.'s systematic examination of the Allen stocks held subject to lien showed that there was much which he would not want to use for years (so it would not matter if the printer refused to release it), and equally there were cases where he could undoubtedly persuade the printer to hand over the stock for less than the amount of the debt. Since it is the owner of the publishing business who alone holds the right to sell the books in question, the printer can be sued if he sells the stock himself. Thus he has a strong incentive to release the stock at some figure well below that of the outstanding debt.

Stanley was particularly adept at this sort of negotiation. Confidently then, he made his offer 'subject to lien', and it was accepted. There were other complications (described in his book), but he picked his way through them and secured his vital stake in the new company of George Allen & Unwin Ltd., formed to take over the Allen business.

He had to gamble on his superior knowledge of publishing to give him speedy dominance over the former Allen directors, for he bought himself into the firm on terms which meant his 'carrying' these three existing directors. At his insistence, all four, including himself, were to draw only £300 per annum, with no increase on this save by unanimous vote of the board. It was essential that they should limit their pay in this fashion if the firm was to be built up, and it was typical of S.U. that he cheerfully accepted this self-denying ordinance, although he had been earning double, and for his last year four times, that amount with Fisher Unwin.

Though the whole arrangement was far from ideal, it fulfilled one

of his important conditions for attempting to run a firm of his own: he
was not starting a new business from scratch, with that anxious first year
or so to get through before he could hope to see any of his money back.
With Allen's, who had been going for over forty years, there was a
useful back list of steadily selling books, including Ruskin's works, which
had continued to bring in about £1,000 a month in sales even during the
period of the Receivership, when no *new* books had been published.

The new Company was formally registered on August 4, 1914, and
at once the outbreak of war reduced the ostensible value of the assets
by about a third. S.U. had to face some years at a much reduced income,
he was considered a fool to have thrown up the Fisher Unwin job, and
among other publishers he found himself cold-shouldered and denied
membership of the Publishers Association, because it was thought that
he had treated William Allen badly. This charge was wholly un-
founded as Mr. Allen, the son of the founder, had left the business six
months before Stanley came on the scene, and at that time they had no
dealings of any kind together.

The former Allen offices in Rathbone Place, off Oxford Street, were
too expensive, so Stanley, attracted by the nearness of the British
Museum, plumped for 40 Museum Street as their new premises.
George Speed, then head of the warehouse and packing department,
was a trusty pillar of the firm who had worked for George Allen in the
Ruskin days. He told me years later how he had stood on the pavement
gloomily surveying the proposed new offices.

'It was one of those terrible, hot, steamy September days', he said.
'You could 'ardly breathe—and there was our new guv'nor, 'e 'ad a
long brown beard then, 'e flung open the street door and it all looked
just awful! Muck and rubbish everywhere. I stood and looked at it.
"Come along, come along," 'e says, and in we went, and 'e was all
over that building like a terrier after a rat.'

With the semi-derelict warehouse at the rear, it provided all that
was absolutely necessary for the firm to develop and flourish for the
next sixteen years (until partial rebuilding in 1930). The George
Allen business was ideal material for Stanley to work upon, because it
actually had three different sides, each of which was susceptible to his
capacity to ferret out unusual ways of making them profitable. For
him, the most interesting was the list of Swan Sonnenschein, with
which Allen's had amalgamated in 1911. It included the very early
books of J. M. Barrie, Bernard Shaw and George Moore. There were
also a number of important Socialist works, including the first English
edition of Volume 1 of Marx's *Capital*.

The Library of Philosophy, edited by Professor J. H. Muirhead, was
another of their treasures, and I was proud to take a hand in its revival
after the 1939 war, under the skilful editorship of Professor Hywell

Lewis. In its early days it was published mainly for its prestige and as a contribution to the wider appreciation of English philosophy; it was to be many years before the vast expansion of university education all over the world would make it a profitable venture. Nevertheless, it was one of his new acquisitions of which Stanley was justly proud, and he never failed to support the Editor's acceptances, though on most of the books in the series the publisher had to wait five and sometimes nearer ten years before he saw his money back.

The *Social Science Series,* including such worthies as Holyoake and Beatrice Webb, was all very much in line with S.U.'s radical views, while another Sonnenschein author, Edward Carpenter, whose work included his classic *Towards Democracy,* was strongly in sympathy with the teachings of Abbotsholme School. Finally, there was the first translation, by Dr. Brill, of Freud's *Interpretation of Dreams,* an author with whom Sonnenschein had pioneered (like Fisher Unwin) many years before the boom in psychoanalysis began.

On the Allen side of the business, Ruskin's books had been dominant, and as I have said, it was their decline in sales which had been the main reason for the collapse of the firm. But there were also such classics as Belloc's *The Path to Rome,* Augustus Hare's *The Story of My Life,* the works of Maurice Maeterlinck and the Gilbert Murray translations of the Greek dramatists.

The third strand was made up of the smaller Bemrose list, which was mainly topographical, but included—surprisingly enough in view of the Unwin religious background—certain Anglican publications.

Senior members of the staff, some of whom were department heads, had been drawn from all three of these once independent firms. An immediate frustration for the new owner was to be told, when he asked one man about what proved to be an Allen book, 'Don't know anything about that, I'm a Bemrose man', or when he asked another about a Sonnenschein book, that it was nothing to do with him, *he* was an Allen man. After a day of this, S.U. delivered his ultimatum: 'The next man who gives me this answer again gets the sack—from now on every book is a George Allen & Unwin book.'

He quickly showed his mettle and that he knew what he was about. I can well imagine the brisk and energizing sense of purpose he would have injected into the staff, and best of all—for them—he saw that their near-starvation wages (£1 13s. for a married warehouseman and child) were quickly increased.

Sartorially, he cast aside the top hat, frock coat and stiff collars of the T.F.U. days, and was later to claim that he had always worn a soft collar from the time he had his own business. He also contented himself with a poky downstairs office—from which, however, he 'could see everyone who came into or left the building'.

Once again, Stanley had a foundation of excellent books, as in the T.F.U. business; but contrary to his experience there, he now had no one else besides himself to provide publishing ideas and judgement. Virtually all constructive ideas, and the drive for new authors, had to come from him. Two of his fellow directors were quickly involved in war service and did not reappear until the end of 1918, while the third was called up in 1917.

A thorough search through the basement of the old Allen premises in Rathbone Place revealed stock thought to be unsaleable. The new managing director's knowledge of world markets enabled him to 'remainder' it (sell it off at a reduced price) successfully and 'turn it into cash'. Years later some of us might smile among ourselves as our 'Guv'nor' insisted on racking his brains to find a remainder-buyer willing to pay a few pence per copy for some outdated book on a forgotten subject which we wanted to pulp; at a time when the firm's cash position was more than ample, we might feel that directorial time could be spent more profitably, but this was yet another of the famous lessons of his youth. The ability quickly to turn old stock into money was vital, however, to the early build-up of Allen & Unwin.

The first deal in a new book was a typical piece of improvisation. S.U. was offered a manuscript by M. Phillips Price (later an authority on Russia and an M.P.), entitled *The Diplomatic History of the War*. As a small boy I remember seeing the book on my father's bookshelf, an imposing demy octavo volume bound in dark red cloth and bulking nearly two inches. The basic text was a short summary of the diplomatic moves leading up to August 4th, but the official white, red, yellow and blue books issued by the various Allied governments, stating their particular case, were obtained free of charge and bound up at the end of Mr. Price's comparatively brief book—hence the substantial and authoritative volume, for which the publisher's production costs were minimal.

The book was highly topical, it was widely reviewed, and it sold well. It was unfortunately a cause of fury to step-Uncle Fisher. Shoals of orders for it poured into Adelphi Terrace, since at that moment, naturally, to the majority of booksellers the name of Unwin as a publisher's imprint at once suggested T. Fisher Unwin. Sad to relate, he let his feelings run away with him to the extent of forbidding his staff to send on the orders to Allen & Unwin. The book was just reported to the booksellers as 'not known'. It is fair to say that whenever an order for a T.F.U. book was received by Stanley, he had it forwarded to its rightful publisher. S.U. was also scrupulous not to 'pinch' any Fisher Unwin author, though some brought MSS to him. There is no evidence that he ever showed any tendency to gloat over his uncle's later lack of success—rather the reverse.

Had Stanley been content to trade simply under the name of George Allen & Co. his former boss would never have worked up the feud so bitterly. As S.U. said, 'To Uncle Fisher it was unforgivable that through my action he was now no longer the only Unwin in publishing.' When I worked for T.F.U. he used to refer to Stanley as 'that confounded relative of yours!' and when Stanley's wife-to-be, Mary Storr, called at Adelphi Terrace to pay her respects shortly before their marriage, she was not received.

Never the conventional 'ladies' man', Stanley's tremendous vitality was nevertheless an undoubted attraction for some women, noticeable at any book trade gathering in his old age. (At his eightieth birthday celebrations, it was charming to see the number of our lady guests who put up their cheeks for a bristly kiss.) On the winter sports parties he organized at Lenzerheide for three years, from 1909, Stanley would have been at the top of his youthful form, skating and dancing and playing the piano for the singers in the evening; and it was there that he fell in love with Mary. Her father, Rayner Storr, at one time a partner in the prosperous firm of Debenham, Storr, was another man of independent views, a Positivist, whose highly individual outlook had kept him and his family somewhat apart from the normal stream of social life. That his daughter was no conventional church-going girl may well have been an added attraction to Stanley, but the upbringing of them both was perhaps one reason why the pattern of a life with little social contact continued on into their married home.

None of us who came to know our Auntie Mary could fail to love her and to admire the close personal interest which she would take, even in the families of her great-nieces, when she was far into her eighties. There could be no question as to the durability of the marriage, but I often regretted that Stanley did not give his wife more encouragement to appear with him in public; when she did so her gentle charm, shrewdness and thought for others won all hearts.

S.U.'s respect and affection for many Germans, and his international outlook and knowledge of European countries, made the whole idea of the war repugnant to him. Though not a declared conscientious objector, he adopted the pacifist standpoint from the start, while undertaking strenuous V.A.D. duties. He was particularly receptive to books by what he termed 'the unpopular minority', notably left-wingers who did not regard all Germans as evil, and those who, later on, favoured a negotiated peace. Moreover, this group of intellectuals did buy books.

The printing numbers might be small and the market limited, but it was reasonably certain. The worthy book of patient merit, sometimes with an author willing to put up part of the cost of publication, also made its useful contribution; and agencies, such as those for the booklets of the Fabian Society (agreement negotiated on tough terms by Sidney Webb), were not despised. By unspectacular means Stanley sought all the time to guard against big risks and to adhere to one of his favourite dicta: 'Avoid losses and the profits will take care of themselves.' In itself, a thundering good discipline for the building-up of a small publishing business at any time.

Though larger risks have inevitably to be faced as a firm grows beyond a certain size, it has always interested me to see how frequently —almost unfailingly—the competent if unexciting specialist book printed in a modest number, and perhaps partially insured by an advance order from some interested party, will make money. The policy of many small risks and seldom a large one, started almost willy-nilly in 1914, continued for over half a century and served the firm extraordinarily well. Among the small risks there will always be some books that develop into big sales.

There was, of course, the inspired dash for Bertrand Russell, whose articles in American magazines, notably *The Atlantic Monthly*, had caught Stanley's attention. His exploratory note to Russell led to the publication of *Principles of Social Reconstruction*, and so began the long professional association between the two men, so very different in background, yet sharing perhaps an independence born of their early conditioning. The great Russell-S.U. saga was one of the most satisfactory and mutually profitable author-publisher relationships of the century, yet they had remarkably little contact face to face, and in the fifty years of their collaboration they seldom had a meal together. Certainly Russell never came to Stanley's house, and he visited Russell in his own home only once or twice, towards the end when Russell, in his nineties, found it difficult to get about. Yet after one of their rare meetings his publisher would be full of the latest story Russell had told him and show every sign of having enjoyed a lively conversation with the great man.

On more than one occasion Stanley was away when important matters cropped up, and I had the opportunity of dealing with Lord Russell myself. The first was in 1929, when he called unannounced on a Saturday morning, in a tweedy aroma of pipe and countryside (it was during the period of his school near Petersfield), to deliver the typescript of *Marriage and Morals*. Contracted for under the title of *Sex Freedom*, it was a book which all the young men in the office were dying to read: I dropped all other work for the rest of the Saturday morning. Well ahead of its time, like so many of his general books, this one advanced ideas which are now widely accepted and it still sells happily in its eighteenth impression.

Another time, in 1956, when the Chief was on one of his overseas missions, there came over the telephone that unmistakable, slightly reedy, gravelly voice, with its effortlessly beautiful diction, saying modestly, 'Oh, Russell he-ah, could I come along late this afternoon and bring you some biographical essays I've written? My wife will be with me.' Needless to say, everything else was again pushed on one side and a phone call home warned that I should be late back. At about half-past five, this distinguished couple arrived and I had the great pleasure of meeting his fourth wife, Edith, for the first time: to me it was all delightful and memorable.

Then, almost casually, he produced the typescript of the book which became *Portraits from Memory*, in some respects a deeply interesting preview of the Autobiography, which followed over ten years later. He had mentioned it to Stanley, but there was no contract for the book, no heavy gunning from an agent and pressure for the highest possible terms. Large advances were not normally paid on signature of the agreement for his books, but it was understood that he was always welcome to have a general advance at any time he wanted money.

A glance at the typescript left me in no doubt whatever of its popular appeal, so towards the end of the meeting, when I asked if any advance payment had been discussed and Lord Russell said 'No', I chanced my arm and said, 'Would you like £1,000 straight away?' (With serial and translation rights included, this was hardly a risk.) 'Oh, really?' he remarked, seemingly in some surprise, and his eyes lit up still more brightly. 'Thank you, that would be very nice indeed.'

I was proud to have been able to please him and to demonstrate in the presence of Lady Russell our immediate willingness to offer cash down upon the new manuscript; but the remarkable thing was that it seemed an entirely new experience for him to have the offer of a large advance. I do not think that Stanley had ever done such a thing with Russell, and he may well have considered my action precipitate when he learned of it later. 'Russell knows he can always have money when he asks for it', would have been the reaction; but that is not quite the same thing.

In the course of that interview, the sales of Russell's earlier books were mentioned and he remarked, 'I must say, your uncle is very good at keeping my older books going. Ones that I wrote more than thirty years ago, I still see them earning royalties for me—and all those foreign editions too!'

It was perhaps no more than good A. & U. routine work, but it was part of Stanley's professional attitude and his almost relentlessly efficient handling of the affairs of our most important author. Every Russell book had to carry, opposite the title-page, the full list of all his other works; and if there was a blank page at the end, it had to carry advertisements of them as well—and woe betide the Production Manager if he ever slipped up on these points! Similarly, every one of his books had to be reprinted as it sold out, even if in some cases the demand was slow and it might take years to recover the outlay.

There was only one time, around 1934, when he was passing through a difficult period domestically, that I can recall any letter of even implied complaint from Bertrand Russell, and then he did publish a comparatively slight and topical book with another firm. We were much upset at the time, but it was an isolated incident and the great man returned to us with his next and all subsequent books. I think he fully accepted one of the tenets of my uncle's faith, that the books of one author concentrated with a single publisher could help to sell each other in a way that was impossible if they were spread over the lists of several different firms. Unquestionably it worked that way with Russell. Booksellers turned to us automatically for any of his books, except the immortal *Principia Mathematica*, which 'everyone' knew was done by the Cambridge University Press.

Rightly he came to occupy the first, and commanding, position upon the A. & U. list. S.U. saw to it that only our best printers were entrusted with Russell manuscripts (though they were so immaculately prepared that almost any printer could have handled them successfully), and under the acute paper shortage in the 1939 war, a generous allocation from our meagre ration always went to his books.

The start, and the enduring success, of the Russell relationship was all typical of Stanley. First, the approach to one whose forward-looking ideas attracted him enormously, then the fearless determination to publish, and to go on publishing, the books of one who was so out of favour with authority that he was imprisoned for a time in the 1914 war. And following this, the forty years of steady, unfailing acceptance of every book as it came along, although for more than half of this time Russell was no popular world figure; many an average reader probably thought of him as a crank with, to say the least, very curious ideas of morality. There was no attempt to persuade him to write any particular sort of book, and no fulsome praise of any new manuscript he sent in. Between these two men, essentially of the Victorian age, the purely business relationship appeared to suit them best. Stanley once admitted, perhaps a trifle wistfully, that he 'never knew Russell very well', but in his youthful approach during the early years of A. & U., he had made the greatest coup of his publishing career.

It was a source of encouragement to Stanley, if embarrassing, to have Fisher Unwin authors offering him their manuscripts, and to have members of his staff seeking employment in Museum Street. For all the 'school mastering' which he had doubtless practised at Adelphi Terrace, he had been popular among his colleagues and I have no doubt that even in his twenties he had infused them with that sense of purpose and interest in the job which was always one of his best characteristics. Stanley did not take on any of the T.F.U. staff at that stage, save for one man who, he thought, had been sacked rather harshly after an irregularity with the firm's cash. He was given a second chance with A. & U. and worked well for a time, but then reverted to his former practice and again had to be sent upon his way. It was the old story of the dishonest traveller who collects accounts, receiving cash payments from customers, and then fails to hand in the money to the firm.

The departure of this man left the young A. & U. without a London traveller. Stanley's solution was a piece of improvisation which would horrify professional management in the 1970s, but which at the time worked remarkably well. Seeking above all reliability and honesty, he reacted against what he regarded as the extravagance of the Jack Crane type of salesman in Fisher Unwin's business, and picked from the warehouse a powerfully built man, rather like a knobbly cart horse, who despite limited education was a genuine reader and could write out orders in an immaculate copperplate.

Stanley believed confidently that what he published would find its market; what mattered was that his traveller should conscientiously carry the new books round London to every bookseller customer of the firm, and they could then be relied upon to order what they needed. No prodigies of high-pressure selling and speculatively large advance orders were expected. There was no special briefing of the traveller before he set out with a batch of new books—and never that time-consuming sales conference! Blurb, jacket and page-proofs were the only advance material supplied. It sounds extraordinarily primitive, yet for twenty years, with the London representation of that one man, and much of the time only a single country traveller, the firm successfully put over their auto-suggestion books in the early 1920s (sales of over 100,000), Arthur Waley's translations of Lady Murasaki's *Tale of Genji*, Laski's *Grammar of Politics* and Emil Ludwig's best-seller *Napoleon*. In the late 1930s came Hogben's great popularizations *Mathematics for the Million* and *Science for the Citizen*, plus the first of the famous Phaidon art books, for which S.U. secured the English agency in 1936. Looking back from the experience of today's more sophisticated sales organization, with its elaborate advance material on each book, the torrential notes and memoranda sent out to at least three times as many travellers (each with his car supplied by the firm), one reflects in some humility upon the results achieved by the Founder with his simple, inexpensive methods.

For years Stanley claimed to be his 'own sales manager' and his not-too-frequent letters to leading booksellers about important new books invariably found their mark and brought a good order. Equally, he would not hesitate himself to give a reasoned reply to any bookseller's complaint; and some of them did not hesitate to complain about his stiff trade terms, that is the scale of discounts on which Allen & Unwin books were supplied. For nearly forty years of his business life, S.U. adhered to the practice, dating back to the early years of the century, of allowing not more than 21 per cent discount on orders for a single copy of a book. It was only under the strongest pressure in the 1950s, in which his son Rayner played an important part, that he reluctantly agreed to what was then the normal minimum of 25 per cent. And our profits, long prophesied to disappear if we ever took such a step, did not in fact vanish overnight—quite the reverse.

This is no place for a dissertation on the thorny subject of a publisher's trade terms. I have mentioned them simply to underline the fact that through all the years of the firm, a steadily rising turnover and big sales for some individual titles were achieved with a minimum of sales organization and no attractive inducements to booksellers.

Of the period around 1916 Stanley wrote, 'my circle of friends was at that time very limited', though he had then been in publishing for more than ten years and had been working in London since 1900. The narrowness of his social circle could have been due to his Nonconformist family life, and the fact that he apparently knew so few authors was probably the result of his concentration upon the commercial rather than the editorial side of the Fisher Unwin business. In many ways, too, he tended throughout his life to hunt alone. Thinking out every problem for himself, independent in his judgement, he had little inclination to turn to others for advice or seek, as lesser mortals might, the chance to 'talk it over' in order to clarify his own mind. But he made good use of the few contacts he possessed.

From one of them—he did not reveal his name—Stanley had the invaluable introduction to R. C. Trevelyan, brother of the historian, who put him in touch with G. Lowes Dickinson. This led to the publication of a symposium, edited by Charles Roden Buxton, to which a number of distinguished men of pacifist leanings contributed. The fact that the firm was willing to publish for this 'unpopular minority' became more widely known and brought in such useful authors as J. A. Hobson and L. T. Hobhouse, H. M. Hyndman and J. Ramsay MacDonald. (Hobson's *Evolution of Modern Capitalism* had appeared earlier, but S.U. acquired the rights, and although twenty years ago it was said by our economic adviser to be out of date, the book still sells.)

A. R. Orage, editor of *The New Age*, a particularly fearless and outspoken weekly of the period, was also a good friend at the time, acting as reader for the more important manuscripts, and frequently introducing young authors. G. P. Gooch was another who respected the new firm's ideals and helped in the same way. No reference to the early years of Allen & Unwin would be complete without mention of

Bernard Miall, a scholarly recluse who lived on the edge of Exmoor—much of the time at Coombe Martin. He was the translator of a vast number of books from German and French and was possessed of the most astonishing range of general knowledge. Originally he worked for Fisher Unwin and from 1914 he was for about thirty years the principal reader for Allen & Unwin, able to turn his hand to almost any MSS for a competent first opinion. Stanley was fortunate also to be able to call upon Edward Crankshaw a good deal during the 'thirties and before we had our own staff reader.

The Congregational connection was not neglected, and when Stanley and Mary were married by the famous preacher Dr. R. F. Horton, at Lyndhurst Roach Church, Hampstead, he seized the opportunity to 'fix up the terms for his autobiography in the vestry' after the ceremony. (What his bride thought of this devotion to business is not recorded!) Through the good offices of his eldest brother Edward Unwin, junior, known always as 'Ted', he also obtained a good and long-lived book by another leading Congregational divine, *The Builders*, by Dr. J. Fort Newton of the City Temple, the subject of which, curiously enough, was Freemasonry.

Robert Saudek, a Czech journalist and London correspondent for a Prague newspaper, and a specialist in the analysis of handwriting, was also particularly helpful to the firm in the early 1920s, especially with the Capek connection. The relationship seemed to begin with his perceptive analysis of S.U.'s handwriting, long before Saudek came to know him well. Besides emphasizing the subject's 'urge towards a pregnant clarity', he observed that 'he always keeps a close watch on his bank balance'! Saudek was consulted by many large firms to analyse the handwriting of applicants for important jobs, and his book *The Psychology of Handwriting* remained in the list for over forty years. Graphology may not be an exact science but there is undoubtedly much in it, and the subject has an enduring appeal to judge by the sales of the four books on it which we sponsored.

This was one more example of Stanley's open-mindedness on out-of-the-way subjects, to which F. A. Mumby could pay this tribute in the first edition of his *Publishing and Bookselling*, published in 1930: 'In proportion to its size, the firm of George Allen & Unwin has probably done more than any other to add to the stock of common knowledge.'

The outbreak of war, which had at first seemed a knock-out blow, proved in reality, thanks in part to the special interests and sympathies of the new owner, to be a definite advantage. Since Allen's had done no new publishing for over six months, they had no autumn list of unsuitable peace-time books to be disposed of: the new firm was free to concentrate at once upon more topical subjects directly related to the war. Also, as in 1939, after the first upheaval, the new war-time conditions, with thousands of men uprooted from their homes and often 'standing by' in a state of boredom, produced an increased demand for books. This grew still further as other articles, especially those suitable for presents, became scarcer. As many of us saw in the last war, almost any publishing firm, unless it was very incompetently run, was able to make money at that time, because the paper shortage guaranteed that practically every book sold out.

Altogether it must be admitted that, added to his considerable personal efforts, Stanley did have his share of luck. Even his operation for appendicitis, which had caused him so much trouble in his Fisher Unwin days, now left him, at the 'call-up', in a lower medical category than the only other remaining director of the firm, a man named Reynolds; so that it was S.U. who was left in peace to run the business on his own—precisely as he would have wished. The absence of any paper ration—owing to Allen's having been in the hands of the Receiver during the period upon which the ration was based—added in some respects to the difficulties. On the other hand, it left Stanley free to buy paper wherever he could, and the number of new books he produced at the time is clear evidence that the firm was not unduly handicapped by the shortage.

I referred earlier to the very small market that existed in those days for academic and specialist books; but this was offset by the much lower standards of living for even skilled workers, permitting what now seem unbelievably cheap costs of printing. These made it possible to print as few as 1,000 copies of a book (where 3,000 is the minimum today), and still arrive at a competitive published price. Such conditions facilitated 'minority' publishing, where a sale of even 600 copies would avoid a loss, and in those early days of Allen & Unwin, with the prospect of three other directors on his back when they returned from their war duties, Stanley was not over-anxious to show profits.

Instead of drawing more himself, which would have meant more for the others also, or declaring attractive dividends, he stuck to his £300 a year and concentrated upon such unspectacular but vital measures as conservative stock valuation and the building up of reserves. So while the firm was immensely strengthened, and the shares became worth far more than they had been in 1914, it did not yet seem a golden prospect in terms of future incomes for the directors.

This, I imagine, was a factor which helped to persuade one of the Allen directors, Reynolds, to allow himself to be bought out by Stanley after returning from his war service. Of the three original directors, he was the one most strongly antipathetic to Stanley's ideas and general outlook. Colonel P. H. Dalbiac, one of the others, who had originally joined Swan Sonnenschein in 1891, was now taking a much less active part, so that Stanley was left in effect with only E. L. Skinner, who had just returned from the War Office; he was a solicitor, who had bought an interest in George Allen & Co. in about 1912.

A good-looking man, whose family owned extensive slate quarries in South Wales, he had private means and the comfortable addition of a wife with money of her own. Some nine years after the end of the war, when I appeared at No. 40 Museum Street on Stanley's suggestion, it was Skinner who interviewed me and gave me the job. Frankly, and in this I was not alone among the staff at the time, I always had a soft spot for Skinner. In the utilitarian, radical world of the Unwins, it was an interesting and refreshing contrast to have a director who always sported his Old Etonian tie, who wore obviously good suits with an easy carelessness, and who worked in a comfortable atmosphere of finest tobacco. He exuded the spirit of *The Times* and *The Morning Post* (the ultra-conservative paper bought by the *Telegraph* in 1937). He was a member of the Travellers' Club; he once took me to the Members' Stand at Lords for the last couple of hours of the Oxford v. Cambridge match (he was an Oxford man), and entertained me and my wife at his home one Sunday evening. His letters occasionally included light-hearted phrases about disposing of certain shares 'with gratifying results', while holding on to 'my prefs' (to our Chief investments were far too sacred to be referred to in such casual terms.)

Skinner's legal knowledge was useful; he had background and taste and could write a good letter when he chose. I have never forgotten one he sent in reply to some wholly unjustified complaint. It had this thundering start:

'Sir,
  Your letter of . . . (date) is incorrect as to facts and offensive in suggestion . . .'

One felt that his genuine qualities, so complementary to Stanley's in many ways, could have been a valuable asset to the firm, but the two of them, with the vast difference in their backgrounds and ideals, were not made to get on together. While he handled a number of authors quite successfully, I do not believe that Skinner himself introduced any of importance, except possibly Richard Aldington. Some would say that by failing to take enough trouble with Aldington, Skinner also lost him, after the firm had published two or three books of his poems. Stanley was inclined, not altogether fairly, to regard him as an incubus. At any rate, the two men finally parted company in 1934 on what S.U. always described as 'onerous' terms, under which he bought out E. L. Skinner, who then took over the business of Williams & Norgate. As the value of A. & U.'s ordinary shares rose handsomely over the next twenty years, under our united efforts, Stanley was richly rewarded, whatever he paid Skinner.

I cannot help recalling that Skinner subsequently published with considerable success a book which A. & U. had declined. It was one of those cases where the simple publisher—P.U. this time—was immediately attracted to the book. It might not have been of the highest intrinsic importance, but it was most interesting, it was in no way disreputable, and it seemed certain to sell. It was a well-indexed American dictionary of Musical Themes, in which the browser could identify, by a line of music, the basic theme of 'everything he'd ever heard of' (and much more besides). It seemed genuinely to deserve that overworked adjective 'fascinating'. Moreover, as a work of reference, it might well go on selling for years. Unfortunately, the expert, in this case a musically well-educated ex-German publisher then working in our office, condemned it for its superficiality, and S.U., ever prepared to attach surprisingly heavy weight to any alleged expert manuscript reader, decided against it. Not infrequently, a useful book designed for the semi-popular market gets condemned by critics because it is not serious enough, in other words, because it is not the book which the author never intended it to be. Anyway, the departed Mr. Skinner's book of Musical Themes is still selling after twenty years.

My own connection with Stanley began, I suppose, in 1923. There had been one or two near pat-on-the-head meetings with him when I was a boy, and in my innocence I had then seen him as no more than just another bearded relative, of whom I always possessed a round dozen. In 1923, however, I met him for the first time on adult terms. He and his wife, our very dear Auntie Mary, had been invited to lunch by my parents to our old home at Surbiton. Unfortunately she was laid up with lumbago and unable to come. I had begun work a month before at Fisher Unwin's and arrived at about half-past one that Saturday, when the family, including my brother Rolf and my three sisters, were already at the dining-room table.

I came in, ready to slip unobtrusively into my place, but Stanley, clad as usual in his brown, double-breasted suit and square-toed shoes, jumped up smartly from the table and shook me vigorously by the hand. He gave his number one greeting, 'Very pleased to meet you', which my etiquette-conscious sister Joyce had told me one should not say; but he uttered it with such energy that it carried complete conviction. I immediately felt myself, rightly or wrongly, to be an object of some interest. Talk veered round to our Uncle Fisher. I raised a laugh, probably, by recounting one of his eccentricities, such as the number of times he had sung 'yes-yes' to himself while opening the post that morning: Stanley held forth on one of his T.F.U. memories, and I realized at once that we had a bond.

S.U. could always be a vivid and amusing raconteur on his own particular subject. On at least one of his visits to us, our maid Doris found his particular story over the dining-room table so utterly compelling, that she stopped dead in her tracks, a vegetable dish in each hand; her jaw dropped, in laughing amazement, at what this astonishing man was telling us all. Until Mother caught her eye with an admonishing nod, all vegetable service was at a standstill.

On that fine autumn afternoon we successfully persuaded him to our standard form of entertainment for the active guest—a bicycle ride. Many visitors must have suffered, if they were out of training, clad in city clothes and on an unfamiliar machine, as we spurred them cheerfully forward over the Surrey hills—all of us good for forty miles a day at any time. Stanley, though admitting he had not cycled for several years, stood up to it gamely after a few uncertain wobbles, and we put him safely over some fifteen miles, tram-lines included, to Oxshott woods and back. Part of the way he and I rode together and naturally we spoke of publishing. I was then too green to be able to put pointed questions to him—about the state of Fisher Unwin's—as I did later, after more experience; but I had the feeling, just out of school as I was, that here was a boss-type uncle who, in spite of being twenty years older than I, still seemed relatively young. I communicated immediately and readily with him, far more so than with T.F.U., sixty years my senior.

As always, S.U. made his mark, and to my surprise said to my mother, later that day, 'If you had wanted Philip to get some experience in my office, I should have been very happy to have him there—but of course Uncle Fisher would not have taken him after that!' It had always been assumed that as Stanley already had one son, there would be no question of his wanting another Unwin in his business. Here, however, was at least a veiled hint which I was not to forget when T.F.U. retired three years later and sold out to Ernest Benn Ltd.

7 Uncle Stan in the Twenties

I spent five months with Ernest Benn Ltd., following their take-over
of the Fisher Unwin business in October 1926, and I enjoyed them.
Under the management of Victor Gollancz, then in his late thirties,
there was a stimulating, explosive atmosphere. I had plenty to do as an
assistant to the production manager, and had some responsibility for
the activities of two most interesting and able young men, Bernard
Glemser, a Jew, from whom I gleaned my first sense of typography,
and Graham Fraser, a Scot, who went on, via Jonathan Cape, to
become the head of Collins's sales effort in Scotland.

My Uncle Stanley had indicated with his customary caution, when I
had run across him earlier, that he 'might' some time have an opening
for me in Allen & Unwin, now that my obligations to T. Fisher Unwin
had ended. And Sir Ernest Benn, in the course of a kind and wellnigh
fatherly interview, had suggested that although I was doing 'valuable'
work for his firm it would be advisable for me to look elsewhere for my
future. His strong opposition to trade union policy had strengthened
his determination never to have any direct connection with a printing
firm. Benn's never owned printing works then and the last thing their
chief wanted was to have on his payroll someone by the name of
Unwin, let alone a son of the managing director of Unwin Brothers.
He was thoroughly considerate to me and made it clear that I need not
regard myself as under notice, but when by chance the second man in
the production department at Allen & Unwin gave notice unexpectedly,
and Uncle Stan asked me to lunch with him, it looked as if my 'star'
might, after all, be in a favourable aspect.

By 1927 Allen & Unwin had been going for 13 years. The hard
initial slog was over. Sales had risen to about four times what they had
been when S.U. acquired his interest in the business. He had managed
to buy—for £10,000—the freehold of the Museum Street premises,
which would show a useful appreciation in the future. He had secured
financial control of the firm. His income was thought to be at least
double of any other Unwin at the time: he had boasted that he could
already 'afford to retire'. He was, at 43, the Financial Wizard of the
Family, even if some of his relatives found his cocksureness tiresome.
He had travelled widely—'been round the world'—he spoke German
fluently, and he had just written and published a book of his own.
Above all, he appeared to know that blessed secret: how to make

money. And at the same time he was that figure of glamour which I hoped to emulate: a publisher.

It was in a Slaters' Restaurant in Farringdon Street that we met—Reform Club membership was yet to come and his (rather premature) application to the Athenaeum had been thwarted, some said by Sir Frederick Macmillan. Though S.U. may occasionally have met his father and other directors of Unwin Bros. at that restaurant, as it was close to their London office in St. Bride Street, it was a long way for him to come from Bloomsbury, and it was typical of his consideration for a youth (myself) that he suggested that venue, close to Benn's office in Fleet Street, where I was then working.

I was, of course, waiting for him at the entrance of the restaurant. Along he came, walking fast, the firm set of his full, straight lips and the keen grey eyes giving him his perpetual air of fox-terrier alertness. I can still see the slightly 'Jamaican planter' appearance he presented, with his neatly pointed brown beard beneath the rather broad-brimmed felt hat, with its braided edge, as was worn in those days. In later years he gave up wearing hats, except for his topper at a Royal Garden Party, and as he was always one to 'make things last', I would swear that it was the same old 1927 hat that came out again in a spell of cold weather during his last winter. He was wearing his inevitable double-breasted suit, for ever unbuttoned, his tie pushed through the curious tie-ring given to him by his mother on his twenty-first birthday and, of course, the famous shoes, square-toed, handmade, with no toe-caps and rather wrinkled—probably because shoe-trees would have upset the 'nature form'.

What we ate at lunch for the first course I cannot now recall, but I chose apple pie to follow and he briskly ordered 'Apple pie for two and *one* portion of cream.' The assumption that his ascetic taste perhaps eschewed the richness of cream, and that it was all for me, was disproved when he at once seized the little cream jug, poured me a generous tot and retained the remaining third for himself.

Crisply and with clarity he outlined the position. He *could* fit me into 40 Museum Street, where—unlike Benns—my name would be an advantage; he was not 'making me an offer', it all depended on me. I must study German, and he would want me to get some Continental experience. While prudently leaving all channels of retreat open, if I proved a flop, he yet gave me the firm feeling that a unique opportunity was being offered, and that with any luck there was a golden future. It was all quite friendly and avuncular.

Here, then, was my big chance: a vacancy in the particular department in which I had most experience. To avoid too gross a charge of nepotism I was interviewed, as mentioned earlier, by E. L. Skinner, the one surviving director of the George Allen Company. Apparently he approved of me. I was given the job, and on March 1st, 1927, I started, at £14 a month, on the third leg of my life's work, as second in a production department of three.

Structurally, Museum Street has remained unchanged, as a good example of early Victorian city architecture, since that bright, cold day when I took the first of some 12,000 morning walks along it. I had once again crossed the Thames, using Waterloo Bridge this time, and walked through the morning smells of Covent Garden, which in memory seem always to have been oranges, celery and beer, then into Drury Lane, past the old Winter Garden Theatre, and so into Museum Street. The dignified, cream-painted stucco building of 'Mudie's Select Library' was on the west corner in New Oxford Street. With any luck one might still see a handsome carriage and pair standing outside, while her ladyship was choosing her books in the Library. Museum Street was no one-way traffic artery then—just a quiet backwater, traffic wardens undreamt of and gas lamps put on individually each evening by the lamplighter with his pole and hook.

The already prosperous firm of Allen & Unwin, though ready to burst at the seams, was squeezed into one small, four-storey house plus basement (actually five floors), and its mouldy little warehouse at the rear. Within the book trade its name was known from London to Tokyo and from Auckland to Oslo with Leipzig and Amsterdam thrown in, but its premises were frankly a bit of a come-down from those of either my first publishing Uncle or the firm which had taken him over. It was all typical of Uncle Stan—spartan and no frills, but a good bank balance and secure jobs.

The shop-front entrance, half of it scantily-stocked bookshop—because it contained only A. & U. books—and half 'reception', plus office boy and invoice clerk, gave no suggestion of a thriving business, and the garret-like stairs, with their noisy, iron treads, did not help. Heating in the offices was by ancient gas fires and along the stairs and passages there was none. It was somewhat ironical that although S.U. had immediately arranged for central heating to be installed at No. 1 Adelphi Terrace, when the Fisher Unwin business moved there from Paternoster Square in the early nineteen hundreds, he had not provided it for himself. By 1927 plans were afoot for rebuilding, so there was a natural reluctance to spend money on the old premises. Besides, my Uncle Stan was—and for ever remained—unbelievably impervious to changes of temperature. In old age he wore neither hat nor gloves, and seldom more than a raincoat on the coldest days, while in the tropics he would never hesitate to 'go out in the midday sun'—if there was a bookseller to be visited, however humble.

But these were superficial blemishes; what really mattered to me was that this was a firm that was making real progress, its chief had just received full recognition throughout the trade both here and overseas for his book *The Truth About Publishing* ('by one of the most successful of the younger British publishers', said Houghton Mifflin on its U.S. edition); he knew the business inside out, he was finding himself overloaded, he cherished the idea of a family firm, his sons were in the nursery or prep school, and he had a lust for imparting information. If I wanted to learn all about publishing, there were no better feet to sit at, and if I made myself useful surely there were prospects.

At nine o'clock on that March morning I was taken up by the office boy—no commissionaire here!—to the dingy little back room on the first floor which housed the firm's production department. My running mate was Howard Timmins, a cheerful, flaxen-haired giant who later migrated to South Africa to become a successful agent for several British publishers, including A. & U. The Production Manager was an extraordinary but entertaining character of about sixty, of whom S.U. had told me 'he knows his job but he has no memory and no system'—he also had no teeth, was very short-sighted—he wore thick-lensed, rimless pince-nez—and had an exceptionally foul pipe. When, at intervals, he dismembered it and blew hard through the stem to clean it out, the stench of the brown spray which emerged was unforgettable. Originally with the little Bemrose publishing business, he had come into George Allen's when they took it over, and so was part of the staff acquired by A. & U. in 1914.

He had a fair knowledge of printing by the standards of those days and he was well read, but his forgetfulness and tendency to imbibe too freely at times caused much trouble and furious rows with the chief. I can still hear them: 'Mr. Z—did I or did I *not* tell you that we must have a good bulking paper for this book?' 'I have said not once and again, but again and again and *again* that we cannot expect people to pay ten and sixpence for a miserable little book like that'—probably on seeing the dummy of the paper.

S.U. was fond of enunciating that there are endless pitfalls for the unwary in book production; none of us escape them entirely and poor old Mr. Z fell into most of them. It was strangely typical of S.U. that he never made any move to find him some other job or to pension him off. The latter would surely have been cheaper for the firm and it would certainly have spared my Uncle's nervous energy for more profitable use. I am not sure, however, that he did not derive some curious satisfaction from his verbal beatings up of the old boy.

I shall never forget one of Mr. Z's escapades which provided an impressive 'object lesson'—favourite phrase of S.U.'s—to his juniors. Soon after my arrival, the firm published Emil Ludwig's biography of *Napoleon*, of which 2,000 copies had been imported from the American publishers, Boni & Liveright. Just as the sales began to develop, S.U. went off on a trip to New York and was not on hand to supervise the reprint, which quickly became urgent. The book was of an unusual size; it ran to 700 pages, and it was not easy at short notice to get just the right paper. In the general rush Mr. Z accepted something far too thick and the result was a squat, fat volume which in appearance was almost a cube. Instructions were given to the binder to 'squeeze the life out of it'—but no binder's press could reduce the bulk by about two inches, which was what was needed.

When the Governor returned castigation followed. After the initial explosion over Mr. Z, he said to me: 'Not your responsibility this time, but it may be next—never forget, there always *is* an answer; imagination plus technical knowledge will solve most problems!' And he ripped off straight away two possible solutions. They involved minor technicalities which I will not go into, but they were both practical alternatives which I made use of on later occasions. The incident led inevitably to another of his favourite dicta, that 'there are more ways of killing a cat than by drowning it in cream'. The capacity to step back, 'to exercise a little imagination' and approach a problem from a different standpoint, was always one of his great strengths.

At that stage all the heads of departments in A. & U. were men of middle age or older, who had been part of the staff of the George Allen Company. Senior amongst them was an incredibly youthful-looking sixty-year-old, Spencer Swan Stallybrass, a cousin of William Stallybrass, who ran the firm of Routledge & Kegan Paul successfully for many years. 'Spencer', as we all knew him, was Secretary of the Company and had come into the Allen complex at the amalgamation of Swan Sonnenschein with George Allen in 1911. The Stallybrasses changed their name from Sonnenschein in the 1914 war. A man of independent views and limited personal ambition, he never hit it off successfully with S.U., but he nevertheless remained for nearly fifty years as an able and trustworthy Secretary and a figure of unfailing kindliness and justice towards the staff. He was short in stature but had very large, powerful hands, derived from his lifelong prowess as a gymnast. I always imagined those hands enabling him to do a superb long-arm stand on the parallel bars. He ran a gym class until he was well into his sixties and always opened the annual display by doubling briskly round the hall at the head of the class, to the amusement of those of our girls to whom he had given tickets.

Another Sonnenschein trusty was J. James, a dour, dark man who presided over the trade counter, possessed an immaculate knowledge of the firm's entire catalogue, plus that of its predecessors, Sonnenschein, Allen and Bemrose, and provided a well-disciplined training for many a junior boy on his way up into 'the office'. Besides him was that remarkable old character, George Speed, who had all but known Ruskin himself. Now possessed of but a single tooth, he was a good reliable stock-keeper, even though constantly at war with his colleague James on the other side of the warehouse. He had worked originally for George Allen when the publication of Ruskin's books was being handled from Allen's house at Orpington. Yet another stalwart was a sergeant-major type, W. J. Ellard, wax-moustached, with hair parted in the middle, a butterfly collar and a perennial buttonhole, befitting the keen gardener, who in his day was one of the fastest ledger posters in the trade. For a great many years he kept all the firm's trade accounts—those with booksellers—prided himself on rendering accounts instantly on the last day of the month, and getting the money in promptly.

All these gentlemen must have looked askance at the twenty-nine-year-old Stanley, when he whisked into the business in 1914; but they quickly realized that in him they had a boss who—unlike their previous directors—knew far more about the details of publishing than they did. Most important, he quickly set the firm on its feet, sufficiently to be able to pay them something better than the sweated wages they had previously received. All of them worked through to retirement; and this says much for my Uncle's capacity, both to shape people to his own requirements, and to instil in them thereafter a remarkable measure of loyalty.

From the standpoint of even a middle-sized publishing house today, Allen & Unwin was small beer in the nineteen-twenties, with annual sales of about one-thirtieth of what they are now. I remember how the daily book deliveries to the carriers went off on a couple of box tricycles, often piled extremely high; only on publication days did we rise to a hired horse and cart. The first Morris van followed about five years later. An enormous advantage to me, of course, was that the small size of the firm enabled one to see pretty well what was happening everywhere, and my Uncle was both shrewd and adroit in ensuring that those of some responsibility, or who were in training for it, should know what was going on.

Once again I was quickly drawn into the morning post routine, sitting beside S.U. to open every envelope—slit on three sides to make certain nothing remained within—and I was free to read every letter, provided I had got a running start on him, to ensure that he was not kept waiting. On the time-honoured principle of being 'shown where the deep end was', I had to plunge in, being given a number of letters to deal with on my own each day. Frequently a hint would be given as to how the reply should run, and if by any chance I had not got it quite right at the end of the day, there was a fresh lesson: he scrutinized every outgoing letter from each department before it was posted.

Stanley himself was a master at the business letter; he could say precisely and clearly what he wanted in the minimum number of words. This sometimes resulted in unnecessary coldness, but if he wished he could also inject remarkable warmth and humour into some of his replies.

He was so full of his subject, and recollected so much case history, that there was a danger of being overwhelmed by his warnings, examples and object lessons; but basically it was a wonderful training. Every form of incoming mail came across that table, the orders from booksellers all over the world, at that time pre-airmail, frequent cables from American publishers, and we thought up ingenious abbreviations to save the shillings charged for every word, printers' estimates, authors' complaints, or inquiries about possible new books, or again, praise the Lord, letters of commendation from some authors, expressing delight with their books.

Continually, S.U.'s encyclopaedic knowledge of every detail of the firm's business was exemplified in his immaculate round-handed notes, jotted on some letter before it was passed over to the department concerned. Another of his funny habits was to scribble on the letter '?S.U.', in which the tail of the 'U' was extended into a balloon round the initials, making them look curiously like a tadpole. As a result, one member of the staff used to say, 'Bad post this morning, lots of little tadpoles!' meaning that the Governor was probably on the war-path. One could never be quite sure whether the presence of a tadpole meant what one of his unregenerate lieutenants might imply by 'What the hell . . .', or whether it merely meant 'Ask me about this and I will tell you an interesting story about this man (or this book).' Occasionally, one gathered a dossier of facts about the transaction in question, only to find that this was an entirely harmless tadpole.

Immediately he had finished the day's post, which was usually at about 9.30, S.U. would make the rounds of his 'checkpoints'. First, into the production dept., to see what Mr. Z—and in the early days his nephew and the aforesaid Howard Timmins—had got up to. Estimates for any new book, specimen pages, jacket proofs, paper samples, binding numbers would all be scrutinized and approved or rejected. I always admired the rapidity of his calculations on an estimate, to decide just what terms could be offered to the author, or what price we could charge for a thousand copies to an American publisher. There was more rule-of-thumb about it, perhaps, than would be the case today, but my goodness, how he got through the stuff and produced the results. 'The best can be the enemy of the good' was another of his favourite maxims, and that is a facet of truth in a commercial business, particularly when allied with another of his favourites, 'Learn to master your job.'

From the production dept. he ascended the second flight of steel-treaded garret stairs to Mr. Stallybrass, to sign cheques and investigate the bank balance, decide how much to put on deposit at Drummonds and perhaps settle some minor staff matter. And *how* minor were staff matters in those days. For a new girl, be it copy typist, filing clerk or potential secretary, we had only to ring up the Secondary School Headmistresses Employment Bureau and along came three or four admirable young women, from whom one could make a pick—all of them knowing that there was competition for the job, and that if they failed to perform satisfactorily they might not find it too easy to get another. It was the same with office boys, clerks or warehousemen. As a result, there was comparatively little staff turnover.

So, on again and up the last flight of stairs to Mr. Ellard's eyrie, on the top floor, where at an enormous old Victorian desk he sat, surrounded by the mighty loose-leaf ledgers of those days, long before machine accountancy; there it seemed to be mainly a question of what action to take about some errant bookseller who had not paid his account. In the days long before full employment, staff shortage, exchange control, paper rationing or overloaded printers, there was an undoubted simplicity to a lot of it; on the other hand, with unemployment, little social security and no education after fourteen for most people, the potential market for books was very much smaller than it is today. In fact publishing was inclined to be a depressed trade.

One of the admirable systems for the newcomer was the circulation of 'yellow sheets'—that is, the office copies of outgoing correspondence —which took place every day. In practice, ninety per cent of it was made up of S.U.'s own letters, plus a few from his co-director Edgar Skinner, and from Janet Marler, who acted both as advertising manager and as a sort of personal assistant to my Uncle until her marriage about a year after I joined the firm. From the daily scrutiny of these letters one learned a tremendous amount, not least something of the workings of S.U.'s mind and his approach to every sort of publishing problem.

In many ways he continued to use, after thirteen years, exactly the same methods as those with which he had started George Allen & Unwin in 1914; watching every detail, lynx-eyed, and taking personal care to see that every nut and bolt of the business was tightly screwed together. All this was vital in the early days, before he had trained the staff in his own ways; but by the late twenties many would say that he was spending more time than was economic, or necessary, on the mechanical aspects of the business. Other publishers in his position would by then have been more engaged in the pursuit of authors, editors and literary agents. Some publishers who adopted this course had more apparent best-sellers on their lists, but I would doubt very much indeed whether any of them built such a sound business; while many, of course, were seen to go down, or at least disappear into amalgamations, after the initial brilliance of their start.

I was lucky in that there was no objection to authors making a direct assault upon the production dept.—dingy though the accommodation was—whereas at Fisher Unwin's they never seemed to penetrate that far. Within my early months I had minor dealings with some authors, including the famous economist J. A. Hobson and handsome, fresh-complexioned, white-haired Eleanor Rathbone, whose book on Family Endowment, *The Disinherited Family*, we were publishing. Needless to say, I shall never forget 'my' first author. This was the late Reginald Hine, a literary solicitor, who produced a stupendous history of Hitchin in two volumes. We were prepared to publish it only 'on commission', which involved his paying the entire costs of production, with us selling the book for him and taking a percentage on the sales. He was a tremendous extrovert, and though of Quaker inclination he had a poetic flow of speech calculated to win over anyone. He gathered in so many advance subscriptions for the book from the inhabitants of Hertfordshire and Middlesex, whose names were printed at the end, that we had to increase the printing number. After Herculean labours on everybody's part, a very fine local history resulted. Mr. Hine, meanwhile, had become a byword throughout the office, and a barely suppressed groan went through the typists' room whenever I announced still another letter to be dictated to 'Mr. Hine of Hitchin'. When the book was published, however, it was well reviewed, and he gave me an inscribed copy with a charming and appreciative note of thanks for all our efforts to 'usher it into the world with a becoming grace'.

S.U.'s own office at that time was a curious room which he had ingeniously tacked on to the original premises. It had a flat roof with a skylight, which was draughty and leaked in heavy rain, but it was all his own invention and he was very proud of it. Another window, which gave on to a lead flat, was adjacent to an opening into the first-floor offices of the National Book Council—forerunner of the National Book League—in the adjoining street. Stanley was the prime begetter of the N.B.C. and he took a characteristic delight in scrambling through that window for quick, surprise visits to Maurice Marston, Secretary of the Council. For many years Mr. Marston worked closely with my uncle and he has given me the following most interesting account of him in the 'twenties and his successful efforts to promote better trade organization.

'It must have been in 1920 when S.U. and I first met. I had just finished a short apprenticeship with the publisher of the poet W. H.

Great-grandfather Jacob Unwin, 'Steam Printer'

Great grandparents James and Louisa Spicer, taken on holiday, snowstorm
and tea things apparently photographer's props

Grandfather George Unwin, Victorian main-spring of Unwin Brothers The Gresham Press

Great-uncle Edward Unwin, brother of George and father of Stanley, flanked by two of his managers. Note Edward's orchid from the expensive greenhouse

Family of James Spicer with their married
partners. Sir Evan and Maria, my grandmother,
seated on extreme left, Sir Albert third from
right, the unmarried Charlotte and Harriet seated
modestly in front

T. Fisher Unwin trotting between
Nos. 1 and 3 Adelphi Terrace

My mother, twin sisters and self about 1908—blue sash for boys shows extraordinary Edwardian habit of dressing boy children in frocks

My father, George Soundy Unwin,
Edwardian and early Georgian mainstay of Unwin brothers (1924)

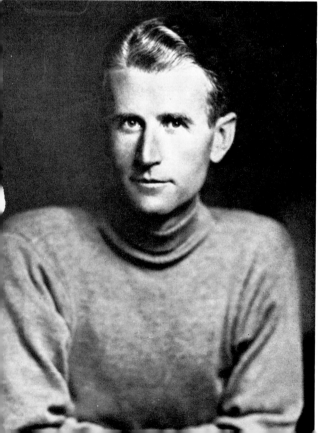

Philip Unwin (1942)

Stanley Unwin in 1920

Philip Unwin at 60 at yet another launching party
(bow tie already askew)

Davies, and that extraordinary personality Dr. Marie Stopes of *Married Love* fame. I was young, with little training, offering nothing but unlimited enthusiasm for books and reading. So, with a more experienced partner, it seemed natural to become a publisher! And then, almost before the office doors were opened, S.U. appeared and offered advice and help. He put us in touch with authors, printers and bookbinders, he supplied us with names of translators and in countless ways lent us his experience. To me he became a valued teacher, a leader of the new thought in the book world.

'How S.U. regarded me is difficult to assess. He certainly approved of my enthusiasm for his reforming mind in book trade politics. I think too he was mildly flattered to have a young, however gauche, disciple. Or perhaps being at that stage in his career a rather lonely man with few sympathizers and not a few enemies from the pre-1914 Establishment Publishers, he was attracted to someone who wholeheartedly believed in what he was trying to do, although not always his methods. He was always a man of sense but not always of sensitivity. Whatever the reasons S.U. set up, with myself as a junior but eager lieutenant, a ceaseless attack on the Establishment Publishers for their stupidity in refusing to face up to the new post-war conditions. His was the kernel of the alliance but it was not until after the formation of the Society of Bookmen that he really came into his own. From the start I was appointed its Secretary and S.U. was a founder member.

'The formation of the Society in 1921 was unique. It was not another literary society. Its membership, limited to fifty, consisted solely of those connected with the authorship, production and distribution of books. Yet it was not in any sense a rival to official trade bodies. It had no money, no position and no office. What it did have was selectivity of membership and, consequently, a gathering together of those who thought along similar lines, a freedom from preconceived ideas and abundant energy and enthusiasm.

'From this rather incoherent but willing assembly, S.U. emerged not so much a leader but as one who was always prepared to encourage the discussion of new ideas. He was no orator, not for him the impassioned appeal, the flow of fine words, the flashing wit. But rather a cold logic, the relentless addition of fact to fact. What his audiences came to admire was his sincerity, his wide knowledge, his conciseness and, most important, his brevity. He never made the mistake of boring his audiences; infuriating them, yes; but they did not yawn.

'So from the meetings of the Society a platform was built and from that platform a very simple gospel was preached—the Promotion of Reading and the Wider Distribution of Books. For five years the arguments of how to do this with the minimal expense went on with a ferocity which today seems ludicrous.

'Then in 1926 S.U. conceived the idea that the Society should send a delegation to Holland and Germany to report on the organization of their book trade with special reference to book promotion and book publicity. Representatives from the trade bodies were named and under the leadership of S.U. (with myself as Secretary) the delegation set forth and, later, produced *an historic report*, upon which the basis of the National Book Council was formed.

'The report, which somehow secured unanimity, was successfully adopted by the Society and subsequently, without enthusiasm, accepted by the trade association. The N.B.C. was in being but not off the ground. In 1927 operations began.

'By this time I was free to accept the Secretaryship of the N.B.C. and from a tiny office in Little Russell Street at the back of, yet part of, and belonging to Allen & Unwin, approached by an outside staircase, work began. The office was certainly easily accessible to a room in which S.U. worked across a flat-topped roof entered through a window. By this route S.U. was constantly in touch with me! I found it amusing at first but later rather irritating particularly if anyone was with me and the entrance of S.U. through a window had to be explained.

'In 1930 the N.B.C. left Little Russell Street, W.C.1, for Henrietta Street, W.C.2. S.U., yearly gathering supporters around him, watched its steady growth. Although under-financed and crippled in other ways, it had come to stay. Not even his fiercest opponents could deny that S.U., almost alone, had with immense skill and courage, created in the National Book Council an organization which the book trade was not prepared to give up. It was his creation and for always will his name be coupled with it.'

A few years later the Chief created another similar office for himself, alongside the first one, but with the advantage of a southern aspect and complete freedom from traffic noise. Its major defect, to which I think he was totally impervious, was its floor level, which was lower than that of the rest of the building, and necessitated an awkward flight of three steep steps immediately inside the door. He always shot down them two at a time, and the thump of his foot at the bottom was some warning of his arrival, if one was in a nearby room. A visitor unfamiliar with the terrain, however, would have to grope his or her way cautiously, and at least one new member of the staff—she who has typed this book—celebrated the first summons to her employer by falling headlong down the steps and scattering at his feet the contents of the file he had sent for.

A Persian rug covered half the floor area, but his own chair and the large, plain oak desk, acquired second-hand with the Swarthmore

Press, when S.U. bought up that little Quaker firm, were on the un-carpeted part, and so it always remained. All-over fitted carpets and an upholstered chair for himself he regarded as totally unnecessary luxuries, and any visitor, including Bertrand Russell, also had to sit on a bone-hard type of 'hall chair' and dangle his feet on the bare lino-leum.

The top of S.U.'s desk was a remarkable indication of some facets of his character. It was always covered with scrupulously neat little piles of old letters, notes, booklets, memoranda and reports of the Pub-lishers' Association and the like. They were seldom referred to because, like most of us, he relied on his secretary to keep all the files of his correspondence and anything else of importance that he might suddenly need. What appeared as almost a nervous reflex action by his continually gesturing hands ensured that those curious little piles were tidied up frequently throughout the day. For the fundamentally efficient businessman behind them, they performed about the same function as Butler's Musical Banks in *Erewhon*.

As a result of this permanent coverage of his desk, the only real working area was reduced to the left-hand flap, which he kept for ever drawn out, and so had to thread his way carefully round it every time he moved to and from the desk. On the precious flap had to be piled all his own letters for signature, and those of everyone else in the office; for he continued to insist—to his last day in Museum Street—on 'seeing' every outgoing letter. It seemed an extraordinarily uncom-fortable arrangement, but it did at least ensure that letters could never be muddled up with anything else on his desk, and avoidance of physical discomfort was never one of his primary considerations.

Another feature of his desk organization which was a constant source of astonishment was the Edwardian device known, I think, as the 'Wall-o-graph Telephone Arm'. It must have been almost the last year of its production when S.U. ordered this Heath Robinson con-traption in 1929. It consisted of a lattice arm, like a miniature lift gate, which at one end gripped the old-fashioned 'umbrella stand' type of telephone, and at the other was attached to the wall, against which the telephone lived when not in use. When the bell rang the phone could be hauled out about three feet from the wall, where it joggled in mid-air, since the lattice arm was far from rigid. The base of the 'umbrella stand' had always to be steadied with one hand while one spoke, and note-taking was excessively difficult; but my Uncle Stan was devoted to it, and it must have been nearly twenty years before the 'Wall-o-graph' was scrapped in favour of a modern instrument on a shelf, with earpiece and microphone in one.

Gesturing during conversation is said to be due to a superabundance of nervous energy. Our Chief was a living example of the truth of this proposition. No telephone conversation of any importance went through without his free hand doing circular receding chops into the air. No reference could be made to another department without a quick stab in its direction; and after my forty years in Museum Street, when he looked into my office to say, 'Can you come through to my room?', he would still point over his shoulder to indicate where it was.

A one-time office boy never forgot his first day, when at about four p.m. S.U. dug out from his trouser pocket the famous tray purse, shook out a coin and said, 'Get me something substantial for a penny.' The youth went off to the nearest confectioner, a humble establishment, and bought the largest thing he could find for the money—a much-inflated cream bun. 'What's the use of that!' snapped the Chief, when it was hopefully laid on his desk. 'Look, it's all air!—air!!' as he jabbed his finger mercilessly into the collapsing bun, demonstrating its lack of substance. I have no doubt that it was instantly converted into an object lesson. Another office boy remembers mishearing the request for 'something to *eat*' and returning with the unlikely tea-time comfort of a pennyworth of *sweets*.

In these days of luxurious offices and mammoth firms it is easy to laugh over the more primitive methods and conditions of half a century ago, but the little publishing business I have been describing already had on its list the names of Ruskin, Bertrand Russell, Gilbert Murray, Radhakrishnan, Gandhi and Harold Laski, not to mention J. M. Synge and St. John Ervine. The rigid economy in 'overheads' may seem tough in retrospect, and indeed we could have afforded a little more comfort; but example in such matters, spreading down through the staff, helped to build up a strong financial position, which saw us safely through the depression years. The same tradition, always allied to publishing the right books—or at least avoidance of the wrong ones—was to guard us against the over-spending and cash shortage which later on led so many others into amalgamations and loss of identity.

In the next chapter I shall try to show more of the methods by which my Uncle Stanley built up the firm and inspired others to prodigious efforts to that end.

8 *Slogging through the Thirties*

In his prime, Stanley Unwin possessed a compelling, almost mesmeric, force in argument. Not only could he marshal his facts and state his case eloquently—often with humour—but there was something in his smiling, slightly glassy eyes which carried you along and left you, at least temporarily, with the conviction that he was absolutely right and that none but a fool would disagree with him. It may have been due to his built-in business sense, which showed him automatically where his commercial interest lay, and his habit, as some have said, of instinctively adjusting facts and argument to serve that interest. 'One of the secrets of my success', he once said to me, 'is knowing how to state my case.' After forty years it still comes to me with a slight shock to realize the innocence and lack of guile which caused me then to marvel that the same basic facts could be set forth in two different ways and so produce very different results.

One effect of this particular skill was his amazing capacity to impress upon everybody the great size and importance of the firm. 'In a business of our size' or 'with a large output such as ours . . .' were frequently recurring phrases in his letters at the time when the entire staff did not exceed twenty-five, including the office boy. A big proportion of the books published were importations from America, sometimes as few as 250 of a title, or odd little agencies he held for various series, such as one with the sobering title *Publications of the Institute for Intellectual Co-operation*. None of these amounted to much in actual sales, but they all had the chance of reviews in the many little specialist journals then published, and office overheads were so modest that these low-priced series could be handled economically.

Naturally, new members of the staff were left in no doubt whatever that they were exceptionally fortunate to have the chance to work in such a firm, and it was another feature of S.U.'s success as an employer that he continued to give everyone the feeling that the efficient performance of his or her particular job, however lowly paid, was of the utmost importance. And pay *was* low in those days.

While A. & U. certainly had not the reputation of paying extravagantly, we were not bad by comparison with many publishers. There were modest annual increases and a small Christmas bonus. The root of the matter was that publishing was a comparatively depressed trade and the country's economy was stagnant, with about 2,000,000 unemployed. I never forgot the shock I had on finding that the well-spoken girl of 20 or so who did my letters, with faultless shorthand and typing, was paid 35s. a week. When she left us to train for nursery-school work her father, a solicitor, wrote a charming note to S.U. to thank him for the good job his daughter had had with us.

There was never any lack of candidates for the humble but exacting task of being office boy at about 20s. a week. He had to be 'in' by 8.30 in the morning and gather up the post from a dark and dusty corner of the basement, where it had slid down a chute into the mail basket. This cumbersome system had been devised because on one occasion some enterprising thief had pushed a treacly stick through into the letter-box (then on pavement level) and extracted some registered letters. As we very rarely received cash through the post, it is unlikely that the wretched man secured anything of intrinsic value, but our ever-practical and ingenious Chief at once devised the chute system. Malefactors with treacly sticks had no more luck, but the hazards for office boys increased. Every so often a letter or two flipped over the edge of the basket and fluttered off into one of the dusty corners of that basement dungeon. Inevitably on some unlucky day the office boy failed to retrieve it, and there the odd letter lay for days, or even weeks—but not beyond the next bank holiday. Why? Because the indefatigable head of the firm invariably came to the office alone on a bank holiday *morning* to open the post (tennis in the afternoons only). He prided himself on having a good look round the basement and several times found an errant letter or two—with ensuing finger-wagging admonitions for all concerned on the Tuesday morning! Later on I used to mark in my calendar for the Friday before a bank holiday—'look in the basement'.

Besides this 8.30 routine the office boy had frequently to wait upon S.U. during the day, including the tea bun responsibility, to deliver by hand all letters within a radius of half a mile *and* not leave until all the day's letters were dispatched at the nearby G.P.O. It could be 6 p.m. before he was free to go home . Yet for this fussy, thankless job we had a steady supply of diligent and responsible boys, at least four of whom rose to high executive positions with us and have put in over thirty years with the firm.

I mention this to show my Uncle's remarkable influence as an employer and a business builder. In part it was simply due to his being there, among us, every day, and to his being seen to do a hard day's work for himself. He never tired of expounding certain of the truths about publishing to every member of the staff, and his explanations were vigorous and clear; while his paternalistic habit of paying out the weekly wages himself every Friday afternoon brought him fleetingly into direct touch with everyone.

Five points he early impressed upon me were:

1. To 'avoid losses and the profits will take care of themselves'.

2. To seek a way of 'insuring' against the risk on a new book by an untried author wherever possible, e.g. by an advance order from an American publisher, or possibly by getting the author to share the risk financially.

3. NOT to be dependent on agents and upon bidding competitively against other publishers.

4. To build up and nurture a 'back list' (the books which go on selling year after year without expensive promotion).

5. To price books realistically in relation to costs.

To the more sophisticated management of today these may seem over-simplified, and there is, of course, more to successful publishing than just these particular precepts; but they were remarkably good principles for Allen & Unwin then, and we have rarely departed from them. As I have frequently told my younger colleagues, most of our success in later and more affluent times has come from adherence to and extension of the ideas laid down by our Chief forty years ago.

Though it is clear from his autobiography that my Uncle led a full and interesting life in the 1930s, the first five years of the decade were in some ways tough and dull within the firm. Though we had the solid 'back list' elements of Edward Carpenter, Maeterlinck and the Gilbert Murray translations of the Greek dramatists—all acquired with the original George Allen business—and Arthur Waley and Bertrand Russell, who had not then made a widely popular impact, we seemed to have nothing really exciting and saleable among our new books. Also we had virtually no 'set' books in our small academic list, while our stiff terms did not make us popular with booksellers.

Thus, with no outstanding sellers, our sales dropped by a seventh at the start of the decade and remained static for five years, until we published Hogben's *Mathematics for the Million*.

Inevitably profits declined and in one year, 1934, we would have shown a loss if the Chief had not refunded part of his salary. During this time we remained adequately buttressed by the cautious policy of the earlier, more prosperous years, in which it had been an article of his faith always to 'plough back' into the business not less than one half of each year's profits.

One reason for the lean times was the Wall Street collapse of October 1929, when share prices also plummeted on European stock exchanges. Michael Arlen, author of *The Green Hat*, super seller of the 'twenties, was one of the few who made a further fortune by selling out just ahead of the crash. There was a general slow-down of the economy, which led on to Britain's financial crisis in the late summer of 1931, still further reductions in Government expenditure, wage cuts and higher taxation. It is difficult for anyone under fifty to envisage that complete antithesis to all the economic and social conditions which we have worked under for the past twenty-five years. Instead of prices rising continually, they actually came down. The price of a good cup of coffee in a Lyons' tea-shop was even reduced from 3d. to 2½d., and dear old Gatti's restaurant just off the Strand, where we used to have the lunches of the Publishers' Advertising Circle, took to giving us an extra (fourth) course for our 3s. 6d. lunch, in lieu of a price reduction. In memory it seemed a better lunch than one has in comparable restaurants today for 50s.

One immediate effect of the slump was the serious decline, almost to vanishing point, of the American market. I still recall the founder of Norton's in New York telling me: 'You can't imagine what it was like to come into your office in the morning and find not one single order from any bookseller' (where normally there would have been hundreds, if not several thousands of books wanted on any one day, which is what a publisher lives on). Up to that time, A. & U. had normally sold at least 250 or 500 copies of every new book to some American publisher. Now this useful addition to profit disappeared. Library expenditure was cut, booksellers went out of business and several London publishers went into liquidation, leaving many of our acquaintances out of work.

The slump struck us at a particularly bad moment, because my Uncle, following the appearance of *The Truth About Publishing*, had been quickly drawn on to the Council of the Publishers Association, and he plunged with great energy into book trade politics. After 1930 fully half his time, and I think much of his creative thought, was absorbed by it. Till then he had been the prime energizer and author-getter for the firm; now much of that power was switched off. Though not yet fifty, and his beard merely touched with grey, he was already becoming an oracle, a sort of Uncle to the Trade; and everyone in need of advice, be it competing publisher, failing bookseller or hopeful seeker after a job, tended sooner or later to be told to 'go and see Stanley Unwin'. Since he never tired of holding forth upon the complexities and excruciating difficulties of the book trade he found it hard to resist these seekers after truth; his book had left no one in any doubt as to his pride in publishing and the fascination it had for him. But, above all, there was his intense professionalism, the fact that in 1930 he probably knew more about the whole spectrum of publishing than anyone else; and in the minutiae of its economics he was unbeatable. No other head of a publishing business at that time had systematically made his way round the English-speaking world by slow boat, dusty trains and even pre-1914 mule-drawn coaches; after that, he could dilate with unrivalled authority upon the mark-up needed by the booksellers of Pretoria, or the subjects sought after in Tokyo (and, some added irreverently, what you could sell in Patagonia).

One certainly could not blame him. The Publishers' Association was badly in need of revival and reform; S.U. had once been refused membership, and now to be cordially welcomed in was irresistible. A. & U. was yielding him a comfortable income for his fundamentally frugal way of life—'my wants are few', he used to say—so there was no particular reason, when the value of money seemed stable, for him to strive especially hard to push up sales, when there were other things that interested him more. He was his own master, with no city financiers breathing down his neck and demanding more 'growth' or a better return on their capital; the firm's preference shares paid their five per cent punctually, and if there was no dividend on the ordinary shares for five years, who cared except S.U.—who owned the lot!

His frugality, incidentally, extended to such little things as the famous stubs of pencil with which he did all his writing. There were always three or four of them kept loose in the side pocket of his coat, and I never knew him to use a decent-sized pencil or later a biro. Adam Helms, that dynamic Swedish publisher, was fascinated by these Lilliputian pencils. He told me how, at Frankfurt one year, at the end of a discussion with him, my Uncle so far forgot himself as to leave his pencil stub behind. Adam promptly appropriated it as a souvenir and set it up on end, sellotaped to something on his desk in Stockholm. It constantly aroused the curiosity, then the admiration, of visitors, until one day an over-zealous new secretary, tidying up a notoriously congested desk, threw it away.

It may be idle to speculate about 'what might have happened if . . .', but one really cannot help wondering how the firm might have progressed in those years if more of S.U.'s time had been spent on it. Inevitably he was apt to infer indirectly that the disappointing results were due to the shortcoming of his young men, P.U. and Charles Furth, another young disciple of the master who had joined the firm soon after me, following a year in Germany. He and I were mainly responsible for much of the 'author-dealings', interviews, correspondence, and generally 'seeing the books through' from manuscript to publication. Since those days we can claim to have played a large part in the growth of the A. & U. list to its present level of prosperity, but in our twenties, we were a bit young to have gathered that peculiar cocoon of varied knowledge and contacts which enables a publisher to get ideas for new books, find possible authors and know just the right outside experts to give advice on specialist manuscripts.

However, the speculation may be idle in another sense, for I have always thought of Stanley as primarily a business man, who was able to do clever things once the books were in his hands, but who was less

inclined to devote his energies to the finding of them and their authors.
He rarely invited an author to lunch and scarcely ever to his comfortable and well-staffed home in Hampstead. It was unusual also for him
ever to go off and visit a potential author. He would say a little wist-
fully sometimes, 'I suppose I should run after these people more', but I
think the Victorian elements in his nature, which served him so well in
some respects, gave him the feeling that right-minded authors, those
worth having, would come of their own accord to a good, sound publisher like himself. Furthermore, it was not in his nature to sit for an
hour or so engaging in that easy give and take, 50–50 type of conversation, in which ideas for good books can be generated. Those authors
of distinction whom we had on the list in the 'thirties—apart from
Russell, who was unquestionably my Uncle's personal 'catch', as was
Harold Laski—tended to be those who had been acquired when we had
bought up various bankrupt businesses. Maunsell of Dublin had been
one such valuable purchase, which had brought us J. M. Synge and the
early plays of St. John Ervine.

However, among the earlier captures he made was a small group of
authors who grew to great stature. One of these was Arthur Waley,
secured by no more than a timely letter to him after some of his translations of Chinese poems had appeared in the *Cambridge Magazine*. The
firm had enjoyed a success with the publication of his famous translation of Lady Murasaki's *Tale of Genji*, but by the 'thirties that was
selling more slowly, and the greatest demand for Waley's work was
still to come. On one occasion some time when S.U. was away, Arthur
Waley came to see me, to say that he had struck a difficult problem
with his translation of the Chinese classic *Chin Ping Mei*, and wanted
our advice upon it. When I asked if I could be of any help, this charming,
gentle, ascetic-looking scholar (the country's greatest Orientalist, who
in fact never travelled east of Austria) said gravely, 'The trouble is
this passage where the hero dies from the overdose of an aphrodisiac—
here's the typescript, I'll leave it with you.'

In the climate of those days S.U. decided, finally, to publish it under
the imprint of John Lane the Bodley Head during the period when he
bad a controlling interest in that firm.

Some authors undoubtedly did come of their own accord, attracted
simply by S.U.'s virtues as a publisher, but I think it is fair to say that
the 'procurement' of authors was not the Chief's strongest point.
Indeed, when they had come or been found, they did not all take kindly
to the masterly lecture to which they might be subjected, on publishing problems, or the singularly unsaleable qualities of their books. On
the other hand, many publishers full of author-charm and lunch invitations have failed to keep a firm solvent and independent over fifty
years, and S.U. was apt to say that one can always 'buy' the literary

expert whereas financial expertise was not so easy to come by. Some would say that a genuine and responsible 'flair' is the vital element in publishing. S.U.'s great strength lay in his acute commercial sense coupled with his sure 'feel' for the viability of different types of books over a wide range of subjects.

After one of those difficult years there was a particularly uncomfortable moment when we were surveying the annual accounts together, and he remarked with devastating objectivity, 'Of course, at this stage it would pay me to sell the firm and let the premises to someone else.' One of his famous 'statements of case'. I doubt if it really held water, because in the trough of the depression he would have found it difficult to get a satisfactory offer for A. & U. The City was not interested in the book trade, and few, if any, publishers had cash to spare for acquisitions—also there were masses of office buildings 'to let'. Nevertheless, it was one of those remarks calculated to shiver the timbers of striving young men, while leaving them at the same time with a sense of the magnanimity of a boss who, apparently for their sakes, would yet keep the business going. He did add, however, that of course he would be a fool to dispose of it, because of its potential; if we could hold on, conditions were bound to improve and in the course of time it must be our turn to have a best-seller. In the event his confidence was proved up to the hilt.

This element of confidence in his destiny, backed up by unceasing work—God helps those who help themselves—'the eternal not ourselves which makes for righteousness'—was a tremendous force in his make-up. His success with books on auto-suggestion, Baudouin's *Suggestion and Auto-suggestion* and C. H. Brooks's *Practice of Auto-suggestion,* in the early 1920s had, I am sure, fortified S.U. in the fundamental belief that he—the firm—was made to progress and that nothing could hold it back for long.

Having galvanized the Publishers' Association into setting up new committees to examine and control certain shortcomings and to develop creative co-operation between publishers, booksellers, librarians and the book-trade paper, he could hardly refuse—nor indeed did he wish to refuse—to serve on the committees himself. Thus there were many days when most of his time seemed to be spent away from the office, when it was difficult to catch him for discussion of any length; and not surprisingly he could be pretty short and sharp when one did succeed in getting his attention for a moment. In one year, 1933, while President of the Association, he had to cope with illness in his own family and no less than three family executorships. It really became a marvel that he had any time or energy left for his own business.

Yet he did; and so long as he was within physical reach of 40 Museum Street, he always acted as if the whole show would collapse without him. With any journey in prospect, whether to Switzerland for winter sports with his family, or to a booksellers' conference for a long week-end, he would contrive to dash into the office, if only for half an hour, and go through as much of the morning's post as possible, neatly inscribing his notes and 'tadpoles' on some of the letters. When he did a six-week trip to the States, and had to catch a boat train at Waterloo at about 9 a.m., he arranged for his secretary to be at the station with as much of the morning correspondence as she had been able to collect. He then dictated last-minute replies and instructions to her in the corner of the railway carriage, while the more devoted members of his family waited on the platform to see him off.

His passion for keeping an eye on every letter was exemplified one year when he was on holiday with his family at Overstrand. Suddenly on a Thursday afternoon I received a telegram which read, 'Are you free come week-end, bring correspondence tennis shoes.' The consideration for my week-end was to be the conveyance of all the office correspondence of the past fortnight, so that he could go through it, pick holes where necessary, and thus reduce the accumulation which he would have to face on his return. When I answered 'Yes, thanks', the telegraphic rejoinder was, 'Meet you Cromer 2.32 luggage in rucksack preferable.' Bulky files of correspondence loose in a rucksack seemed a hazardous arrangement, but I risked it and we had a good walk along the very pleasant cliff path from Cromer Station to Overstrand. After a bathe, I did my best to give satisfaction on the tennis court.

Another of his famous telegrams came from Iceland in 1934. In search of solitude in the midst of exceptional pressures, he had gone there as almost a pioneer holiday-maker. With no air service in those days, it meant a long and potentially sick-making trip in a small boat, from Aberdeen or Leith. Naturally his family was anxious for his welfare, when he set off for this possibly cold and misty island. But in sending news he wasted no cabled words on a long home address; instead, the missive came to the office, so as to use our code *Deucalion*. It just read, 'Happily arrived sunshine'. The fact that it had been handed in at Reykjavik naturally told the story. The cable prompted a memorable comment from Charles Furth: 'I never thought of that as a nickname for S.U.'

This was the first occasion on which Stanley had gone off without having his former co-director E. L. Skinner available to leave in charge, as they had parted company earlier that year, when Skinner took over the Williams & Norgate business, which A. & U. had owned since 1928. Almost without a word of warning, Charles and I were suddenly accorded not, alas, the status of junior directors, but a neat arrangement under which in S.U.'s absence abroad we held a joint power of attorney, able to commit the firm to engagements up to the sum of £500. This seems ludicrously small today, but in the 1930s it was ample to enable us to accept and put in hand the production of a quite large book. Nowadays, when it seems reasonable for almost every member of the staff to have some high-sounding title, and when directorships of various degrees proliferate, it is strange to recall how the head of the firm could then get by perfectly well, according the minimum of status to anyone else.

For years, I suppose, I traded on the name of Unwin when confronting authors, and would-be authors, including disappointed recipients of rejected manuscripts. They would angrily demand to 'see a director', but when they asked me who I was, I had only to say 'Philip Unwin' for them to assume that I was at least a junior partner. Another favourite designation from the Chief would be 'one of my assistants at this office', or 'my nephew', but of course it left one's actual position with the firm quite unspecified. Though we seemed to have a long time to wait for directorships, yet as profits increased, salaries and bonuses grew, and in retrospect, according to the general conditions existing then, we had no cause for complaint. It is fair to say that S.U.'s policy towards his senior staff was not unusual in the 1930s. Such egocentricity, and the implication that he 'did everything himself', was frequent in many a firm during the active life of the founder.

My Uncle's outside preoccupations meant of course that Charles and I had excellent opportunities to deal with authors and with visiting American publishers. In my case, one of the very early developments was the Indian side of our list. For me this began with my first meeting with the almost mythical C. F. Andrews. Stanley has devoted some space to him in his autobiography, and it is certainly no exaggeration to say that in appearance, and in his general nature, he was quite literally a Christ-like figure, with his long, flowing beard and penetrating, but incredibly gentle eyes. The first book I handled for him was *Letters to a Friend*, a collection of letters that had been written to Andrews by the famous Indian poet Rabindranath Tagore. In the course of our dealings, Tagore paid a visit to London and I had to go and see him one day, with the proofs of the book, when he was staying in some Kensington hotel. There he sat in an armchair, clad in what seemed to me an exquisite silken robe, with his ivory-smooth, café-au-lait complexion, and this wonderful silky beard spreading out from it. With beautiful diction, and quick, slightly disapproving hand movements, he emphasized his disagreement with some point which Andrews had introduced into the book. However, it all passed off satisfactorily and *Letters to a Friend* proved quite a success.

We published a number of books for Andrews himself, the most successful of which were his edited versions of Mahatma Gandhi's long, rambling work *My Experiments with Truth*. Andrews secured Gandhi's authority to extract sections from this and to preface them with a long, explanatory introduction, and all of them enjoyed a good sale in India at the time. On his many fleeting visits to London, C.F.A., who rarely seemed to possess any clothes beyond a thin tropical suit, and occasionally a mackintosh, relied on the devoted services of Miss Agatha Harrison, who acted as his unofficial secretary, seeing amongst other things that he did not double and treble book himself for the multiplicity of speaking engagements he undertook in different parts of Britain. It must be remembered that in the 1930s India was chafing desperately against British rule; there were many sympathizers in this country for the cause of Indian freedom, while at the same time it had such formidable opponents as Winston Churchill. As my Uncle was to write later, 'No man did so much to help Indians and the English to understand one another. It is difficult to exaggerate how much the friendly relations between our two peoples is due to Charlie Andrews.'

Through Agatha Harrison I first heard the name of Jawaharlal Nehru, and learned also that he was at work on a book and hoped to visit England shortly. When he arrived I had the chance of attending a talk which he gave to the Friends of Indian Freedom—or some such organization—and was immensely struck by the way in which everyone present seemed to hang upon his words. At Miss Harrison's suggestion, he subsequently came to 40 Museum Street: I saw him and received the typescript of his autobiography. We made an offer for it, but as at that time Nehru was *persona non grata* with the British Government in India, there was every risk that the book might be banned by the British authorities there. We therefore wanted to make the amount of advance royalty we paid dependent upon whether the book could sell freely in India. Nehru's name was not then particularly well known outside India, and there seemed no certainty that the book would necessarily enjoy a large sale in Britain; but while the matter was under discussion I set off on my first trip to America and was bitterly disappointed on my return to find that Krishna Menon, who was acting as unofficial agent for Nehru, had swooped in, carried off the manuscript to Allen Lane and accepted his offer of, I believe, £150 advance, which we had hesitated to make. It was equal to £750 today.

Later, the situation developed two aspects of monumental irony; first, interest in the book was so great here that the sales would have been ample to justify the advance asked for, while in India it did in fact sell freely. Second, the firm of John Lane was then in very low water and went into liquidation the following year, with the result that the royalties on the first year's sale were unpaid, and the distinguished author thus ended up a great deal worse off than if he had accepted our original offer of a £50 advance. I consoled myself, as one is apt to under such circumstances, with the thought that had I been in London I could have persuaded Miss Harrison to intercede on our behalf, as I knew she had considerable influence with Krishna Menon. But that, perhaps, is a case of 'what might have happened if . . .'

With these Indian affairs came the beginning of my dealings with that very great man now known to the world as Sir Sarvapelli Radhakrishnan, former President of India. The connection had begun almost casually, at a time when he was just a Professor at Waltair University, by his submitting to us his two-volume work on Indian philosophy for publication in our Muirhead Library of Philosophy. That had led on to *The Hindu View of Life*, a classic which we have been selling for over forty years, and then his famous translation of *The Bhagavadgita*. He had a quick and somewhat abrupt manner, often accompanied by a strumming of his sensitive brown fingers upon one's desk, and would conclude a discussion with the words, 'Well, see to the thing, will you?' But behind it was great warmth and kindliness. His brief hand-written letters about business affairs rarely concluded without an inquiry after my health and that of the Chief's.

In later days, when he was India's ambassador to the U.S.S.R. and subsequently her President, his visits were most memorable. At the surface level, it was impressive, to say the least, to see two or three motor-cycle policemen sweep up Museum Street and close it to all traffic, until the great Cadillac flying the flag of India had drawn up and deposited our distinguished guest upon the doorstep. Then, accompanied by an aide-de-camp in the uniform of the Indian navy, complete with epaulettes, he would slowly ascend our steep office stairs. I am still touched to think that he frequently asked for me first and I would often enjoy a talk with him, only partly on business matters; then I would ask my Uncle to join us, and the two of them would launch into a survey of world affairs, on which S.U. was always extremely well informed.

It was amusing to see them together: both men spoke rapidly and with force and conviction, and were accustomed to having their point of view accepted; also both gestured freely as they spoke. There was one splendid occasion when they were going at it excitedly together, probably about the problem of Kashmir. For emphasis, each shot a hand into the air simultaneously and involuntarily grasped the other. This seemed to bring the whole operation to a standstill; they both laughed, shook their heads and agreed to differ.

Radhakrishnan was a very fine business man where his publishers were concerned: to this day, he remains the only author who has succeeded in persuading us to let him have six free copies of each reprint of his books. As they all sold well, and were reprinted continually, he gained a large number of copies in this way. I only hope they did not find their way eventually on to the second-hand market in India.

In connection with Nehru, I referred to my first visit to America. This was one of the more pleasant surprises of the 'thirties, which developed almost by chance. Some years before, Stanley had said that of course I must 'do a trip to the States' some time; but, like the longer period which I was supposed to have in Germany, to improve my rather sketchy knowledge of the language, it somehow did not material-ize. Then, suddenly, one Saturday morning in November 1935, an author connected with the Institute of Pacific Relations, New York, with whom I had had some dealings, and to whom I had mentioned vaguely the possibility of a trip to the States, wrote in the course of a letter, 'and when are you coming over here?' That seemed to stop Stanley dead in his tracks. 'Yes,' he said, 'that is a thing I want you to do. Well, you know, it might be possible this year. I've got no plans to be away for the next couple of months—it might be an idea for you to make a late autumn trip, when other English publishers have got out of the way and when Americans are back from their various travels. Why don't you go round to Cook's this morning and see what boats are available?'

In an incredibly short time I was fixed up with one of the cheapest first-class cabins in the *Laconia*, one of the slower, and therefore cheaper, Cunarders sailing from Liverpool; and after letters to sundry American publisher friends, I was off in a fortnight.

Today, when New York can be reached from London within six hours and trans-Atlantic crossings are comparable to a bus service, it is difficult to imagine the excitement which such a journey could hold for someone like myself, thirty-five years ago. The mere fact of going off from Euston Station on the Irish Mail, with two coaches specially labelled 'Liverpool Riverside', was something in itself, especially when it included a splendid breakfast *en route*, with bacon, egg and grilled mushrooms. Then came one's first impression of Cunard ser-vice and food, the sense of being an honoured guest in an extraordinar-ily comfortable hotel—even though it was rough enough for two days to make even me come within an ace of seasickness. One morning I was delighted to find myself the only passenger at breakfast; on that occasion, when the ship took a tremendous roll, two stewards had to rush to my table with one accord in order to hold things on to it. Ships were, of course, quite unstabilized in those days.

Owing to the rough weather, we were a day late; having started at midday on a Saturday, we did not dock until the following Monday week. Waiting on the quayside for me, with the typical kindness of Americans, was Daniel Melcher, who had worked in our office for six months in the previous year. He most kindly escorted me along to the

Harvard Club, where one of the directors of W. W. Norton had secured me 'guest privileges' for my stay. Then dear Fred Melcher, Dan's father, gave me lunch at the famous Algonquin Hotel, on my first day.

Fred Melcher, who as a young bookseller's assistant could claim to have discovered Arnold Bennett's *Old Wives' Tale* for American readers, was then editor of the *Publishers' Weekly* in New York. He 'knew everyone' in the American book trade and was the unfailingly kind guide and philosopher to any newcomer.

Since the general standard of living and way of life in England has come so much nearer to that of America, it is impossible now for anyone to experience the really tremendous contrast which existed in those days. The Clean Air Bill has made London's atmosphere tolerably clear even in winter, but real sunshine was then rare for us in December: in New York, though it was bitterly cold, the sun shone brilliantly, partly of course because of the more southerly latitude. Again, we now know rather too many skyscrapers in London, but one's first sight of them rising thirty or forty storeys into that bright air was literally breath-taking. The utter comfort of central heating was a boon, coupled with great log fires in the Harvard Club, their best, strong Brazilian coffee, such as I had never tasted before, and superb porridge—or rather 'oatmeal'—and thin cream for breakfast. There was too that remarkable, and to us then unknown, operation of the cafeteria, which seemed to produce such good food, by comparison with the average London teashop. In that pre-deep-freeze era it all had so much more flavour than one finds in most American food today.

The typical publisher's office also became an eye-opener to me, because few if any of us had decently furnished and carpeted rooms to work in before the war. It struck me as quite remarkable to hear publishers claim that since they spent a third of their lives in their offices, it seemed only sensible to make them really comfortable. There was also that charming professionalism about the office receptionist and their automatic telephone greeting, 'The Macmillan Company, good morning, can I help you?' This has become almost universal, but at the time all that most of us could manage in London was a gruff Cockney ''Ullo', and for the visitor, almost certainly a hard seat in some draughty corner, instead of an armchair beside a book-laden table, on a carpeted floor.

The hospitality of Americans in general, and most certainly publishers, has become a by-word; but I cannot pass over this point without recalling the extraordinary kindness of so many of them towards a young man they had never met before. No doubt it was partly on account of my uncle, but it was so good of busy men like Fred Melcher to have me out to his hospitable home at Montclair, and let me drive what seemed then his gigantic Chrysler car; of Warder Norton and his wife to entertain me two or three times in their beautiful apartment near Grammercy Park; and of Ferris Greenslet, of Houghton Mifflin, to drive me on a Sunday morning round the historic parts of Boston and its neighbourhood—and not least, to place orders next day for the importation of nice little editions of two of the books I had on offer. It always remains a thrill for a young visiting publisher to be able to send back to his home office orders to help cover the cost of his trip. Not for one moment that the value of a publisher's visit to America, or any-where else, is necessarily to be calculated by the business done at the time, but it does give him particular satisfaction if it works out that way. Since, in this instance, my whole trip was done for no more than about £70, the chances of covering expenses were perhaps propor-tionately better than today.

Another aspect of American life in those days, which in retrospect seemed to add to its attractions, was that cars and aeroplanes had not yet come to dominate the transport situation so far as to knock out railways. A journey such as that from New York to Boston by the famous 'Yankee Clipper Pullman Express' could be a real joy, with well-served meals in charge of coloured waiters and, of course, the famous Pullman porters, who took your hat away and put it in a bag (to protect it from the smuts from the engine) and cleaned your shoes before you alighted. I was able also, on a return trip by the night train known as the 'Owl', to experience the more doubtful pleasures of the American sleeping-car, in which you climbed from the open centre aisle into an upper berth behind a heavy curtain, and heard the veiled grunts and snores of other sleepers around you. But it was all a part of the American tradition and it had a charm of its own. It was not every young man in publishing who had American experience behind him at my age, and I was once again grateful to Uncle Stan for the opportunity.

After it, of course, came the return match, with an increasing num-ber of visiting American publishers asking to see me. My appointment book became fuller, and there was more 'modest entertainment' to be done 'in the firm's interest', as S.U. put it when granting me an expense allowance of £25 per annum. What some of our visitors thought of my teetotal habits in those days I do not know, but they were too polite to complain and I hope I made up for them after the transfer of my life insurance from the 'Temperance' to the 'General' section.

Besides the Indians and the Americans with whom I had dealings in 1935, the year was memorable to me for my meetings with a most colourful character. This was Prince Lieven—a genuine White Russian Prince—who had a life-long interest in ballet. He had been a personal friend of Alexandre Benoît and the famous Colonel de Basil, and he possessed some very interesting correspondence with the former. This became the basis of the Prince's book, *The Birth of Ballets Russes*. The Prince himself had plenty of money and entertained me, and the translator of the book, Leonide Zarine, royally at the Savoy and elsewhere. He was an enormous man, about six feet three, and partially blind; but he had what he frankly termed his c*rrr*ystal eye, a glittering blue optic which stared at one fixedly, and he wore on his wrist a small clock, which he claimed was part of a Russian cavalry-man's equipment. His knowledge of the ballet, and by his own account of ballerinas also, was considerable and he was enormously good com-pany. I remember his description of some famous old director of the Russian ballet, who, he said, had false teeth, a wig, a wooden leg, and wore button boots, and yet, 'He could have *any* girl he wanted *at any time!*' When I asked him, more or less, 'How?', he said with delicious mystery, 'It was just his s-e-x-u-a-l nature, they could not resist him', which, when you come to think of it, is just about the whole truth. His book did quite well and I sold the American rights to Houghton Mifflin.

One of our major 'might-have-beens' at that time was the publica-tion of Hitler's *Mein Kampf*. It had been offered to the firm quite early in Hitler's career, but my Uncle very naturally could not believe that the Germans, for whom he had such respect, could ever follow such a mountebank as Hitler.

However, 1935 marked the end of our lean period, sales showed a tendency to rise, and by 1936 there were two highly significant events. One was Lancelot Hogben's *Mathematics for the Million*, and the other was S.U.'s masterly deal by which we became publishers of the Phaidon Art Books. Through a series of skilful moves, he 'Aryanized' the Jewish Phaidon Verlag in Austria and thus saved it from Nazi clutches.

Our connection with Hogben we probably owed to the late B. N. Langdon-Davies. Stanley had come to know him when Langdon-Davies was Manager of the Labour Publishing Company, and S.U. subsequently appointed him to manage the firm of Williams & Nor-gate when A. & U. acquired it in 1928. Langdon-Davies was not a natural business man, and did not ultimately hit it off particularly well with Stanley, but he was a barrister and a man of considerable culture, with wide contacts among the younger intellectuals. It was he who pressed Stanley to agree rather reluctantly to the terms Hogben wanted for his scientific books, to be published by Williams & Nor-gate; and when that business was sold subsequently to E. L. Skinner, S.U. most shrewdly insisted that Hogben should be taken over by us, little knowing then that he would write a popular book on mathe-matics which was to become a world best-seller.

The complicated production of *Mathematics for the Million*, and the nurturing throughout of its somewhat demanding author, was largely the work of Charles Furth, and the enormously successful launching of it was greatly to his credit, though it is probably fair to say that the author himself put up as many bright publicity ideas as anybody. At all events, its publication in the autumn of 1936 signalled the end of the long night so far as A. & U. were concerned. That book alone put a welcome ten per cent on to our sales, though I can never in my mind disassociate the excitement of its publication from a most painful attack of shingles which I endured at the time, and which foreshadowed a serious decline in my own health.

9 A Personal Setback

Early in March 1937 I took to my bed with what appeared to be a bad dose of 'flu. I had a high temperature and a cough, which at times exhausted me to the point of not caring whether I lived or died. After a week of this, Lindsey Batten, of Hampstead, a family man, outspoken, human and a very good doctor, ordered an X-ray and by so doing probably saved my life. The plates showed severe damage from pulmonary tuberculosis in both lungs, and there was nothing for it but absolute rest in bed for the next three months at least.

It is not easy for anyone now to realize the total knock-out which such a diagnosis could seem to be over thirty years ago. T.B., the 'White Scourge', was one of the great killers of the day. There were no antibiotics, and apart from physical rest—to give the lungs as little as possible to do—the only treatment was chest surgery of various kinds, involving partial collapse of the lungs. The purpose of this was to put the whole or part of a lung out of action for a long period, in the hope that the tissues would knit together again and thus close up and heal the dangerous cavity caused by the disease. At best it was likely to be close on a year before a patient could hope to get back to work. Whether, without my wife Evelyn, I should ever have come through it to lead an active life again in publishing is decidedly questionable.

My happy marriage in 1932 had been the outcome of one of the more familiar patterns, falling in love with a sister's best school friend, as my own father had done forty years before. Indeed, it was Surbiton High School, where I had once so irreverently kicked a Bible twenty years earlier, that was responsible for my meeting Evelyn Rawson. Her family background was similar to mine; she had taken a social science diploma at the London School of Economics, and so had a feeling for much that A. & U. stood for, and she was prepared to risk marriage on £360 a year. 1932 was just about the trough of the world depression, the unemployed figure had reached 3,000,000, our firm did little more than break even that year, and I thought it very decent of Uncle Stan to have produced even a modest increase in salary to celebrate my nuptials. For £80 a year a roomy, unfurnished flat was to be had at the top of a Victorian house in Hampstead, and we seemed to live comfortably enough on a housekeeping allowance of thirty shillings a week.

When I began to know Evelyn well, I had someone really close to whom I could confide my inmost hopes and fears, and for whose intellect I had great respect. A situation not unique, but it does not happen to every man in marriage.

The pressure of working with an exacting and Argus-eyed perfectionist, though enjoyable and stimulating, had taken a toll of me. S.U. set a standard in commercial acumen and meticulous attention to detail (over-fussy, some would say!) which I had neither the capacity nor the temperament fully to emulate. Not that he nagged anybody unreasonably, but one was apt to feel at times that whatever one did, it might have been done better, and whatever one had learned so far, there was no end to what had to be mastered if one were to be any good as a publisher. Inevitably I had before me Stanley's own account of all that he had achieved in the Fisher Unwin business (profits increased tenfold in as many years), and so far I was a long way behind. For all his avuncular consideration for me in many ways, I experienced times of despondency.

Into this the loving counsel of a good wife brought a burst of fresh air and common sense. Without under-estimating S.U.'s ability and drive, she saw him more objectively, and so could buttress my self-confidence; while her favourite Shakespearean maxim, Polonius's 'To thine own self be true', made me realize that I possessed qualities complementary to those of my Chief. I was able to make my own particular contribution to the welfare of the firm, and especially of its authors and staff.

By 1937 I had begun to feel that I had found myself. My salary had crept up to £500, plus a few expenses allowed by the firm—but no free cars in those days. I had a little new home in Belsize Park, and our standard was not far short of what £2,500 a year would be today. Partly because of the beginnings of rearmament, the economy was picking up, unemployment was slowly declining, and A. & U. had taken a definite upward turn in sales and profits. S.U. had finished two of his most time-consuming phases of Association work, his Presidential years 1933–35 and the International Publishers' Congress in London in 1936, in the organizing of which he had carried the lion's share of responsibility. Also, we had recently taken on, from Chapman & Hall, Malcolm Barnes, who quickly helped to ease some of my pressures in the office, and who in the course of the next thirty years was to become a tower of strength in editorial problems over general books. So it was all the more infuriating that I should fall ill just as prospects were beginning to please.

Some people thought that the particular conditions of the job might have been a factor in my illness. The disease was not in my immediate family, though it cropped up with cousins in two other branches. But there was so much tuberculosis infection about in those days; pasteurization of milk and tuberculin-tested herds were by no means general; a beloved and far too thin kindergarten mistress of my childhood had died of the disease. Another possible factor, mentioned by one of the doctors who dealt with me later, was the strain of my longdistance running at school. But there was never any complete explanation of where or whom the disease might strike.

Over the previous year or so I had suffered recurrent intestinal upsets, with no idea that they could be in any way related to my having rather more colds than usual, followed by a loose cough. Add to this loss of weight and a tendency to tire more easily, and one has a classic T.B. case; but I had imagined that nothing short of severe haemorrhage could be any indication of lung trouble. My comparatively Spartan upbringing and my mother's interest in Christian Science had made her family reluctant to fuss over illness. I would be the first to recognize the benefits which that faith has brought to many people; but on the other hand, the outlook it engenders can lead to the deliberate ignoring of dangerous symptoms, and that is what had happened in my case.

So there was I on that bright spring day, the 'Home X-ray' plates just developed and still dripping into the bath, and Dr. Batten saying, 'Well, I'm afraid there *is* a good deal of trouble in both lungs and you'll have to take things very quietly for some time.' In the next room was our pretty little daughter, Judith, born three months before, a fine strong child; and it was the supreme irony that we cautious family planners, who had deliberately postponed parenthood, should have brought her into the world just as her father's health broke down. Some blessed impulse of maternal intuition had brought my mother, for the first time uninvited, to visit us that day. She had been uneasy to hear that I had been in bed for a week—such a thing had not happened to any of her children since they had had mumps in 1917. It was providential that she was with us when the blow fell.

Her reaction was immediate: we must come to the family house at Milford, in Surrey, where she and my father had moved after I had left the old home at Surbiton five years before. The spare room, with good windows facing south-west and a glorious view to Hindhead, was better than any sanatorium, and there was another unused bedroom for Evelyn and Judith. She still had a cook and a housemaid, everyone must turn to and it could all be done. The fact that my mother would not at that time have accepted medical treatment for herself was not for a moment allowed to stand in the way of a local doctor for me.

After the first shock I experienced profound relief. I thought I knew the worst. After months of pushing myself when already ill, total rest was heavenly luxury. Quite soon the cough disappeared, temperature declined, my appetite returned and I had no more digestive troubles. My stomach had not been so comfortable for years. What I did not realize was that the state of my lungs had been such that neither Lindsey Batten nor the excellent specialist he called in, F. H. Young, was by any means certain that I should rally. At that stage there was nothing to be done but to rest and wait for a couple of months, while my Christian Science relatives prayed earnestly for my recovery. I would never suggest that it was not a factor in helping me through at that early stage, and probably my earlier interest in the Faith helped towards my inner conviction that I *would* get well.

At the end of the time another X-ray showed dramatic improvement and I was allowed to be driven down to Milford. Of course I assumed, feeling so well, that I should soon be allowed to get up, but was firmly told that I had to think in terms of months rather than weeks, and so far I had done no more than begin to work off an overdraft; I had yet to build up a strong credit balance. Left to myself, without medical science, I expect I would have struggled up after two or three weeks and then gone down with worse and probably fatal damage to my lungs in the following winter.

How my brave wife got through those two months in London I do not know. She was breast-feeding our baby, and was now determined to keep it up for six months—which she did.

Even at our modest level, however, we had in those days another pair of hands in the house, in the shape of a pretty fifteen-year-old girl, and a marvellous private nurse came in every morning at about 5s. a visit, to perform that skilful ritual of the 'blanket bath' and making the bed round the recumbent patient. With no experience of such things, I at first dreaded the prospect of unimaginable embarrassment. The upper works, the feet and knees, 'Roll on your side', and the back and behind are all done easily and so comfortably with that beautiful warm flannel, damp enough to refresh but never so wet as to cause an invading trickle—but oh, Lord, what about the middle? Not to worry —no pause in the flow of easy talk, just a quick upward flick of the blanket for a sidelong glance to see how the land lay, then the firm gentle flannel pursued its way and I returned the talk. A monograph could be written on the psychology of patient-handling from the patient's point of view. Some nurses do it superbly, with sensitivity, getting on swiftly and efficiently with their professional job of work, but still leaving a sick man with the feeling that he is a real person, worth talking to, and that he will live and love and work again. Some, insensitive and over-hearty, polish you up like a piece of furniture; yet others will dab and dither and perhaps leave bits unwashed. To this day I never smell methylated spirits—usually in a secretary's room after her typewriter has been serviced—without a vivid reminder of blanket baths and a sense of gratitude for the skill and hard work of the nurses who helped me back to health.

Mother was a marvellous manager in domestic matters. There was never any doubt as to who was boss in strictly home affairs, though she would always defer to my father on major matters. She and I had had our tussles in the past, but we had always got on well together, and never so well as after I married. She and Evelyn, both strong characters, had taken the measure of each other, 'spoken out' on one or two occasions and settled to a relationship of real affection and mutual respect. I felt sure we could all work in together, especially as my father was fond of Evelyn and doted on his first granddaughter.

It remained a generous and courageous gesture by my parents. Though they were fit, my father was 68 and my mother 65; each was beginning to feel the years and to be at a time of life when one wants to take things a little more easily and to have less expense, rather than more. None of us realized that I should monopolize that spare-room bed for nearly eight months, with meals to be brought up on trays; and the continual presence, first of a baby, then a toddler—however sweet —in an essentially adult household was an upheaval, not least for my twin sisters Nora and Nancy, who were living there with my parents.

The day I was driven down to Milford was the only time in four months that I had my clothes on, and it was humiliating to find how useless leg muscles were; to mount stairs was impossible without help. Then began that long spell in one room, broken by just two visits to Brompton Hospital for X-ray and examination by my specialist. Yet, what a room, with its view over a pleasant garden, across the edge of the village, and on over gorse and heather-covered common, with the back-cloth of Hindhead six miles away!

Before he had agreed to 'home nursing', Dr. Batten had made sure that Evelyn and I both knew what the routine must be, and that we should have the strength of mind to keep to it. (Only one visitor per day and leaving the bed only to use the commode.) When, in an astonishingly short time, one felt and looked so much better, it was wellnigh impossible to believe that there was still an unexploded bomb in the chest, for which the fuse had not yet been removed. The temptation to say 'To hell with it—let's get up and live', was too much for some people, and later on I heard of many a patient who had started off well and then suffered a fatal relapse after trying to force the pace.

I was desperately sorry to have let S.U. down in this way. He very decently said at the outset that I must not 'worry about anything'— without, however, making any specific reference to cash; but he was one of the few people in the family circle to realize that it might well be a year's job at least. After four months I was put on half pay, 'until we see how things are going to work out'.

It must have been maddening for him after the trouble he had taken with me, and after I had reached the stage of being able to relieve him of a great many things; moreover, I believe he had an idea of trying to re-visit members of his family in New Zealand at about this time. My collapse, with war following two years later, put paid to that for another ten years.

One of S.U.'s favourite sayings was that 'Kind words butter no parsnips', but as an old publisher friend of mine once said, in this particular connection, 'What a difference they make!' A word from him of genuine sympathy, coupled with the hope that I should get well and return to the firm again, would have meant a devil of a lot at that particular stage; but like so many of his generation, I think he found it difficult to give expression to personal feelings of that sort. Anyway, he could reasonably have pointed out that genuine 'butter' was being provided in the shape of my half pay.

The first break in the quiet of my rural retreat was a visit to Brompton Hospital in July. Now plump of face and quite sunburnt, I was convinced that I should be pronounced fit to start getting back to normal life. The great Freddie Young examined the X-rays and then came to my room to deliver judgement upon them.

'Well,' he said, 'you're going along quite well, now it's back to the country for another couple of months and then come and see me again in September.' I was thunderstruck. Then so deeply depressed that I almost contemplated a leap out of the second-floor window into the traffic of the Brompton Road. The thought of a return to that bedroom, surrounded it is true by care and affection, but far removed from my man's world, was devastating. Although one lung had cleared up completely, the other still had the cavity that was the danger point, and it was hoped that another period of rest would enable it to close up.

The next two months were psychologically the toughest for me, not that I was bored—the endless hours for reading peacefully were still a joy—but for the first time I began to wonder whether I should ever resume a normal working life, and I know that Evelyn imagined I would be obliged to seek some form of country occupation. By then, too, we were aware of the increasing strains upon my parents' household, in having us there for so much longer than had been expected; but bless them, neither Father nor Mother ever suggested for one moment that we should go elsewhere. As they generously refused to take a penny from us, I was able to save all of my slender resources towards what we feared were going to be the heavy expenses of the future.

So September came, and my next visit to London. Once again the immaculate Freddie stood at the foot of the bed and made his pronouncement. Now I was as well as could be from rest alone, but a small cavity was still there and I must go to a sanatorium and have a so-called 'A.P.' (artificial pneumothorax, the lung-collapse treatment). When I asked, 'Well, where does all this end? Shall I ever get back to normal life?', he said cheerfully, 'Oh yes, you can expect to be back within three months of having the A.P. Then you have to have extra air pumped into it about once a month, to keep the lung collapsed. It's quite simple, you will just come along to me in Harley Street at the end of the day on your way home. Otherwise you can lead a normal life.'

He then went on to make the personal disclosure which must have encouraged so many of his patients. 'Actually,' he said, 'I've got a double A.P. myself, one in each lung, and I have to have "refills" regularly; but as you see, I'm able to lead a full working life.' This was a revelation. It had never entered my head that this apparently suave, all-capable specialist in the T.B. world could possibly have suffered the disease himself. In fact, I learned later that he had had two very bad doses, but had fought his way back to full activity; and he lived on until well into his seventies.

Rather than face the problems of the two distant sanatoria suggested, Montana or Mundesley, we pressed for the King Edward VII just above Midhurst in Sussex, as it was comparatively near to my family at Milford.

Founded with the aid of a munificent endowment from the late Sir Ernest Cassel, long before any National Health Service, Midhurst had been intended all along for middle-class people who could pay something but not the full costs of a private sanatorium; and who were likely to recover.

Dr. Geoffrey Todd, the Superintendent of Midhurst sanatorium (long since knighted for his distinguished service to this branch of medicine), was prepared to accept me, and after taking my turn upon the lengthy waiting list, I was admitted in January 1938.

Though both Evelyn and I had dreaded the prospect, our first view of the King Edward VII was a revelation. Beautifully built of brick and sandstone, on the southern slope of a hill facing the South Downs, the whole layout and design of the building is magnificent. It reminded me at once of a splendid country hotel, the suggestion of which was enhanced by the appearance of a party of half-a-dozen cheerful young men and women who came in from a walk (medically prescribed) and dropped their walking-sticks into the stand provided for the purpose just inside the hall.

The operation I eventually had was an elaboration of the ordinary A.P. known as the extra-pleural pneumothorax. This was more complicated surgically and involved much more frequent refills. As a technique it was somewhat experimental, and I do not believe that it was generally successful. However, my 'extra pleural' worked splendidly, and closed down the cavity; at the end of it all, exactly ten years later, I had two sound lungs once more.

No one who has not been incarcerated in a so-called sick bed for a year can know the sense of pure joy and exhilaration which comes from one's first walk abroad when the sentence is over. At that time one of the essentials of T.B. convalescence was strictly graded walking exercises. It happened to be a sunny February morning on the day I was allowed out for my first half-mile—a short walk through the woods. The smell of fresh air and the pine trees and the jewelled appearance of frost on the grass and dead bracken were unbelievably good.

It was very fortunate for my little family that Evelyn was able to get rooms in a farm about one mile from the sanatorium. There, she and the now-toddling Judith lived happily for the six months of my open imprisonment, and she could visit me regularly. She loved the surroundings and did not hesitate to drag the pram along steep paths through the woods, to see the country she wanted, nor to walk up and down the dark road to the sanatorium to spend the evenings with me. I was lucky to be able to keep my family life intact. Some marriages fell apart while one or other partner was in that strange and artificial sanatorium life.

The confining together of over a hundred mainly young people of different sexes, away from the world, rather as on a ship at sea, inevitably had its problems, and there was no shortage of sanatorium romances. Most of us were well on the way to a fair restoration of health; we all had plenty of food, and none of us was allowed to get physically tired, so the sexual pressures built up. This the Medical Superintendent handled skilfully. There were two lounges through which there was a constant traffic of doctors and nurses, and here girls and boys could sit and talk, or play cards, to their hearts' content. They were not supposed to go for walks together, though pleasant dalliance could occur through a chance meeting in the woods. When we had a weekly film show in the main dining hall, the sexes were firmly segregated.

One of the great virtues of the sanatorium was that it taught a patient how to live and survive after he had left the place and returned to work. Not to push himself to the limit, to take if possible an hour's rest on his bed before his evening meal, not to attempt to work through a cold—to take everything in moderation; and as for alcohol, Dr. Todd used to say, 'It isn't the drink that does you the harm, but what you think you can do after you've had it.'

As well as the chances for further reading, with a good library at hand, I had tremendous enjoyment and stimulus from endless talk with other patients. We used to gather after breakfast in one of the garden alcoves and discuss the events of the day, with close argument over whether Anthony Eden was right to have resigned from Chamberlain's government, or how soon could we get rid of the Conservatives (or no, they were England's only hope!). Would Hitler or Mussolini go mad, would there be war, etc., etc.? This whole experience helped me to take stock afresh and to find myself. It did for me a little of what university life might have done ten years before. Also, I think it taught me to relax.

Having reached the stage of walking my measured mile both morning and afternoon, I was pronounced fit to leave at the beginning of July 1938, and to start a shortened working week in September. It seemed rather appalling that after eighteen months I should still not be able to report for full duties, but the standard form in all T.B. convalescence was graduated progression, and finally, not to allow the successful patient to plunge straight from the easy, healthy country life of the 'san' into a 5½-day working week in London. Even if one planned to keep strict office hours—no overtime or taking work home, no working lunches and no late nights—the change in effort was inevitably very great, and there was always the chance of a cold or 'flu infection once you were back in general circulation.

Since I still had to have the 'refills' of air twice a week, it seemed a good idea to remain within reach of Midhurst. The 'san' performed the job for ten-and-sixpence a time, half the sum charged by the London specialist, though even his guinea fee was very reasonable for Harley Street. I could have had it done free at a London hospital clinic, but that would have meant a much longer absence from the office during the working day. After the expenses and the reduced income of recent months, we had to keep down our living costs, so we found an old cottage near Shottermill Ponds, a mile to the south-west of Haslemere, which was to let for 22s. 6d. a week.

It was primitive, only one 'loo', and that on the ground floor, no hot-water system and no proper bath, but an extraordinarily considerate landlady. She took an interest in us and provided an 'Ideal' boiler, while I managed to procure a good secondhand bath through the engineer at the 'san'.

That stone-built cottage had a pleasant garden, with a lovely view over Bramshott Common to the west, and though only a mile from Haslemere Station, it was right on the edge of beautiful country. I took it for three years initially, thinking that we should eventually move back to London, but the onset of war a year later discouraged one from deliberately taking a young family into London; we became extraordinarily fond of the place and stayed on until some years after the war. The Southern's electrification of the Portsmouth line in 1937 had given Haslemere a magnificent train service, so that commuting from there was easy.

To come out into the world again was, of course, the attainment of a goal yearned for and dreamt of over months. Yet I was suddenly reminded that it is only in the country of the blind that the one-eyed man is king—only inside the sanatorium was I an exceptionally active, healthy person, one who had done well, and who had talked confidently and been able to encourage new patients. Now I was faced by the realization that I was *still* far from taking my full part in the workaday world. I was supposed to rest on a bed for an hour before lunch and before my evening meal, and I was not to lift anything heavy, or do anything strenuous with arms and shoulders which might possibly upset the section of my lung that was artificially collapsed. Above all, I had not to get over-tired. But there were great compensations; we were a family unit again, friends and relations dropped in to visit us once more in our own home. And the summer weather was lovely.

After two months of this rather lazy life, during which the Nazi shadow was growing over Czechoslovakia, I started back at A. & U. on my four-day working week, just as Chamberlain undertook his first flight to confer with Hitler.

To obviate a daily journey, at first I spent three nights a week in a small Bloomsbury hotel, which then charged about 10s. 6d. a night for dinner, bed and breakfast. Not surprisingly perhaps, S.U. had resented this 'short week' and had pressed for me to wait a bit longer, until I was allowed to work full time. That, however, was completely against the Midhurst doctrine of gradualness, which also took account of the need for progressive build-up of one's resistance to the hazards of London life. With so much at stake, I felt obliged to stick to the medical recommendation, and so I began work again under something of a cloud with the Chief, though the kindly welcome of members of the staff, some of whom had written to me regularly, was heart-warming.

In retrospect, my first six months through the winter of 1938–39 was not a happy period. Though there were plenty of odd jobs for me to do in the firm, my future was still seen as precarious, and there was reluctance to entrust new books and their authors to me again on any scale. I had to live quietly, and of course very economically.

There were good, long week-ends from Thursday night to Monday morning when Judith, Evelyn and I could be together, but she disliked and resented the lonely winter days between, especially as we had no local friends in Haslemere at that early stage. It was a strange transitional period in which it was difficult to adjust from the sheltered institutional life (and I had still to revisit the 'san' every Saturday morning) to the normal working day. Also, one was apt to feel resentful that nearly two years of impaired earning capacity had inevitably lowered one's standard of living.

Two remarks made by friends at that time stuck in my memory for ever. One was by that ebullient and open-hearted American publisher Storer Lunt. On a trip to London, he most kindly visited me soon after I came out of Midhurst, and on taking leave of us he said, 'Well, Philip, it's good to see you looking so fit; but never forget that health is the first wealth.' Trite perhaps, but utterly true. The other was made by a fellow patient—then a medical student—who had been at Midhurst and who later became a close friend. One day, when I was cursing the nuisance of my frequent 'refills', he said, 'Well, old boy, you've got to remember that we're both *lucky to be alive!*' He was so very right, and it put the situation in its proper perspective.

Part of my luck had been to have first-class specialist treatment available during the illness and for the ten years of chest 'refills' after it. Midhurst has been described as the 'Balliol' of T.B. sanatoria; I managed to stay within reach of it and of Dr. Young in London from 1938 to 1948. One other lesson has stood me in good stead: get a doctor you trust, then *do what you are told*.

That first winter passed; I survived with nothing worse than one bad cold; best of all, I was allowed to work a five-day week from January 1st, 1939. The primroses, violets and bluebells of the nearby Sussex woods enchanted us, and though Hitler invaded Czechoslovakia in March and Mussolini bagged Albania at Easter, we dared to hope, like so many others, that war might yet be averted. In the event, my eighteen months' absence from the firm was to be the means by which I was free to put in 'six years hard' for A. & U. while three other key colleagues were on National Service.

10 Publishing at War

Throughout that fine summer of 1939 I began to live again. I now knew I could survive a working life in London. I was taking on more responsibility for authors in Allen & Unwin, and Evelyn and Judith were flourishing at Haslemere, where I joined them every Friday evening. We had still to keep within a modest budget, and our summer holiday of one week that year was taken at home with the aid of a borrowed car. I had some over-conscientious notion of trying to 'refund' the firm for my long absence by reducing my holiday to less than the normal fortnight. (Our Chief, though not as reluctant over holidays as Fisher Unwin had been, came only slowly—and many years later—to the idea of an automatic three weeks for his senior staff.)

When Hitler invaded Poland, my wife and I were thinking it would be good if we were to have another child. Fortunately, as it turned out, our wish was by then already on the way to being granted. After the previous upheavals in our family life, we would probably have thought it unwise to have another baby in all the uncertainties of war, but our second daughter Lynette arrived safely just before the battle of the Low Countries, and neither she nor her mother allowed the subsequent air-raids to disturb her successful progress. According to our cautious outlook in the 1930s, we would not have had either of our fine healthy girls had we known that my T.B. would follow the birth of one, and that the arrival of the other would be succeeded by five years of world war and about ten years of scarcity.

In the last fortnight of August 1939, my ever-prescient Uncle Stan made one of his few bloomers by taking his family to the Continent. Several of his relations expressed anxiety, and in his autobiography he writes: 'Unlike 1914, the Second World War took few people by surprise.' But he had a sort of refrain: 'I am not going to let Mr. Hitler disturb my holiday plans', and this was even repeated triumphantly on a postcard he sent to the office just after he had arrived in Liechtenstein. In the event, he and his wife, with David, Ruth and Rayner (then only fourteen), were stranded in Switzerland for three weeks, and had a distinctly hazardous journey home—slow and crowded and ending with a Channel crossing where U-boats were already on the prowl. Thus S.U. was away from the office on the declaration of war and out of reach at the stage when important decisions had to be taken quickly.

Charles Furth, having earlier joined the Territorials, had been called up a week before September 1st to man his searchlight post. So Malcolm Barnes, our editor, who had now been with us three years, Walter Beard, our ever-resourceful Production Manager, and I formed a triumvirate to decide all publishing, as distinct from purely commercial matters. The most important thing we did was to buy up all the paper we could lay hands upon before rationing clamped down, and another was to warn some authors that we might have to ask them to release us from contracts to publish certain new books which now seemed unlikely to sell. We had a good basement below our modern steel-framed building in Little Russell Street, part already commandeered as a public air-raid shelter, and we had decided against any general evacuation of the firm.

Most publishers regarded any removal to the country as totally out of the question. A few firms made a start at it, but they mostly drifted back to London a few months later. Certainly in Allen & Unwin it was thought impossible for all the usual reasons—inaccessibility, staff problems, break-up of families, etc. Little did we realize that in another twenty-five years we, and half the publishers in London, would be moving anything up to three-quarters of our staff thirty or forty miles away from the capital, paying all removal expenses and much of the cost of equipping the new homes. But *then* we had no conception of the social revolution which was to come upon us after the war—and which would put into practice so much that Allen & Unwin and its predecessors, Swan Sonnenschein, had stood for: a fairer distribution of the country's wealth, a better regulated economy, wider educational opportunity, the ideas of Karl Marx, Hobson, Keynes, Laski, Beveridge—each of whom we had published! For all its high taxation and regulation, it was to result in an explosion of book-buying which was unthinkable in 1939.

The pleasantly rising A. & U. sales curve of 1936 had continued healthily through 1937 and 1938. Hogben's second masterpiece of popularization, *Science for the Citizen*, had made a big contribution in the second of those years. 1939, however, with its anxiety and uncertainty, was a poor one for the entire book trade. Once again our profits dropped.

It seemed obvious to me that even in wartime there must be books that would be wanted, but we could not expect to survive on those about world peace, international affairs and India, which had bulked large in our recent lists. I had learned from those with memories of the 1914 war how great a demand there had been for well-written practical books on specialist branches of training for the various forces, to supplement the official manuals. Over a month before the outbreak of war, we had been approached by a naval man with the idea of a series of handbooks on aspects of navigation, meteorology, etc., all designed for junior officers. Acting on the advice of a service officer, for whom we had already published, we commissioned one or two titles, and with the quick production possible in those days of the 'phoney war', before printers began to lose staff and became permanently overloaded we launched the series in the first two or three months. The jacket, with its neat, coloured reproduction of the junior naval officer's cuff design, helped to get it off to a good start. Similar series followed for R.A.F. and Army trainees, and they sold in thousands, mostly at 2s. 6d. a copy, after 1940.

Few of us had any real conception of the increase in book reading which this war would bring. First, there was the extraordinary condition of total black-out, in which there was no street lighting whatever and no house might show any gleam of light. Otherwise the air-raid warden soon banged on the door and a fine could be the result. Cars groped their way along with no more than small slits of head-lights. (The average sensual man must be forgiven if he recalls the spurious charm of the ladies of Soho who, in those pre-Wolfenden days, advertised their presence by friskily waving their dimmed electric torches at the ground.) Naturally, most people stayed at home, and a book could be the answer to boredom.

Secondly, much National Service involved 'standing by' for long periods, after the traumatic months of the Battle of France and the Battle of Britain. So again the book came into its own, especially as most other commodities became rationed. Tolstoy's *War and Peace* was one of the monumental sellers, following a B.B.C. serial on sound radio. Television ceased on the outbreak of war. Jane Austen and Trollope found new readers by the thousand, while that four-year-old trouper *Gone with the Wind* was still popular, and at a tougher level, *No Orchids for Miss Blandish* scooped up sales by the hundred thousand.

On his return to London, S.U. fully endorsed our actions to date. Though war books were far outside the stream of his interests, he supported them fully; they did after all represent a real contribution to the war effort, and later had the great advantage that it was possible to secure for them an extra grant of paper, over and beyond the firm's normal ration. I was interested to find, however, that in the main S.U. favoured carrying on with the publication of almost every book then in preparation. He reckoned there would be time for them to be absorbed by libraries and the public before the war reached an acute stage. And in the event, he proved right. Actually, any new books which 'stuck' at the start almost certainly came to be wanted as the later book famine developed.

History may say that all of us who worked in London through the last war were luckier than we knew. The margin for the survival of ordinary activity was perilously narrow in the autumn of 1940 and the 'flying-bomb' summer of 1944. But for Stanley, his decision to remain in London came out right. His home in Hampstead was virtually undamaged throughout. It *was* better that the firm stayed in London, as our premises escaped bombing and we kept our main staff together. It *did* prove sensible to continue putting out new books in the first few months, even though they were not designed for war conditions. Our major oversight was to leave the unbound sheet stock of about ninety per cent of all our books in one warehouse, belonging to our binders, at Edmonton. A single oil and high-explosive bomb set light to the lot one night in November 1940 (and gave Uncle Stan one of his best stories for years to come!).

To be wise after the event, if we had swapped a part of this stock with another publisher in some other part of London, we should at least have spread our risk; but even that would have involved a massive and costly cartage operation. A bare one thousand sheets of an average book make several heavy and cumbersome parcels, and at the beginning of the war, in the absence of the heavy bombing we had half expected, few people realized that without involving the destruction of all London, there could still be devastation and total loss in certain areas.

Stanley burst into my room with the news on that November morning, adding the doom-laden words, 'It will affect our profits for years to come.' Theoretically he was right, because all that stock of older books had been prudently written down in our balance sheet and would therefore have shown a good profit when it sold. Now it had ceased to exist, and as he wrote later, 'We received [from War Risks Insurance] only a few thousand pounds for stock which over the years would have yielded more than twenty times the amount.' Actually, since book buying improved so much during the war, sales were bound to increase if one had the appropriate books. In the light of his warning, I was determined to do everything possible to make good this loss of potential profits, and in the event they advanced far beyond our pre-war level.

Also, truth to tell, I was not alone in thinking that much of our destroyed stock—many years old—might never have sold out, and I wanted to see it replaced with more saleable books.

At that moment, in late 1940, I was feeling rather elated at having contrived my first war-time 'seller', and was confident of producing more. In that unforgettable summer of 1940, when day after day of the most glorious weather was punctuated by appalling war news, culminating in the collapse of France and the withdrawal of the British army from Dunkirk, nothing seemed to go right. Then, one Saturday, travelling up from Haslemere for the morning stint (which A. & U. and its indefatigable Chief were to keep up for another twenty years!),

I saw in the *News Chronicle* a vivid article entitled: 'I fought in the sky over Dunkirk'. It was the most welcome and invigorating thing I had ever read about the war and showed that our pilots and Spitfire planes had actually beaten the Germans and their Messerschmitts in the air at Dunkirk. Efforts to make contact with the author revealed that the article was one of a series of 'first person stories' being done for *Life* magazine, New York, by two of their correspondents in London, Allan Michie and Walter Graebner. Pleased at the chance of more permanent publication, they quickly gathered thirteen of their articles and some striking photographs to make up a book, for which we seized the title, *Their Finest Hour: The War in the First Person*. This, of course, was many years before Winston Churchill wanted to use the immortal phrase for one of his own books. It went through several impressions and later was widely distributed by the Ministry of Information. There was something specially heartening in the fact that these two widely experienced men were finding among us a succession of 'almost unbelievably dramatic personal experience stories . . . of the men of Britain's fighting and civilian services'. The exploits of soldiers, sailors, airmen, merchant seamen, firemen, and ordinary citizens were all in it, and their stories were appearing as top features in this leading American magazine. It was perhaps breathless journalism rather than great literature, but it was utterly genuine and at that time a valuable morale raiser.

We published three or four more collections of the *Life* stories—two with Churchillian titles—and three substantial books on later phases of the war by Allan Michie. All of them sold well. Particularly useful was the fact that others came to us with similar books of personal war stories, such as those on the hospital services and the Polish forces in Britain. However, it was the series of so-called *Observers' Books* for the R.A.F. which began for me one of the most interesting and stimulating associations of the whole war, the introduction to Francis Chichester.

He was then connected with a firm of air navigation instrument-makers and was later prominent on the R.A.F. instructional side. He put up to us the idea of a first book on astro-navigation, a subject to become of enormous importance as our bomber crews trained for night flying—their major occupation for the next four years. It grew to four books as the subject became increasingly complicated, and the sales were very large.

We must have met first in my office and I was slightly awed by the coolly appraising look of his grey eyes behind the steel-rimmed spectacles. He weighed his words cautiously and the almost hesitant speech belied the clear thought and determination behind it. At some stage, when there was the suggestion of a joke, a boyish smile emerged, but there was a serious job to be done and he wanted it done quickly. I had the feeling that we could work together and Francis must have come to the same conclusion, for it led to a happy collaboration which lasted for twenty years.

Directly bombing over Britain became a reality, he organized for his firm the first team of factory roof-spotters in the country, well ahead of the government regulations which later made roof-spotting obliga-tory. The 'spotters' had to be on the look-out for enemy planes, and directly they were sighted, give the take-cover warning throughout the factory. Only then did the workers leave their benches and go to the air-raid shelter. Before this system was adopted, hours of industrial time had been lost because factory staffs had been told to stop work and take shelter as soon as the air-raid siren sounded, although no bombers might come within miles of them. It was essential that spotters should know a German plane when they saw it, and not sound the alarm for a British one.

Late one afternoon in September, just after the Battle of Britain reached its climax (and we had, as usual then, let our staff go off early), Francis Chichester strolled into the office and put up his idea for *The Spotters' Handbook*. It was to show how to set up and train the team, and it would give silhouettes of all the likely planes. With his charac-teristic ability to see ahead of others, he was convinced that every factory in the country would soon have to adopt the system. We signed up after momentary hesitation, rushed the book out in about two months, and had the enormous satisfaction of a *Daily Mail* feature review on the day of publication, with the banner heading 'Every Factory Manager Should Buy this Book'. I had very soon to redeem my light-hearted promise to stand the author and his wife a good lunch, when the sales passed 10,000. Before long, they rose to double that number.

Of course, the book quickly had competitors, but Francis was first off the mark and we had the best and simplest of the titles. Uncle Stan had not been particularly enthusiastic about the book at first, but was now much impressed by the author's originality of mind and his evident capacity for foreseeing a demand ahead of events. Though the further ideas which Francis put up to us, for Planispheres, Star Compasses and other ingenious aids to the learning of astro-navigation, were highly unconventional in book terms, S.U. was ready to support them all. He fully shared our enthusiasm to find ways to fashion each of these ingenious devices so that they ended up in the form of a book, and thus escaped purchase tax.

It was in this early period of the war, as I came to sponsor an increasing number of books on subjects hitherto unknown to A. & U., that I began to appreciate particularly my Uncle's readiness to let us 'have a go' at almost everything, so long as it was an honest treatment of its subject and had a reasonable hope of paying its way. The war-time atmosphere was throwing up new subjects and giving us the chance to meet new writers, some of whom one hoped would go on to become established authors for future years. This open-mindedness on the part of our Chief was to be especially encouraging for me after the war, as the opportunity came to branch out into fields which the firm had not attempted to cultivate previously.

As the friendship with Chichester developed, I learned with enor-mous interest of his early life, of his dissatisfactions with his family and his determination to leave England, go to New Zealand and 'not come back until he had made £20,000'. He told me how he achieved this target by imaginative land development, and then went on to his daring solo flights in the little single-engine Gipsy Moth plane, culminating in that epic piece of air navigation which brought him safely from New Zealand to Australia. During the war we re-published for him, under the title *Alone Over the Tasman Sea*, his account of that most memorable flight, which depended upon his accurately locating one tiny island in the middle, where he had to re-fuel.

Years later, we were delighted to handle the stories of both his lone voyages across the Atlantic. Subsequently, the literary agent at that time acting for Francis gave us the opportunity to bid for his auto-biography, on the strength of a synopsis and one specimen chapter. The advance payment asked was a big one, and since it was more than a year before his famous round-the-world voyage, the author was not the world-renowned figure which he later became. Also, we did not then know that he was planning the new voyage. We discussed the book long and earnestly—in the office.

Having known Francis for many years and been deeply interested in his life and adventures, I was extremely keen for A. & U. to have his autobiography, but my colleagues had grave doubts whether sales would be sufficient to justify the terms asked. (Comparing notes later with several other publishers, I found they too would have taken the same view *at the time*.) I could probably have won my fellow directors over—including the Chief—if I had 'set about them', but I was un-easily aware just then that I had let the firm in for a large unearned advance upon a book I had recommended strongly the previous year, and I hesitated. It was a mistake I shall never forget. Hodder & Stough-ton snapped up the offer at once, and under that perfect title, *The Lonely Sea and the Sky*, the sales were soon into six figures.

Ever philosophical, Stanley would only remark, 'Well, we were all in it together', whenever I kicked myself for having let slip this prize best-seller. It seemed quite extraordinary how many people, both in and outside publishing, talked to me about the book and asked, 'Why didn't your firm publish Chichester's new book?' My family cringed instinctively whenever visitors mentioned it!

All one can say is that over the years we have probably made more money by resisting the temptation to gamble on large advances. Everyone sees only the glittering successes, the glowing reviews and boldly advertised sales figures, of the 'large advance' books which have come off; the world never knows how often Messrs. X have been left with an unearned advance of several thousands of pounds, when sales have fallen far short of expectations.

As more and more of my friends disappeared into the forces, I felt increasingly the unheroic nature of my position. Since the partial collapse of my left lung was to be continued for as long as possible (and I must never fail to have the weekly 'refill'—the air pumped into my chest by the specialist), I was classed as Medical Grade IV, which put me beyond the pale for any sort of war service, including even civil defence. Unless I kept to a regular early-to-bed routine, I was warned there might be another breakdown, and then I should again be a burden to others. With the calling up of many of the A. & U. staff, it seemed clear that the firm was the place where I should be of most use. Hesitantly, the government recognized books as 'essential'; I was finding books that were directly valuable to the war effort, so to put all one's energies into it became the obvious course. The Excess Profits Tax ensured that every pound of profit we made over and above our immediate pre-war level went to the government, so one's work was at least helping to pay for the war.

In his autobiography Stanley has described at some length his efforts to convince the government of the need to allow adequate paper for books during the war, and R. J. L. Kingsford, in *The Publishers' Association 1896–1946*, provides an admirable account of the skilful and devoted work of members of the Association during those years. The battle to free books from purchase tax, in which S.U. and Geoffrey Faber took a major part, was the great achievement of 1940. It gave the P.A. deserved stature and influence, which made it the envy of other and larger trade associations. As this side of 'publishing at war' has thus been so fully documented elsewhere I am not repeating the details here; but it remains a most important part of publishing history and of my Uncle's life at that time.

To me it was always astonishing that the exacting routines of publishing in war-time, and the infinite variety of dealings with authors, seemed never to be enough to absorb his energies. Though nearing sixty, he battered away ceaselessly in letters to *The Times*—I don't think he ever lost a youthful pleasure in seeing his name there!—and in direct appeals to government departments.

Behind his public arguments that literature and the trade was being crippled disastrously for want of more paper, he retained in private an amazing optimism and inner confidence that all would be well in the end. Part of this, I think, derived directly from his religious up-bringing, 'All things work together for good . . .', etc.; but it was an undoubted tonic at times. He could also be accurate in his prophecies.

Soon after the Munich agreement in 1938, some German publisher friends wrote saying, in effect, how very satisfactory it was that Hitler had been able, after all, to settle the Czech crisis without a war. S.U.'s acid comment was: 'He may have succeeded this time, but Hitler is a gambler, and does a gambler ever know when to stop? Did Napoleon?'

His belief in Britain's success was total, even during the most devastating times after the fall of France. To a correspondent he then wrote, 'Though things look black at present, we shall come through in the end. Of that there is not the slightest doubt.' In a similar way, it might be added, he confidently assumed that 40 Museum Street, or at least our more modern building behind it, would never receive a direct hit, and that his Hampstead home would remain unscathed. It is difficult not to believe that in the case of a powerful mind some element of extra-sensory perception does not operate!

As paper and binding materials became scarcer, and our better printers turned increasingly to government work, which took priority over ordinary books, we had to seek out fresh printers, some of whom were totally without experience in book work. In those days, production operations were far from straightforward; each needed more supervision by hard-pressed staff, and we were always devising new methods to economize in paper or cloth or binding boards. In all of this, Stanley played an energetic part and accepted without complaint the curious-looking books which sometimes resulted.

While we did our best to be fair to authors already on our list, I considered it essential to find new ones, and those who could be expected to carry their writing on into the post-war years. Attracted at once by the first issue of Cyril Connolly's brilliant monthly *Horizon*, 'Review of Literature and Art', I subscribed to it and read each one with loving care. It seemed a miracle that such a magazine, a real piece of literature, beautifully printed by the Curwen Press, in that incomparable type Caslon Old Face, could have been successfully established in the days of the 'phoney war' at the beginning of 1940. I have a copy in front of me as I write: 80 pages of text as well set as a fairly expensive book, blessedly few advertisements—from the reader's, if not the proprietor's, standpoint—and a list of contributors which includes Calder-Marshall, a youngish don called Crossman, Laurie Lee, Peter Quennell, Anne Ridler, Dylan Thomas, and a fine robust piece by dear old Frank Richards, defending *The Magnet* and his Billy Bunter stories against a recent attack by George Orwell.

In an early issue I came upon Alun Lewis—not his poems, but a penetrating and extremely funny story of army life called *The Last Inspection*, describing an incident on what I took to be the Longmoor Military Railway. Writing off at once to find out whether he had sufficient such stories to make up a book, I learned that he cared much more to get his poetry published. One's normal reaction to such a suggestion was tempered by the thought that here perhaps was the Rupert Brooke of the new war—his work had already appeared in several literary reviews—though in background and style, Alun Lewis was very different, closer perhaps to Edward Thomas. In his poems, most of them written on active service, he spoke for thousands of the more sensitive young men then in uniform, and his little collection, *Raiders' Dawn*, went through five impressions before the end of the war.

In appearance he was all that one might have imagined of a young Welsh poet born 'in the valleys'—soft, lilting speech, deep green eyes, gently humorous outlook—the one incongruous feature was the rough khaki of his corporal's uniform. Besides the writing, which he kept up regularly in a corner of whatever tent or noisy hut he found himself in, Alun took his soldiering seriously, and a little later got a commission in the South Wales Borderers. What with his young wife, Gweno, and his parents in Wales and much of his service on the east coast, his visits to London were rare, and I wished we could have met more often. In due time, his volume of short stories did well—he called it *The Last Inspection*—and I longed for the day when he would have time to come for longer talks and peaceful lunches, and to write a novel. One felt that character, passion and atmosphere were all there, waiting for further development; but it was not to be. The day I learned of his death—through an accident on active service in India—was for me one of the saddest of the war. Though Alun Lewis's sales declined after the end of the war not surprisingly, his work is constantly asked for by anthologists—twenty-five years later.

After the initial anxiety, I was not alone in experiencing a time of intense stimulus and interest during the first two years of the war. First came the colossal relief of finding that it did not mean the instant destruction of London, then the 'Britain Can Take It' mood of the bombing phase in 1940, followed by the entry of Russia and the U.S.A. in 1941, which led one to realize that Germany could not win. In my case, there was, too, the thankful discovery that I was better in health than I had been for years, and within the prescribed limits, felt full of energy.

As night air raids began, and I could be of no practical use in London during them, I started to travel daily from Haslemere. The Portsmouth line maintained a cleaner and more punctual service than any other at that time, and particularly important, the 'Southern' evolved a form of lighting in the blacked-out carriages far more effective than many other lines, so that one could read and work in them on dark winter journeys.

The Southern Railway, as it was then termed, before that amorphous word 'Region' was substituted, covered the south-east corner of Britain, and was thus the most severely damaged of all lines. The resourcefulness of its track engineers in effecting quick repairs after bomb damage was altogether admirable. Thanks to the bountiful provision of suburban branch and loop lines, built by the old London and South Western—the Victorian predecessor of the Southern—there is such a profuse network of railways into South London that from Haslemere a train can travel by no fewer than six different routes to reach either Waterloo or Victoria. In the course of the war, my usual train, at one time or another, made use of every one of them. Occasionally the journey terminated at Wimbledon or Clapham, but always one got through finally, to emerge sometimes upon streets where broken glass crackled under foot and one picked one's way across great lengths of fire hose. Courageously our staff appeared each morning, sometimes grey and tired after a night in some crowded shelter—perhaps even in the Tube—but always miraculously neat and clean, and ready to tackle another's day's work. The spirit of the average Londoner was above all praise.

Typical among them was Stanley's secretary, Doris Davis, who, with sole responsibility for her ageing parents, with whom she lived in a north London suburb, never failed all through the war to reach the office punctually, and still put in overtime on many occasions. Moreover, she kept her garden immaculately tended and full of flowers, though her neighbourhood was badly damaged. Miss Davis began exceptionally well-earned retirement some years ago, and the garden of her bungalow in the Book Trade Provident Estate at King's Langley is one of the very best there. After more than forty years of a pretty exacting boss she remains wonderfully unbowed!

Besides a 9.30–5.30 office day, I would do an hour's work in the train morning and evening. The rest the ex-T.B. patient was supposed to have before dinner had to go by the board—it was enough to have to dash off to Harley Street once every ten days or so, to have the long, hollow needle plunged into one's chest for the 'refill'. If it were not done at the right moment and at the correct pressure, serious trouble could ensue; I sometimes marvel at the risks involved and the good luck by which I was never prevented from getting to my doctor or his locum.

In case any T.B. specialist of that generation, or his nurse, should ever read this, may I add my humble tribute to the professional skill and scrupulous care which saw to it that through all those war years no 'refill' of mine ever went wrong. Once—and only once—did the long needle break off, leaving nearly two inches inside me. I dared not look down, but I guessed what had happened, particularly when the doctor said slowly and quietly to me, 'Keep perfectly still', and very quickly to his nurse, 'Get me a pair of no. 2 pliers.' He had it safely out at the second attempt, but it could have caused a great deal of trouble and a spell in hospital. Once more I was thankful for the expertise which dealt imperturbably with that little incident.

Not surprisingly perhaps, even my time in the sanatorium was turned to publishing account. We brought out two successful books by ex-fellow-patients. One was by Alan Dick, a top reporter for the *Daily Telegraph*, who had contracted the disease while covering the Spanish Civil War in 1937. He too had the artificial pneumothorax treatment, involving 'refills', and when we happened to meet, early in the war, congratulating ourselves on being back at work, I asked him if he would not consider writing a book on his T.B. experiences. The idea was to make more people aware—as neither of us had been originally —that it was possible to have this beastly disease and yet, with proper treatment, come safely through it to lead a normal life again.

He produced a seriously informed, but at times very amusing account of it all, including particularly Midhurst Sanatorium. The book was entitled *Walking Miracle*, the phrase which one of his Fleet Street colleagues had applied to Alan Dick when he first learned what had been done to his lung. The book sold several thousand and was constantly recommended by one patient to another, until the new drugs revolutionized treatment and the long sanatorium era was at an end. The sales of the book ceased almost overnight, but seldom could an author or publisher have rejoiced more genuinely that it was then out of date.

The other book was by the artist Adrian Hill, who later achieved national fame with his 'Sketch Club' programmes on B.B.C. television. It was called *Art versus Illness* and told the story of how, from his own experience at Midhurst Sanatorium, he came to pioneer art therapy. Today, of course, this aid to treatment is widespread, not least in mental hospitals. At the same time he campaigned successfully, by quoting Florence Nightingale at the authorities, to get pictures on to hospital walls. This led to the formation of a lending library of prints run by the Red Cross. After the war, we had the pleasure of publishing another of his illustrated books, *Adventures in Line and Tone*.

It may be thought from this chapter, because it contains little of the general description of war, that S.U. and I spent the period in a quiet corner of publishing. This is deliberate. Scores of others, far better qualified than I, have paid their written tributes to the matchless feats of the men and women of the forces; this is merely an attempt to describe some of the effects of the war on publishing.

It did so happen that neither of our immediate families had members on active service. Stanley was in his late fifties. His eldest son David was medically unfit from a heart condition and worked in our production department for part of the war. He ably took the place of our designer Ronald Eames when he went to work temporarily on the land. I always enjoyed David's company and was very sorry when he decided against publishing in favour of authorship but he went on to achieve a marked success with the writing of children's books. Rayner was at school, old enough to join the Navy only after 1944; and their sister Ruth, married in 1940, began her family the following year. While war casualties, then, did not touch us directly, my Uncle was deeply concerned for the fate of European publishers, especially the Czechs, and he did much to assist those who came to England as refugees. No one, be it A. & U. staff or some acquaintance suffering war-time hardship over accommodation or employment, ever turned to him in vain.

Much has been said of S.U.'s commercial acumen, but behind his passionate appeals to the government for a larger paper ration for publishers there was far more than a mere wish to make money by selling books: he saw it as one of the essentials of free speech—so easily a casualty in war-time. In 1940 one felt one should be lucky to be able to keep a publishing house going at all, and maintenance of food and shelter for one's family was all that could be hoped for. I think that many of us lost all interest in 'making money' as a serious objective— for one thing, there was so little to spend it on.

The variety of odd chances by which a publisher secures a good book have always interested me greatly. I am thinking of the general rather than the academic book, for the line of approach to the latter is more of an established routine, particularly today when zealous young editors are constantly visiting universities, to persuade members of the various faculties to write textbooks.

A chance meeting with a Hampstead friend of mine, whom I had known before the war, led to his suggestion that we ought to get Barbara Ward to write a book. She was then foreign editor of *The Economist* and our only contact had been through a pre-war symposium to which she had contributed. My friend and I persuaded her to come to dinner in Soho, with one or two others, and I suppose—like all men who ever met her—I was at once enchanted, if awed, by her astonishing amalgam of beauty, feminine charm and vitality, coupled with her easy mastery of economic and international affairs. Miraculously she was not under contract to any other publisher—yes, she would like to do a book some time—she would let me know later . . .

A year went by. Then suddenly she could spare half an hour for tea at the Waldorf Hotel, terms were discussed and a contract signed. (Amusing to think now that I wondered if Uncle Stan might regard my offer of a £50 advance as a trifle reckless—but he did not demur.) Two or three more years elapsed, during which Barbara Ward achieved a nationwide reputation by frequently taking part in the famous B.B.C. Brains Trust programmes, with Joad and Huxley. Still no book—until suddenly, about five years after the original contract, she felt inspired to write for us the manuscript which became *The West at Bay*. The advance was then suitably revised, and the book did extremely well.

Another strange chance was a letter to Reginald Reynolds, after I had been enormously attracted by a winning poem of his on some aspect of the war in the *New Statesman* week-end competition. Was there here a possible book of light verse? No—this time it was the direct opposite of Alun Lewis—prose not poetry. It was a vastly entertaining yet erudite book on lavatories through the ages entitled *Cleanliness and Godliness* which Reynolds was longing to write. We encouraged him to go ahead, and though its benefit to the war effort may not have been immediately apparent, it gave pleasure to a lot of people and it must have raised morale. At any rate, it quickly sold out. We could have disposed of double the number and more, if we had been able to provide the paper for immediate reprints. Reggie Reynolds, the husband of Ethel Mannin, was a handsome man and himself a most attractive personality, a Quaker with a great 'concern' for the under-privileged and with an original turn of mind. His comparatively early death was a loss to authorship.

The firm's long association with that great humorist Basil Boothroyd dates from another lucky chance of the early war. One morning in the train, I happened to hear Oliver Warner, a former publisher friend, and two others recounting the comical attempts at soldiering of our local Home Guard. The particular incident had ended in an accidental gunshot through the roof of Haslemere Town Hall; but there were also others which thirty years later might have gone straight into the TV feature 'Dad's Army'. Surely, there should be a book in all this. 'Have you seen the articles appearing in *Punch*?' asked Oliver. 'They are by a man named Boothroyd.' And there, after some weeks, was a ready-made, highly topical 'funny': *Home Guard Goings On*. An inspired jacket design, which the author helped us to get from a *Punch* artist, showed a retired colonel-type Home Guardsman, smoke emerging from both barrels of his shotgun, over a caption 'Who Went There?' We continued to publish collections of Boothroyd's *Punch* articles for years, and were proud to be able to encourage him to do one of the most successful of all his books, *Let's Stay Married*.

The radio talks 'after the nine o'clock news' at that time were to me a prolific source of book ideas, of which two were particularly memorable for the compelling quality of their broadcasters' voices. One was Group Captain Helmore, who gave a monthly commentary through 1941 and 1942, of which Sir Emrys Williams wrote, 'I have never heard a more moving tribute than the one Helmore paid to the men who fly in the R.A.F.' Illustrated with the superb Eric Kennington portraits of flying men, and helped by a broadcast review on the morning of publication, the collection of talks was an instant sell-out. The other broadcaster was, in his way, one of the most remarkable men for whom we published during the war, Frank Laskier.

His rather sensitive, North-country voice was first heard over the air one Sunday evening after the news—a peak listening time—when he began: 'I am a sailor, an Englishman and my first name is Frank. I am quite an ordinary sort of individual—all we sailors are.' He spoke in simple, near-biblical language of the everlasting pull which the sea exerts on seamen, despite the horrors even of submarine warfare, and he went on, 'We are a race apart, we are the sailors. And do you think that a nation like the Germans could ever drive us from the sea? . . . We are British, we are they who go down to the sea in ships and occupy their business in great waters . . . we see the glory of the Lord. And we always will and that is why we are sailors.'

He spoke directly into the microphone—without a note—when Terence de Marney and Eldon Moore, then working for the B.B.C., found him in the Seamen's Home at Liverpool—and his book, entitled *My Name is Frank*, was printed straight from the transcripts of the recordings. It quickly sold 35,000 copies. Frank Laskier spoke at a Foyle Literary Lunch, then disappeared back to sea, and we lost touch with him. No one who ever heard him could remain unmoved by his sincerity and the natural poetry of his speech.

Of course, much of the pace and profitability of war-time publishing was highly artificial. The rapidity of sales ensured that a high proportion of new books sold out, at once, and we had to spend a lot of time rationing our supplies to booksellers, when we faced advance orders of 5,000—often more—for a book of which our paper ration enabled us to print only 3,000. It could not be done mechanically because we wanted to give genuine booksellers, our regular customers, preference over the many new shops which sprang up—suddenly, in order to cash in on the demand for books. Either S.U. or I would often carry home the bulky 'dues sheets' at the end of the day, for the unprecedented task of cutting down the orders which travellers had striven to build up.

With shortages of staff and paper, there was an inevitable reduction in the number of announcement lists we could produce—one or two only in the year, instead of three or four—and our overseas travellers would cable anxiously for news of the latest books, before setting out on their long journeys across Canada or round South Africa. Often some earlier parcel of advance information had been torpedoed at sea. Frantically—perhaps over lunch—I would make notes, and then, immediately after, dictate a long letter high-lighting the coming books, often in near 'cablese'. But men like Howard Timmins in Cape Town knew us well enough to interpret these missives correctly, and soon one had the satisfaction of seeing their precious export orders coming in, based directly upon the letter of 'latest news from war-torn England!'

Mention of our overseas representatives reminds me how much we owed to them and their amazing generosity in the way of food parcels. Not that we were ever near starvation, but our diet was pretty dull and any extra fat and sweets for children, or dried fruit, were as rain on parched soil.

Throughout the war, thanks entirely to a regular Christmas gift from Howard, my wife was able to offer some form of South African crystallized fruit at the festive dinner table, when it had become totally unobtainable in England. Our Australian man, Stanley Bartlett, began by sending me Christmas parcels, and then got his wife to arrange for friends of hers to send us, over a long period, a regular *monthly* parcel, which contained the supreme luxury—it sounds extraordinary today— of a pound of good beef dripping. It meant much to be able to give a growing family a piece of fried bread again for breakfast and to share the extras with friends. These came from people we had never met, they cost money and trouble (the parcels had to be sewn up in linen covers), and they were continued for some time after the war, while rationing was still in force here. This is something one never forgets.

One effect of the boom in book sales was that publishers' cash 'flow' became a torrent. Their customary pre-war position of too much stock and not enough cash was completely reversed, as books sold readily and money piled up—much of it to be drained away in the Excess Profits Tax. At the height of the war it was difficult to believe that we in the book trade might ever be short of cash again, but I do recall saying to a colleague that after the war we should go completely into reverse. Paper would become freely available, and as we started to reprint our back list, we should once more have plenty of books; but then the cash would run down—which indeed it did, partly because the books we then produced were slower selling.

Stanley meanwhile addressed the Society of Bookmen on the subject of *Book Trade Prosperity: Is it Illusory?* He pointed out with unassailable logic all the factors, such as exceptional government buying for the services and the fact that export consignments were being duplicated and even triplicated, because of loss by enemy action at sea; this could mean that the original order eventually bumped up the publishers' sales to three times what they would have been worth. Though he accepted that the war was creating a new book-reading—and buying —public, especially among young people, I do not think he altogether believed that publishing and book-selling would grow permanently out of the small depressed and static affair it had been before the war.

I fancy that Basil Blackwell, though fully recognizing the war-time artificialities, took a somewhat different view. In a talk he gave later to the same Society, there was a delicious moment when he said, 'If Stanley Unwin is to be believed, and who shall dare to disbelieve that formidable man? . . .' and then went on to hint that *some* of the trade's prosperity might not prove quite so illusory.

S.U. was not ungenerous in handing out Christmas bonuses to the staff on a greatly enhanced scale during the war, but he continually accompanied them with a douche of cold water about 'not expecting it next year'. Personally I considered that in an editorial sense A. & U. had broken fresh ground, and that we were moving permanently on to a higher plateau of sales.

I have mentioned only a few of the new authors—there is always the risk that a publisher's own book may become too much of a catalogue— but L. T. C. Rolt must be included among them; I am proud that we should still be selling one of his finest books, *Inland Waterways of England*. Then, towards the end of the war, in 1944, S.U. himself captured a best-seller with Beveridge's *Full Employment in a Free Society*. This was just after the author had become a national figure following the publication of his *Report on Social Insurance*, the foundation stone of all our later social insurance legislation.

The advance in A. & U.'s sales and profits had been achieved in spite of a shortage of experienced staff and in spite of temporary assistants, some refugees. The more responsible of us each had to keep about six balls in the air at once; as a result, improvisations and short-cuts were inevitable. I felt sure that once we had the place shipshape again, on a peacetime basis, we could consolidate on an altogether higher level. Meanwhile, with all its shortcomings, we had brought through the war a thriving and secure firm, ready and able to offer jobs back to all our former staff as they were demobilized.

11 Post-war Hopes Deferred, 1944–1948

Of the 41 years in which I worked for Stanley Unwin, from 1927 to 1968, that hard, tough war-time was in many respects the time of our most valuable collaboration. From the personal standpoint it was the most satisfactory. We worked closely together and on all editorial matters there was no one to consider but ourselves; the other key man on the publishing side was Walter Beard, our Production Manager. From a difficult home background, leaving school at the age of fourteen determined to 'work with books', it was he who on his first day as office boy had received the famous object lesson from S.U. on the failure of cream buns to qualify as 'something substantial for a penny'.

Beard was one of the first of the firm's early office boys to reach managerial status, and his quickness of mind, amazing memory and qualities of friendliness and integrity fitted him ideally for the task of persuading paper merchants and printers to produce for us the maximum number of books with the minimum (often substitute) materials. He made an enormously valuable contribution to the firm in those war years, and it was sad that declining health led to his death in middle age. Ronald Eames then became his admirable successor.

S.U. and I always communicated easily, and so throughout the war we could quickly get on with the vital jobs of deciding upon manuscripts, and on which were to have priority for paper. In Walter Beard we had a Production Manager whose approach to every problem was positive and who would collaborate to the utmost, even when it was essential to produce quantity at the expense of quality. Paper rationing automatically ruled out serious consideration of a wide range of books —those commercially borderline cases which can involve lengthy discussion in normal circumstances. (She who has typed this book, and was my war-time secretary, once asked, 'What reason for declining manuscripts shall we give to authors when there *isn't* a paper shortage?') One had the constant stimulus of battering away hard at the essential jobs which produced direct results, while spending a minimum of time on the fiddling, laborious tasks which show no direct result, though they are important to a well-run firm in the long term.

Like most Londoners, I look back upon the summer of 1944 as an ambiguous turning point, when the thrill and relief of the successful

Allied landings in Normandy were quickly followed by the fresh crunch upon London of the V-1 rockets—the 'doodle-bugs'—which for about two months created almost more anxiety and disruption than the bombing of 1940. To have this hellish flying bomb approach, with the noise of a gigantic 'raspberry' blown from obscene lips, was horrible enough in itself, but it was worse when its engine stopped; then one was supposed to get away from any windows and stand in a doorway. Once, in the middle of a dictating session, I rushed my secretary to take cover as the Thing cut out above us—and it dived down to kill one of our authors, dear old Sir Percy Alden, half a mile away, as he waited for a bus near Goodge Street in Tottenham Court Road.

Once more, too, after three years of comparatively reliable, if desperately crowded railway travel, one found the poor old Southern seriously hit and its trains badly delayed. At home, our small cottage was filled to its utmost capacity with three adults and five little girls. It was a duty to fill any spare room in a technically safe area, so we shared our home with the family of a serving naval officer. There were ups and downs and tensions, but we survived and remained good enough friends for me to be asked to propose the health of one of the girls at her wedding sixteen years later. To be able to introduce myself as the man her mother had lived with during the war got the speech off to a rousing start.

Added to the pressures of domestic life was the fact that many of us were distinctly run down physically after years of food rationing, so that colds and tummy bugs now seemed more plentiful—certainly in my own case. On top of this, there was a depressingly long spell of particularly wet and humid weather during that summer, and the risk of a chance flying bomb on the Albert Hall even stopped the famous Promenade Concerts. Sir Henry Wood had kept them going there ever since their old home, Queen's Hall in Langham Place, had been destroyed by a bomb early in the war.

I was cheered to some extent by the occasional visits of American servicemen. Some were publishers in uniform, others the friends of U.S. publishers who had been told to 'look us up'—they were all in their ways a refreshing whiff of a pre-war way of life, with their well-nourished bodies, good clothes, American cigarettes and often the generous gift of a bottle of Scotch, or some other unobtainable luxury. Though we had kept up correspondence with New York publishers, we had had no personal contact for five years, and it was cheering to feel remembered in this way—even if we knew that they were fast pushing American editions of books into the Dominion markets—hitherto the exclusive preserve of British publishers.

Through all the vicissitudes S.U. had remained extraordinarily fit and totally uncomplaining of our 'short commons', though to one with a sweet tooth such as his, sugar rationing must have been a serious deprivation. His famous motto 'my wants are few' stood him in good stead; shortages of alcohol and tobacco naturally meant nothing to one of his austere habits, and clothes rationing could have been a positive satisfaction to him. There was the cheeky office boy—not one who rose to managerial level!—who was to say somewhat later, to a little group of our junior staff, 'D'you know what Sir Stanley does with his old clothes?' only to rap out in reply, 'Wears them!' Though S.U. paid a good price for his suits, he liked to make them last to their well-worn and shiniest end.

During 1944, in his sixtieth year and from his exertions on the tennis court, he suffered a torn cartilage in his knee—a young man's complaint, as he enjoyed telling everyone. With his usual imperturbability, he had the necessary operation performed 'in room 60 of University College Hospital on my sixtieth birthday', while V-2s, the so-called rocket bombs, were crashing down on Central London at frequent intervals. This mishap naturally kept him away from the office for some time, while my pressures built up. It was only by inflexible determination that he forced himself to keep up the distinctly painful exercises needed to regain the unfettered use of his leg; but in record time for a man of his age, he was back on the tennis court.

His one complaint during the war was about the disturbed nights on fire-watching duty, in which he shared both in Hampstead and at the office. Holiday postcards always mentioned that he was 'catching up on sleep', though one from the Lake District also spoke proudly, if menacingly, of having 'climbed fourteen peaks in thirteen days'. As yet there was not the slightest chance that he would not daily ascend the garret stairs to those departments on the top floors of 40 Museum Street!

Besides his energetic work for the Publishers' Association and the British Council, fully described in his autobiography, my Uncle laboured to keep the International Publishers Congress in being, corresponding continually with Swiss colleagues. At times he complained of this extra burden, but he obviously enjoyed it—it was his nature to keep more than fully occupied at all times—and it ensured that the organization remained intact, until the day when it became possible to plan another Congress for Zürich in 1954. It was typical of his capacity always to look well ahead that in the middle of war he should have concerned himself so fully with this essentially peace-time project. With his fluency in German and his personal acquaintance with so many European publishers, the whole atmosphere of an International Congress was ever meat and drink to him. Always an effective committee man, he was adept in successfully putting over his points to foreigners—in fully gestured German and French, or carefully enunciated English.

After 1944 came a period when I seemed more hard-pressed than at any time during the war. Stanley was naturally delighted to accept an invitation from the Spanish publishers to visit them in May 1945—just before the end of the war in Europe—and the British Council came in on the act, so that he ended up by visiting their centres in both Spain and Portugal, and was away for about a month in all. On top of this, the sheer volume of correspondence and the increasing number of visitors became overwhelming, at a time when none of our former colleagues had yet been demobilized.

And in a minor sense there was worse to come. As we were to learn over the next ten years, S.U.'s forays overseas always gave him a tremendous lift. After three weeks of endless parties, excellent un-rationed lunches and dinners in his honour, and receptive audiences to his stories of British publishing at war (not forgetting how 'I lost 1,400,000 books from a single bomb'), S.U. returned brimful of energy, and with a zest for every aspect of publishing that might apply to the country visited, in this case Spain. 'Now we must get busy and offer them our books', he said. Lists of our recent publications had to be ransacked to find what we could sell to Spanish booksellers, or what translation rights might appeal to their publishers—all splendid if one's hands were not already over-full with day-to-day affairs. I envied the Manager of John Lane, which firm S.U. was running at that time, when he told me (with a wink), 'I've put a special man in charge of everything to do with SPAIN!' I was a fool not to have said straight out that I was already pushing myself to the limit, and Dictator Franco's neutral country could stew in its own juice; but it was difficult ever to oppose, or blatantly fail to share S.U.'s personal enthusiasm.

By 1945 we had a growing number of accepted manuscripts waiting for paper and an increasing quantity of important back-list books demanding to be reprinted. Publishers Association figures at the time showed a total of 52,000 titles, new books and reprints, waiting in the production queue. We were also trying to save up paper for a large first edition of Bertrand Russell's (now classic) *History of Western Philosophy*. His popular reputation had grown enormously during the war and we were convinced that we should have a huge demand for this new book, his first major work for several years. Thus we had to cut down our acceptances of new manuscripts still further, and this reduced the creative and more rewarding side of my own work.

I found myself fighting against deep depression, due in large part to physical tiredness, then sleeplessness, dyspepsia and all those symptoms which make one fear nervous breakdown. It was not until I had submitted to a hernia operation the following year and enjoyed a particularly delightful holiday after it, with my fast-growing daughters on the North Devon coast, that I began to feel myself again. I fancy that with the end of the war, and its long period of tension and maximum effort, there came a similar reaction of weariness and disillusion for many people.

Disillusion struck in several forms. Publishers had expected a speedy end to paper rationing; indeed one of Stanley's few false prophecies from his 1918 experience had been that, 'directly the war is over the paper position will improve overnight'. Though the amount of the ration rose from 42½ per cent to 75 per cent over the next four years, and extra paper could be secured for broadly educational books, rationing in fact continued for four years, and even after that paper was by no means plentiful. Happy, too, as we were to welcome returning staff as they were demobilized, endless difficulties arose. Some who had left us as junior clerks came back with the well-earned rank of captain or major, and were far from content with their former positions.

While it was true that some of them had to re-learn a job which had changed somewhat in six years, I think S.U. laid unnecessary stress upon the need for the ex-serviceman to 'make good' in the firm *afresh*, before he could expect a really satisfactory salary. With this fundamental distrust of anything savouring of 'army methods' in a private business, Stanley overlooked the fact that someone who had been a good A. & U. chap in 1939 would have gained in character and ability if he had done well in the services.

I had no doubt that given a year or two of normal trading conditions, we could soon expand the firm to the point when there could be decent jobs and pay for all the returning warriors. Meanwhile, in my capacity of part-intermediary between staff and Chief, I seemed continually to be soothing down ruffled, or cheering up discouraged feelings on the one hand and pressing upon S.U. the need to raise salaries more quickly on the other; while he would point to the grave uncertainties ahead of us, and the dangers of letting overheads rise too quickly (a subject upon which his eloquence never failed).

There was, too, the old bogey of Saturday morning work. Even before the war many offices no longer worked on Saturdays. From the blitz days of 1940, with its hazardous travel conditions and often sleepless nights, a majority of publishers had decided to work a five-day week, and for a very few weeks A. & U. actually remained closed on Saturdays, but directly air raids lessened in we came again. It was easy enough for my Uncle, who had but a fifteen-minute drive from Hampstead—it was only for a year or so that he was unable to get a small petrol ration—and he really was lost if he could not come to the office on Saturday mornings. Tennis took care of the afternoons, but in the mornings he had to go to Museum Street, to open and go through the sacred 'post' in order, as he would say, to avoid a 'huge accumulation' on Monday morning. By the end of the war, besides being one of the very few to open at all on Saturdays, we must have been the *only* publishing house which gave no sort of Saturday concession whatever. It was becoming increasingly difficult to get staff, and girls and employment agencies in particular were shocked when I had to tell them that we gave no Saturdays off.

I should have issued an ultimatum earlier, but S.U. could become so emotional and unpleasant about it that one hesitated, and he was a good boss in so many other ways. An argument on this subject, or any matter which involved comparison with other firms, always closed with his unanswerable proposition: 'If I had been content to do what other publishers do, A. & U. would not be where it is today.' Finally, in 1947, I confronted him with a chart showing how each department could still be adequately staffed while allowing everyone to take off one Saturday in three. After 24 hours, and not quite in his most gracious manner, he dropped it back into my basket saying curtly, 'Very well, on that basis I am prepared to agree.'

In such circumstances he could give the impression of having received a body blow. I doubt if he had any conception of how much it meant to anyone. By painfully slow stages over the years, and a tough argument every time, we advanced to where the merest skeleton staff came in—making it about one Saturday in six for the individual—until, praise God, in 1964, the hated Saturday work was abolished. Even then S.U. came in alone, and with the help of his retired secretary he still opened the post! It was perhaps fitting that this should have been his final act for the firm, when he came to the office for the last time on a Saturday in September 1968.

The immediate post-war years brought Stanley deserved honours, which gave him enormous pleasure. First was the honorary LL.D. in 1945 from Aberdeen University, which was a pretty tribute to the amount of academic publishing he had done. With his amusing tendency on occasion 'to render unto God the things that are Caesar's' (the Englishman's besetting sin according to Harold Nicolson), he at once gave instructions for news paragraphs about it to be sent out as widely as possible to the press, in order to get publicity for his award 'for the sake of the book trade'.

We had barely got used to seeing him addressed as 'Doctor' when there came the greater thrill of his knighthood, given under the Labour Government in the New Year Honours for 1946. This was a fair reward for the ten years he had put in for the British Council, during most of which he had been Chairman of the very important Books and

Periodicals Committee. In 1935 it had been a revolutionary idea that the government should sponsor an organization whose purpose was to tell the world something of the British way of life, and all S.U.'s inventiveness, imagination and adroitness in committee had come into full play. Books were early recognized as having an essential role in the Council's objectives, and this led to the building up of British Council libraries in all the countries where they were able to work. Stanley devoted a chapter of his autobiography to this important part of his life; altogether he did a very fine job, both for the Council and for publishers in general, since the growing effectiveness of the British Council was a substantial help to book exports.

It occupied a lot of his time; when one asked where the Chief was— if he was not in his office—one seemed again and again to be met by the doleful refrain from his secretary: 'British Council.' It was one more activity which kept him away from A. & U.—and there were a great many of them: directorships of Methuen, Chapman & Hall, John Lane the Bodley Head, and Unwin Brothers, our family printing firm; and until the early 1950s he still served on the Council of the Publishers Association and on several of its committees.

I must admit I had always assumed that S.U.'s British Council labours would bring him a knighthood in the end, but seldom can anyone have enjoyed it more. A genuine sense of pleasure and enhancement went through the firm on the January morning of the news. The immediate nuisance was that one felt it was only decent to add to our labours by prefixing SIR to all the office memos, which hitherto had been addressed simply to S.U.

The year 1946 duly gave us our first post-war best-seller in Bertrand Russell's *History of Western Philosophy*, and though, as I have said, it presented a serious problem for our paper supplies, and we had to allocate all of our first edition to the export markets, it represented a breakthrough to an altogether higher sales level for its distinguished author.

He was now broadcasting more frequently and a year or two later he gave the first Reith lectures, which attracted wide attention. A problem over their publication arose just after Stanley had set off in 1949 on his second trip round the world. He had gone away with the expectation that Russell would enlarge the text of the broadcast lectures by about 30 per cent, to make a book of reasonable size, but the carefully-worked-out scheme of the lectures made expansion difficult. So, on a busy Monday morning, his unmistakable, authoritative, but always courteous voice came on the phone to say that he could not see how to do what my Uncle was expecting—could I come and discuss it with him? He really seemed rather worried.

All of a publisher's post-weekend accumulation was cheerfully left behind, and I dashed off to see him in the pleasant, sunny flat near

Baker Street where he was then living with his beautiful young wife Patricia, with a ravishingly pretty secretary in attendance. As before, he appeared to me charming and the picture of healthy old age, as he stretched his slippered feet towards the gas fire, with a rack of six pipes at his elbow. As I have noticed with other really great men among authors—including Radhakrishnan—on the comparatively trivial technicalities of publishing, he deferred to one completely as the expert. There was really no problem. If we did not press him to expand the lectures, I saw that we could offer a 'new Bertrand Russell' at the attractive price of about six shillings, and the bigger sales we could hope for would compensate for our not having a larger book. We printed 35,000 and soon sold them.

The Russell titles were a pleasant development to set against the gloom of the post-war slump in sales of many classes of books. Towards the end of the war booksellers had often ordered recklesly—some because they assumed the inflated demand would continue indefinitely, others because their orders were in any case likely to be rationed by the publishers. Suddenly the position—unlike paper supply —*did* 'change overnight'. Interest in war books dropped away (the escape stories and war-adventures were yet to come); the hundreds of thousands who had been engaged in reserve, stand-by, ARP and fire service duties were able to return home to normal life, and no longer had the same hours to fill with reading. Also, the end of the nightly 'black-out' in the streets encouraged people to go about more in the evenings.

So one found booksellers writing in day after day to cancel their advance orders for those books not yet published—and often this happened after a first edition had been printed, based to some extent upon the number of orders originally placed. The work of a publisher's trade department became enormously complicated, because of the need to write to booksellers ahead of publication to find out whether they still wanted the number of copies they had ordered, perhaps, owing to production delays, well over a year before. As the replies came in, dues records had to be corrected, and the number invariably reduced. Many booksellers would write asking for ALL their unexecuted advance orders to be cancelled; the clerical work involved was trebled and, of course, trade correspondence multiplied formidably. There were times when we feared the number of booksellers' cancellations on a given day would exceed the orders placed.

Another blow which struck us after the war—and I am sure many other publishers must have suffered similarly—proved to be self-inflicted. This was our failure to put up published prices sufficiently to meet the higher manufacturing costs. *Under*-pricing is, of course, a classic reason for a publisher's failure. Up to that time, one of S.U.'s basic tenets had always been that we should never fix the published price of our books at less than three times the unit cost of manufacture (if typesetting, paper, printing, binding—10s. per copy, then the published price—30s.). This we still aimed to do, but we had all of us—including the Chief himself, it must be admitted—overlooked a vital new element. Thanks to delays in production, due to paper shortage, the interval between the time of the original printers' estimate, upon which the published price was settled, and the completion of printing and binding was stretching out to a year or more, and in this time costs were rising steadily.

Disconcerted as we were by a sharp fall in our profits one year, though sales were going ahead well, we closely investigated costs. Charles Knight, one of our clever young men of the 1920s, now Managing Director of our Hemel Hempstead operation, was then heir-apparent to the Accounts Department. He has the gift, somewhat rare among those with accountancy training, of being able to see the reality behind the figures. He came up with the pertinent fact that for many of our recent books the published price had been well *below* three times the unit cost, due, of course, to our having settled the price on what had become an out-of-date estimate. Without realizing it, we had been letting our precious margin slip away—the crucial difference between cost and selling price—the only thing upon which a business can live.

The remedy was obvious: to prepare a later and up-to-date estimate of final costs before the published price was settled; and before long we also raised the formula to $3\frac{1}{2}$ times the unit cost. Within a year or so this began to have a very beneficial effect on our profits. At first, we thought our new level of book prices looked dangerously high, but the public absorbed them and there is no evidence that our sales suffered—quite the contrary. Today those higher published prices of the late 1940s look ridiculously low—novels at 12s. 6d. and elaborately illustrated books at 30s.—yet still the sales curve rises.

During that exceptionally bitter winter and early spring of 1947, when we suffered continual electric power cuts and reductions of gas pressure, making our office life colder than at any time during the war, Stanley treated himself to a visit to his beloved Swiss resort, Lenzerheide, scene of his courtship and many winter sports holidays. But his first visit there for over ten years was not a success. He was disappointed in the changes which had taken place, and instead of reappearing in London with the famous red-Indian complexion which used to be his form, he crept miserably back with a virulent 'flu germ that kept him at home for a month. It was probably a sinus infection which caused his continual headaches, made it difficult for him to read and, for good measure, induced a sub-normal temperature, which left him fearfully depressed.

Apart from a couple of surgical operations, which are an occupation in themselves, it was the first time in twenty years that I had known him be obliged to abandon all his normal activities. He was totally unused to idling and to the very light reading which he might have managed, and radio just for entertainment meant nothing to him. There were dark hints about a Red Light, and that he would have to slow up in future and change his way of life; but it came to nothing. After about four weeks he perked up, returned to Museum Street and carried on precisely as before—upstairs two at a time, walking fast or trotting, hatless, to the Reform Club for lunch, and tennis at the week-end. Except that he walked less latterly, when he had a chauffeur, these routines continued virtually unchanged for another twenty years —to the end of his life.

Although the first three years after the war were in many ways a time of awkward readjustment, we were shaking down again as a firm, and my own load began to lighten. Charles Furth returned from highly responsible duties with the Control Commission in Germany, to take charge once again of all our educational side, and quickly to start on its regeneration. Malcolm Barnes came back from Senior Press Censorship duties at the Ministry of Information, greatly to strengthen our editorial department; while Charles Knight succeeded to the secretaryship of the company, on the retirement of Mr. Stally-brass, and proceeded to an overdue reorganization of the entire accounts department. For me, the year 1948 was a turning point. Ten years after my chest operation at Midhurst, I was pronounced fit to have the lung 'let up'—re-expanded—to resume its normal state. This meant no more of the tiresome refills, no more rushing along to Harley Street at lunch time, and above all, I could now go abroad and if necessary fly (the *un*pressurized cabins of the earlier planes would have been a hazard to my former condition).

I received the good news in May, and a month later my wife and I had fixed up through friends of friends to exchange our cottage at Haslemere for a month with the flat, just outside Oslo, of a Norwegian family who wanted to come to England for the Olympic Games at Wembley that summer. Sharing with my author-cousin, Ursula Moray Williams, and her two younger boys the hazards of a rough North Sea crossing, and housekeeping in a still-rationed foreign country, Evelyn took our girls with her and managed to surmount the domestic prob-lems. Milk, rye bread and goat's cheese bulked large in the diet. I followed ten days later, travelling in via Stockholm and its publishers and booksellers.

English visitors were then very few in Norway and we were most kindly received. The July weather was perfect and we all revelled in the warm bathing of the Oslo Fjord, and in the beautiful mountain surroundings. Unknowingly I took the first step towards our greatest publishing coup when, a bit reluctantly, I donned formal suit, collar and tie, one hot morning and left the family to swim alone, while I called upon that great Norwegian publisher Harald Grieg, the head of Gyldendal Norsk Forlag. With his handsome head of white hair, strong colouring and blue eyes, he looked to me all that the leading Norse publisher should be, and I was more than grateful to him for sparing time to see me, when he was just about to start off on a holiday. That meeting, and my subsequent friendship with his stepson, Stefan Grieg-Gran, brought the offer of *Kon-Tiki* to Allen & Unwin. But the outcome of that morning's work in Oslo belongs to the next chapter.

In October of 1948 my new freedom to travel enabled me to visit America for the first time since the war. Compared with shabby, bomb-scarred Britain, [still] rationed for most of her food—no luxuries—scarcely any new cars, and petrol for only about 90 miles a month—short of electric power, and no bright streets at night—New York appeared to wallow in luxury. Right at the start, it was the flashing electric advertising signs, seen from the deck of the ship as we reached the Hudson, which struck me so forcibly—we had not seen such things in England for nine years. The proverbial hospitality was never greater nor more generously offered. The only problem was the tiny capacity of my shrunken war-time stomach, and that kind hosts again and again gave me a portion of meat equivalent to our entire week's ration in England.

Though I could claim no major best-seller from this trip, invaluable contacts were made, not least with some of the new refugee publishers from Austria and Germany, and much new business resulted. While on the one hand it came as a shock to realize how very little the daily lives of Americans had been touched by the war, on the other it was pleasant to think how many minor luxuries might be added to our lives when we became a little more prosperous.

That year of 1948, which was the half-way point of my years with Uncle Stan, marked the start of a fresh and altogether more affluent phase for A. & U.—and for me.

The year ended most satisfactorily for Charles Furth and myself by our each being accorded, at last, the status of director. This made little practical difference, since we had held a joint power of attorney in Stanley's absence and had 'signed for the firm' for over ten years past; also, most of the authors and others with whom we dealt had no doubt assumed that we were directors. Yet this promotion removed an understandable grievance. I knew that S.U.'s long struggle to be rid of the original Allen directors had made him excessively reluctant to make any additions to the board, and even now, as Governing Director (shades of T.F.U.!), he still retained absolute control.

12 Best-sellers at Last

Ten days after my return from Oslo, Stefan Grieg-Gran cabled me offering to submit proofs of *The Kon-Tiki Expedition*. It was a moment of profound significance for A. & U. Though we could not know it immediately, that offer was to alter the course of our lives. *Kon-Tiki* played the dominant part in enabling us to change into an altogether higher key of success and prosperity.

While S.U. had his unassailable position as the most professionally knowledgeable of publishers, and A. & U. were respected for the solid quality of their list, no one associated us with a big best-seller. There was more than a tendency for other publishers to say that while we were good for 'difficult' books we were not the firm for a popular success, regardless of the fact that it takes more skill to sell the former. Man cannot live by best-sellers alone, but after the years of solid bread and butter, sometimes thinly spread, I longed for a good big chunk of rich cake.

It must be admitted that we then knew scarcely anything of Thor Heyerdahl and his astonishing balsa-raft voyage. The exploit had little or no mention in our press, because in 1947 newspapers were still severely rationed for paper, and most consisted of no more than six pages. *The Times* gave twelve lines to the start of the voyage from Callao, in Peru, but published no report of its successful conclusion.

Nevertheless, we at once took up Stefan Grieg-Gran's offer and received proofs of the Norwegian edition. The late F. H. Lyon, our routine reader for all Scandinavian books, reported favourably upon it, but we thought it essential to have a second opinion. It was literally such an outlandish subject and the author was quite unknown in England. I had an inspiration and consulted the Royal Institute of International Affairs at Chatham House for another reader of Norwegian, and they recommended one of their members, Robert Gathorne Hardy. In his report, warmly recommending the book, he wrote: 'The mixture of dare-devil courage, forethought and resourcefulness . . . with never-failing cheerfulness and humour makes the whole book such delightful reading that it leaves me bubbling over with enthusiasm.' That was enough for us. We cabled acceptance and the agreement was soon signed.

I sometimes think that getting in touch with Mr. Gathorne Hardy was the best single thing I ever did in publishing. Here was a mature, distinguished, scholarly Englishman—not one to be easily swept off his feet—who nevertheless praised the book in superlative terms. His opinion gave us complete confidence, with the added bonus that his report itself provided a wonderful advance opinion for subsequent advertising. To find the right publisher's reader for Norwegian is not too easy, and at least one American publisher lost *Kon-Tiki* through relying upon a reader of Norwegian nationality who appeared to advise against the book because he thought it would never interest sufficient American readers.

We knew from the start that we had something good, but no one could possibly have foretold the hurricane success that the English edition would enjoy, and the way in which it would light up the demand all over the world for editions in other languages, many of which were translated from our English version, not from the original Norwegian.

Not until the following summer was the translation finished. Only then could we read it for ourselves and savour the magic of Heyerdahl's writing and the compulsive quality of the whole adventure. Stanley returned from his world trip and quickly entered into the spirit of grooming a best-seller. His crucial move at that stage, after confirming our view that—contrary to the travellers' wishes—the exotic words *Kon-Tiki* should be in the title, was to commend the book very strongly to Compton Mackenzie. He was then a leading member of the committee of the Book Society, and their order for a First Choice in those days was worth 18,000 copies.

One Friday morning we received the first supply of complete galley proofs of *Kon-Tiki*, and I learned at the same time that if six sets could reach the Society by midday, they could be sent out at once to members of the Committee, and the book would then be considered at their next meeting, at the end of the following week.

Warned that they were not very fond of reading cumbersome 'galleys' I settled down with my secretary to cut each of the 400 long strips in half and then re-collate and staple them together, so that the proofs became far easier to read. Just by twelve o'clock, I rushed them down to the Book Society's offices, and as I got out of the taxi I remember the thought came to me very vividly: this must be our Choice. We had never had a Book Society Choice, and it had always been an ambition of mine to land one for A. & U. As we learned about two weeks later from Alan Bott, then Managing Director of the Society, this was IT.

Here at once was the first indication that a group of distinguished literary critics were prepared to back the book, and that we were not alone in our enthusiasm. We straight away doubled our printing number for the first edition.

In his autobiography Stanley gives a full account of our launching of *The Kon-Tiki Expedition* in England (based largely upon an article I wrote for W. H. Smith's *Trade News* at the time), so I will not repeat all the details here. Some points, however, are worth recalling. We made every possible effort to act upon the dictum of a one-time American publisher, George Stevens, that 'an ounce of imagination before publication is worth a pound of advertising after'.

Looking back on it after twenty years, I think it was the finest hour of Stanley's and my work for any one book. He was then sixty-five, with about the same degree of bounce and energy he had had at forty—plus all his considerable prestige among booksellers and reviewers. I was forty-four, with reasonable status and contacts, and prepared to go anywhere and do anything to build this book up to the highest possible sales; to show that A. & U. could do as well as any other publisher, and better than most, when we had a really popular book. In organ terms, every stop was to be drawn and the swell opened out to the full.

At first we concentrated upon getting the book talked about, and the words *Kon-Tiki* mentioned in book trade circles as often as possible. The unusual way in which we had come by it was one point, others were the Book Society Choice, the sale of translation rights and the interest being shown in other countries; while all the time we rammed home the extraordinary subject of '4,000 miles across the Pacific on a raft!' We had, of course, the advantage that in those days the fashion for bizarre voyages had not yet developed, and a book about brave and resourceful men, pitting their courage against the elements, not in an attempt to kill or escape their brother man, but for a scientific theory, was a refreshing change from the many violent war books, though these continued to be deservedly popular. It was the first great peace-time adventure.

Every advance in publicity or news of the author's movements we relayed to our travellers all over the world, and as widely as possible spread the idea that something quite exceptional was cooking. Then came those wonderful moments when people in other publishing houses began to say, 'I hear you've got an important book coming. . . .'

Twenty years ago it was rare to have a pre-publication party at which an author lectured about his book and to which one invited *booksellers*. The ordinary meet-the-author cocktail party was familiar enough, but in deference to our Chief's views on alcohol, and the wish to do something special, when we heard that Heyerdahl could come to London, we laid on a series of three lectures. Three were needed because of the difficulty in those days of finding any large hall with a projector which could take his size of film. For one of the shows we combined with the Royal Anthropological Society, to whom he had promised to lecture, and for the others, booksellers, critics, and friends of the firm filled up the seats without any difficulty. A particular encouragement came when our London traveller, Leslie Berry—to whom we owed much for his enthusiastic and tireless work on the book—was able to tell me, the day after the main booksellers' party, 'This morning the whole trade is talking about *Kon-Tiki*.' It meant an enormous amount at that stage to have scores of men and women, 'on the floor' of their shops, who were keen on the book because they had been gripped to see and hear the author in person. This man in the neat blue suit, speaking in excellent English, had been one of those bearded half-naked Scandinavians, filmed in mid-Pacific on the wet and wallowing deck of the raft.

My first meeting with Thor Heyerdahl had been at the Hyde Park Hotel, Kensington, and never did any author live up more completely to one's expectations. He and his most attractive wife Yvonne had just flown in from a holiday in Corsica, so they were both looking extremely well. He has the typical fair hair and clear complexion of a Norseman, and I was particularly impressed by his determined mouth and his powerful shoulders; one could visualize his wrestling successfully with that steering oar on the raft or easily swinging a long-handled axe to cut down the balsa trees. He was one of the most co-operative authors we have ever had and was completely reliable and helpful over anything we suggested he should do to help publication of the book.

We had commissioned a young architectural student to make a large-scale model of the raft, suitably set on a plaster sea (which Harrods were to display in one of their main windows), and this we carted up to Alexandra Palace, where the B.B.C. then had their main TV studios, so that it could appear in an interview with the author. Preliminary chat first with the interviewer, then a run through, followed by a break for some food. Finally the actual interview before the cameras—then the press photographers afterwards. It was all intensely interesting but fearfully tiring, as altogether we were standing around for about five hours, and in those days the terrain was distinctly rugged. Thor and Yvonne bore it with the utmost patience and good temper. As for me, I was happy that we should be making history for A. & U., and that our expensive raft should have a well-displayed photograph in the *Daily Express* the next day.

Through his friendship with the Foreign Editor of *The Times*, Stanley had arranged for them to print an article about the expedition ten days ahead of publication, and I had been able to get the book serialized, not without some persuasion, by the old *Sunday Chronicle*. The author was not then sufficiently known for any of the larger papers to want it, and the price paid was about one-tenth of that offered by the *Observer* for Heyerdahl's latest book *Ra*. However, these two treatments just before publication of the book were enormously valuable as a reminder to editors. When I phoned a number of them about some minor change in the arrangements for the launching party, I was delighted to hear more than one say, 'Oh yes, we've arranged for a good review of *that* book.'

On that thirty-first of March 1950 every daily paper I picked up had its review of *Kon-Tiki*, three of the literary weeklies followed with it on the Friday, and The *Observer* and *Sunday Times* praised it to the skies two days later. All absolutely splendid—author and publisher delighted—cables whipped off to tell foreign publishers of this resounding evidence of its appeal to English readers!

But it is one thing to land a best-seller—quite another to exploit it to the full and to avoid going out of stock. Here Stanley took a bold decision which few, if any, other publishers would have been in a position to do at the time. Scenting the sweet smell of success, with advance orders of over 33,000, we had put in hand a reprint of 27,000 about a fortnight ahead of publication. It was not much of a risk, because we reckoned normally that any book would double its pre-publication orders in time. When the repeat orders began to pour in, S.U. at once plumped for yet another reprint, which gave us nearly 40,000 copies in hand, over and above our immediate sales to date.

When I raised an eyebrow, half fearing that in the first flush of success we might risk burning up our profits in unwanted reprints, Stanley enunciated what proved to be a Great Truth: 'When a book starts off like this and is praised by everyone, you can be sure it will still be selling in ten years' time.' 'I believe we shall want all the copies in the next couple of months, but if we *don't*, we shall certainly sell them in the end. It will all be good stock.' Though there had been cases when his reprint policy on other books had run away with him, and produced unsold stock, it worked out perfectly with *Kon-Tiki*. We aimed always to reprint 20,000 at a time, and we were never out of stock of the book, which is rather exceptional for a run-away seller. This fact alone must have added thousands to our total sales.

Paper merchants and printers also took a tremendous interest in *Kon-Tiki*, and many a time made just that extra effort which enabled us to secure 'the next reprint' in record time.

Stanley entered into the whole spirit of the thing with enormous gusto and thoroughly enjoyed his bargaining with the reprint book clubs, of which there were then four large ones. Never before had they all been persuaded to take the same book; normally each one claimed exclusivity for any book which it chose. But our Guv'nor's insistence that '*Kon-Tiki* was different' carried the day. It was one of those situations where his bland, exultant confidence brooked no thought of refusal.

Suddenly we found ourselves the acknowledged experts on the

super best-seller and I was invited to speak about *Kon-Tiki* to various groups both within and outside the book trade. There was great fun, after nearly a year, when Collins had a double-page advertisement in *The Bookseller* displaying a magnificent Giles cartoon. This showed *their* current best-seller, *The Wooden Horse* by Eric Williams, on a race-course nicely in the lead from a *Kon-Tiki* raft, rowed by two bearded figures ('Why two beards?' asked *The Bookseller*. 'Surely everyone knows that Philip Unwin's countenance is unwhiskered?'). At that time, two years after its publication, British sales of *The Wooden Horse*—that great story of escape from a German prisoner-of-war camp—were certainly ahead of *Kon-Tiki*, but Messrs. Collins exposed their flank by advertising 'World sales 749,766.' We had a hunch that with all its foreign editions *Kon-Tiki* might have done better than this, so I immediately cabled to American and Scandinavian publishers for their latest sales. Sure enough, the grand total came out at 875,000, and within a matter of days we were able to get an amusing cartoon from Vicky—then on the *News Chronicle*—which now depicted the *Kon-Tiki* raft at sea, sailing nicely, and behind it *The Wooden Horse* struggling in the water.

This was also done as a double-page advertisement in *The Bookseller*. It gave the trade a tremendous laugh and engendered good will towards each book; in many a shop the two cartoons were displayed side by side. *The Bookseller* columnist was now good enough to congratulate us upon our 'sheer virtuosity in the exchange of custard pies'.

The saga of our *Kon-Tiki* adventures would fill a book. After sales of nearly half a million in our hard-cover edition that number was doubled with the book club sales; then the *Reader's Digest* paid handsomely for its use as a condensed book, and—remarkable tribute to the quality of the translation—it was set for G.C.E. English, and this ensured the sale of tens of thousands of our school edition. We still sell two thousand or so per annum in our ordinary edition—to confirm Uncle Stan's dictum more than twenty years ago!—and the Penguin version has been reprinted several times. It was a monumental case of nothing succeeding like success.

Naturally, we had the pleasure of earning large sums for Heyerdahl, and rarely can any best-selling author have put his newly acquired wealth to better or more generous use. Directly his royalties had enabled him to pay off loans incurred for expedition costs, he gave each of the five other members of the crew a very substantial payment in cash. He later gave further help to one or two of them who temporarily encountered difficulties, and he has spent a great deal of his own money in the promotion of further expeditions and research into Pacific migration.

For Allen & Unwin the book came at an ideal moment. The vast

sales ensured that as paper became more plentiful, and we reprinted more of our slow-selling back-list titles, we did not suffer, as many other well-established publishers did, from cash shortage, though we had earlier begun to feel the pinch. It also made it easy for A. & U. to put down the large sum needed to establish a proper contributory pension scheme, to include those who were already in middle age. It is fair to say that although the whole concept of retirement was entirely alien to S.U., and only one member of the firm had ever retired—that was Mr. Stallybrass at eighty!—he accepted the idea without undue pressure. We had some argument over the age; he wanted it to be seventy and I said sixty-five would be expected—little realizing the supersonic speed at which my life would appear to cover the next twenty years.

Best of all, *Kon-Tiki* acted as a great tonic throughout the entire firm and gave us increased confidence to tackle other potential best-sellers, though it can be truthfully said that it did not lead to neglect of our normal business. Through all the excitements we still maintained a good flow of normal A. & U. books.

In this time of bumper profits, S.U. lived up to another of his sayings of the leaner years, namely that *when* we made good profits he would begrudge no one a share of them. Handsome bonuses for all, and the principle of company cars for some, began that year. With characteristic prudence Stanley of course avoided vast and permanent increases in our overheads. We all had a nice cut from that year's profit, but rises in salary were virtually at our normal level, and he certainly did not draw any more himself. We managed to avoid the fate of which one famous publisher laughingly warned us in convivial mood: 'Look out, Philip, *Kon-Tiki* could be the ruin of you!'

Through the nineteen-fifties we had our share of luck. There was Anthony Smith who, just down from Oxford, gave a most entertaining lecture to the Anglo-Iranian Society about his University Scientific Expedition to Persia. My brother-in-law, Ronald LaFontaine, heard it and put me on to what became one of our most successful 'first' books, *Blind White Fish in Persia*. Its delightful and prolific author brought us many more books, including *The Body* and *The Dangerous Sort*. Malcolm Barnes, through his excellent Paris connections, secured for us the offer of *The Red Balloon*, that haunting children's book based on the film by Albert Lamorisse; and S.U. himself suggested the idea of a party and special showing of the film, which we were able to organize at the French Institute in South Kensington. The personal appearance of the little boy, Pascal, and his parents was of course a guarantee of success.

Then in 1958 Thor Heyerdahl produced his second popular and most attractive book, *Aku-Aku*, the story of his expedition to Easter Island,

and we went at it again. That booksellers were ready to say, 'Of course, you can't expect another *Kon-Tiki*', made the going a little hard at first, but the superb value for money of a 21s. book with 40 pages of coloured plates, backed up with a rather good and fully illustrated prospectus, carried the day. We achieved an advance sale of close on 100,000 copies, which is good enough for anyone.

During these years Charles Furth's earlier spade work, with both secondary school and university textbooks, was coming to fruition and building up strongly the less spectacular, but utterly essential, bread and butter side of our list. Another of S.U.'s major decisions was taken astonishingly quickly, after he and Charles and I had together heard an after-lunch speech on the developing school and university book market in West Africa. He suddenly said, 'Well, one thing is clear, we must do a trip there as soon as possible.' As Charles put it later, 'S.U. decided suddenly that he wanted to go to Nigeria and a shift in the firm's policy had to follow—no one had thought seriously of it until S.U. went to that lunch.' There was no market research in advance, no weighty board discussions—a visit to Cook's and in a very few weeks they were off, S.U. taking care to see that the British Council offices were alerted in any city he visited. This usually ensured that he was met at airports and had the use of the Council's cars. He did, of course, devote a good deal of his time to visiting all the Council's premises wherever he went and reporting on them when he returned.

The result of Charles's thorough coverage of universities and schools enabled him to commission several new textbooks—for some of which the sales were tremendous, though sudden changes of government personnel or economic climate can disrupt such business suddenly, as we and other publishers discovered later.

For a number of years, however, that impulsive trip of Stanley's undoubtedly paid off, handsomely supported as it was by my fellow director's skilful work and his follow-up visits to Ghana and Nigeria. The books he commissioned and often largely re-wrote himself, added much to our prosperity in the late 1950s and early '60s.

In 1954 came the culmination of a long chain of luck and good judgement—for which I can claim little credit—when we published Tolkien's immortal *The Lord of the Rings*. Luck, because originally it was utterly by chance that Susan Dagnall, the very delightful young woman who was then managing our advertisement department, visited her old tutor, Professor Tolkien, one week-end in 1936. He showed her a story he had written for his children and asked if A. & U. would be interested. She, of course, seized upon the typescript, was much attracted, and brought it to Museum Street. Stanley, as was his wont with the few juvenile manuscripts which we received, took it home for one of his own children to read at the locally negotiated fee of one shilling. Eleven-year-old Rayner, his younger son, now Chairman of Allen & Unwin, was the operative, and he was in no doubt that *The Hobbit*—for that was the manuscript—should be published; so here was his first stroke of good publishing judgement. *The Hobbit* was well reviewed; its sales were by no means spectacular, but they built up slowly, though steadily, year after year.

The enormous typescript of *The Lord of the Rings* reached us just after the war when Rayner was still in the Navy. An outside reader reported unfavourably, the book was said to be 'too Celtic', and we actually declined it. Tolkien then tried another publisher who *was* interested but who wanted changes which the author was not prepared to make. He withdrew the book and put it aside. Some five years later after Oxford and Harvard, Rayner joined us, learnt of the existence of the book and persuaded Tolkien to send it in again. After reading it himself Rayner had no hesitation in saying that it should be published. As we wavered over the enormous outlay involved—one could irreverently call it a Fairy Story for 75s. (at the value of nearly twenty years ago)—I put in my vote in its favour, on the reckoning that at worst another and bigger book on Hobbits surely could not be a total flop. Meanwhile, Charles Knight, then Secretary of the Company, suggested publication in three separate volumes, to give us at least the possibility of drawing back, after incurring one third of the costs, if the first volume proved a failure.

Again, on the final issue, S.U. took the broad view and gave his assent, even if, as he has written, 'it involved a loss of as much as £1,000'. Here was a really bold publishing decision and—dare I suggest?—an echo of Fisher Unwin's belief that 'a really good book will always make its way in the end'. At that moment, whatever its intrinsic merits, and however high the literary judgements upon the book, no one could possibly be *sure* that it would ever sell the three thousand needed to cover costs, much less become the subject of a world-wide cult, with sales running into hundreds of thousands.

Descending somewhat from the sublime, further good evidence of the Chief's readiness to support what must have seemed to him 'way-out' subjects was his acceptance of my ideas for three entirely new categories of books, on railways, cars and yoga. Those on railway history, and general nostalgia for the great days of steam, began with the discovery of C. Hamilton Ellis. This was in 1946 when, in the belief that all variety and colour would soon disappear from railways with their nationalization, I invited him to write *The Trains We Loved*, which he illustrated with eight of his inimitable oil paintings. Conceived as a once-and-only item on our list, the book has sold for years and is now appearing as a paperback. The extraordinary feature of this idea—seen originally as something of an indulgence of a schoolboy enthusiasm—was that it brought in more books on other aspects of the subject, and excited more enthusiastic letters from purchasers, than anything I can recall, apart from major best-sellers. The appearance of Hamilton Ellis's books left no doubt as to the truth of the theory that a love of railways—especially of steam—is shared by clergymen, organists, university dons and schoolmasters, as well as many other able and highly intelligent citizens, who *are* book buyers and who have accounted for well over 100,000 of our railway books.

Well-illustrated books on motor-car history formed our second new departure, headed by some good ideas put up by Richard Hough. The third, rather different, consisted of the many books on yoga, and also Buddhism, for both of which we were indebted to Gerald Yorke for his advice and encouragement.

In breaking fresh ground in this way, two points always struck me. First, that in no time at all specialist booksellers of whom we had not previously heard would suddenly appear and start ordering in very satisfactory numbers; in a sense they 'beat the path to our door', and we had soon added a valuable group of new outlets to our sales organization. Secondly, that before long, after we had done only two or three such books, we would begin to get a reputation for that particular subject. For a while, then, one could safely go ahead with any competent book on, say, railways or Buddhism, confident that it would sell out at least its first edition. After that, the fatal danger of overproduction must be resisted.

Our crowning best-seller of this period crossed my path when I read in the *Sunday Times* that James Pope-Hennessy was about to begin work on the most important book of his career to date, the official life of Queen Mary. One merely thought, '*What* a book for some publisher—I suppose it's already contracted for.' But the very next morning Stanley came into my room, sat down, leaning back in characteristic pose, his behind right on the edge of the chair, hands clasped behind his neck, and said, 'I've just had Spencer Curtis Brown on the phone with an interesting proposition. James Pope-Hennessy . . .'

'Don't tell me—Queen Mary?' I burst in.

'Yes, how did you know?'—and for once I was a jump ahead of S.U., since he read only the *Observer*.

The big advance payment asked was by no means unreasonable, as we quickly realized after a swift check on the sales of Harold Nicolson's *George V*. This was in 1955, only two years after the death of the venerated and much-loved Queen, known to have been a great character in her own right, of whom the American soldier in London is reputed to have said, 'I guess she was like everyone's Grannie.'

Within the firm we had no doubt about it and S.U. soon had the contract signed. Though our 100,000 sale—more than double that of any other recent royal biography—was very much a team operation, the offer of the book was entirely due, I think, to S.U.'s position at the time. It was said that Palace circles were particularly anxious that the book should have the widest possible sale overseas, and that our Chairman's reputation for Dominion travel, which was to lead to our 55 per cent export sales achievement, was an important factor here. It was a proud moment when, with James Pope-Hennessy, he and I received the Princess Royal and the Duke and Duchess of Gloucester at a party we gave in the Royal Commonwealth Society. The author's delightful talk on the writing of the book was followed by the showing of a special film that had been prepared for us, made up of 'news-shots' of Queen Mary, from the time of the Indian Durbar in 1911 up to her eightieth birthday.

So that decade of the 1950s closed with a rosy glow for A. & U., and though the firm was to grow larger and more profitable still, for some of us it was the period of the greatest fun, when we spread our wings into a freer air, but had not yet entered the less personal age of the inevitably larger organization.

13 Uncle Stan as Grand Old Man

It was a curious feature of my Uncle's rule that while he prided himself upon overseeing every detail of the business, and was apt to give the impression that every decision was his, he would depart upon his long journeys abroad with scarcely any last-minute instructions—on what was to be done in his absence—and assume, quite fairly, that all would be going well. Few if any bloomers occurred at such times, and he could safely turn his back with the confident assumption that the business would not founder. He half believed that this was due to some built-in quality of 'this wonderful business' (which he had created), rather than to the abilities of the people running it. He would not readily have subscribed to the idea that a business is *people*. I believe this outlook is not unusual with men who have founded and built up a firm.

During his last twenty years, S.U. was free to spend plenty of time away from Museum Street, and very sensibly he made good use of it. He had a tendency, however, usually about a week after his return, to pick minor holes in various directions. One incident, after his return from West Africa, infuriated me at the time; but it had its funny side and was so typical of him. We had arranged that during his absence some quite extensive plumbing, carpentry and decoration should be done in the fairly primitive ladies' 'loos' of 40 Museum Street. The primary object was to enable more of our girls to powder their noses in comfort simultaneously and thus not have to waste time queueing up for the previously very limited accommodation. The work, with all its noise and mess and general disturbance, was completed just before the Chief returned. In some pride, I showed him the improvements and said how fortunate it was that we had got the work finished before he came back. His only observation was, 'Now I suppose the girls will simply spend more time in there gossiping.' Partly he resented money being spent on such frills—he never saw any need for the water heaters which I had put into the lavatory some years earlier, and he continued always to wash in cold water himself.

After the war he made three separate journeys round the world, plus trips to Scandinavian countries, U.S.S.R. and South America, to Israel and, of course, many times to the Continent, including Frankfurt about every other year. Publishers and special booksellers would be called upon, British Council offices inspected and a rather pre-war lecture on book production given to any receptive society. He adored it all, and his mind and physique were wonderfully well adapted to changes of language, food and temperature. The ginger-beer drinker— if possible a large Schweppes, iced, and woe betide the wine waiter who brought two small ones instead—they cost more!—was of course never troubled by even the mildest hangover, which can add to the weariness of lesser mortals on a prolonged round of business entertainment in foreign cities.

To some, the act of constant talking, viewing, showing appreciation and moving on the next day becomes immensely wearying after a week or two, but like a good politician Stanley throve on it. He never, never tired of expounding the eternal truths of publishing, whether as to its economics ('the present high costs of production' was a phrase which echoed through two generations), the irrationality of some authors or the meanness of successive governments in regard to books. He drew strength from the circle of admiring foreign faces, from which the same questions would come. And always he returned home in good form, sometimes with the manuscript of a local author; though in later years none equalled the distinction of *Salka Valka* by Halldor Laxness, the fruit of his visit to Iceland in 1934.

He was, as I have said, an Englishman who never hesitated to go out in the midday sun. Charles Furth recalls one blistering afternoon in Nigeria when our Chief triumphantly located some little bookseller who owed the firm £25. S.U. had been hoping to collect it, but the poor man proved to be in a desperately low state of health, having suffered elephantiasis and only recently survived a serious operation, so that his one-man business had suffered accordingly. Touched by the extreme difficulty of his situation, S.U. agreed to cancel not the *whole* of the debt, but £20 of it.

'But why,' asked Charles Furth, when they had made their hot and sticky way back to the hotel, 'didn't you cancel the whole amount while you were about it?'

'Ah,' said our Chief, 'I did not think I had the moral *right* to release the man of all sense of obligation to us, so I thought it better to leave £5 still for him to pay.' Casuistry some might say, but I think it was a genuine expression of a facet of Victorian ethics.

Until well into his seventies, he was always delighted to do a 'traveller's job' wherever opportunity offered. Equipped with the firm's latest catalogues, he would be ready to go through them with the bookseller to make up an order for A. & U. books. And proper details of terms and the method of transport would be filled in too, just as he would have done if on his Fisher Unwin journeys half a century before. He could not himself perform every single office routine—he did not type, and I never knew him to post a ledger—but every job he *could* do, including sometimes the most simple correspondence, such as answering an inquiry for one of our books, he loved to seize upon at times and deal with as immaculately as possible.

Stanley was indefatigable in attending and taking part in the meetings of every single organization of which he was a member, and of those in which he had been accorded honorary status. No elder statesman—President or Vice-President—could ever have appeared more regularly at meetings, and not only the Annual General but the normal business meetings as well. He would have done his homework thoroughly, and never would he take part in any enterprise unless he felt able to make a genuine contribution.

Occasionally one might feel that he accepted such invitations just to keep busy and to be in the swim; but, as ever, he exerted himself for the benefit of the cause and invariably left it better than he found it. The capacity to take pains over quite small matters never deserted him. He was seventy-five when my wife asked him to make a Sunday evening broadcast appeal on behalf of The Friendly Almshouses. This is a small charity in Brixton founded by my great-great-grandmother, of which Evelyn is Chairman of the Committee and Stanley was a trustee. He agreed, so long as he did not have to write the broadcast himself (after his autobiography he became curiously reluctant ever to write anything longer than a letter to *The Times*). I accordingly produced the script and Evelyn sat in on the actual broadcast, including the rehearsals for it.

The producer took infinite trouble to get the timing just right and put S.U. through it three or four times, always with a further suggestion for some minor improvement of style. As each fresh point was added, Stanley never forgot the earlier ones and the final performance was faultless in relation to all of the producer's recommendations—an achievement for any amateur broadcaster, let alone a man of his age. To his great satisfaction the appeal brought in £1,500, which is good for a small cause on a regional basis.

A few years later, when he was close on eighty, he devoted a great deal of his time to a closely detailed study of all the funds held by the Almshouses, with recommendations for their reinvestment. Though it was completely his line of country, I know he found it a chore at the time—but, for the good of the cause, he saw it through. In the same category of personal effort and care taken for others were the months, if not years, he spent upon the negotiations for the amalgamation of two trade charities to form the Book Trade Provident Institution. Again, his contribution was very much more than a name on the notepaper or a formal presence at an A.G.M.

The fact that Stanley's beard was nearly white from the age of about fifty-five gave him an exceptionally long run as an allegedly grand old man. At first sight many took him to be about seventy and were naturally astonished at the speed with which he walked and ran up and down Museum Street, one hand clasped upon his middle to hold the unbuttoned double-breasted coat together; but the remarkable feature was the way he kept it up until he was nearly eighty. Tennis, of course, was far and away the most important part of his physical activity. Frankly, it was an obsession. It dominated his week-ends and only very rarely was any social engagement permitted to come in the way of the sacred game. I took it as a mark of exceptional favour that he gave it up to attend my own wedding on a Saturday afternoon. On the infrequent occasions when he drove his wife down to Little Missenden on a Sunday morning to see Rayner's young family, there could never be any question of staying for lunch; the visit was overshadowed by the need to be back in Hampstead by one o'clock, so that tennis could begin sharp at two.

It was something of a ritual. As one of the regular players, Mr. A. J. Macdonald, has told me, once you were on S.U.'s list for tennis you were committed to his private court at Oak Hill Park every week-end for two or three months at a stretch. Then, suddenly, you were dropped for no apparent reason, and again, after some weeks, you were as mysteriously restored to favour.

Virtually no climatic condition, save heavy frost or thick snow, was allowed to stop the programme. Wet or fine—in drizzle or fog—you were kept at it, and many a racquet was ruined. Mr. Tom Todd, a director of the scientific publishers, Francis Hodgson, regularly partnered Stanley in the one-time annual match between W. H. Smith and Sons and the Publishers. He frequently played at Oak Hill Park and has given me this wonderful description of those days:

'The Saturday and Sunday matches counted for a great deal with S.U. and nothing was permitted to interfere with them. I had heard, and I suspect it was the truth, that when abroad attending some function at which he was expected to speak, S.U. made it plain that his week-end tennis was essential and that without it he found difficulty in after-dinner speaking. The weather had to be more than impossible to make him call off the game. I remember telephoning him one Sunday from Wimbledon, saying that I assumed the game was off as there was thick fog. I got the delighted reply that although Wimbledon might be in fog, Hampstead was above the fog and the weather was fine there. It took me hours to drive through London in the fog, but, true enough, Hampstead was free, and we played.

'Those who had not played at Hampstead before found the first time rather embarrassing. Whenever a ball was hit outside the court nobody moved except S.U., who ran to get it while the others of us rested. The fact was that, such was his energy, he just could not stand still while another player fetched the ball. If somebody else tried to get there first, S.U. would indicate his displeasure with a wave of his hand as he sprinted for the wire door.

'He was one of the most generous men. He showed many, many kindnesses, but never made a fuss about helping people. There was, however, in him a "careful" streak so far as tennis balls were concerned. Those supplied for use at the Hampstead court were frightful. The "regulars" often brought a box of six new ones, but not too frequently, as S.U. liked to supply his own.

'On one occasion he announced that he had purchased six from Woolworths, as they were going cheap at the end of the season; and another time he found some very old and dirty balls and washed them in Lux. On one week-end, I remember S.U. produced a box of balls that must have been ten years old; however, they were "new" and we started to play. It was like playing with blancmange, and after a few minutes it was S.U. himself who said, "I think these balls are a bit soft."

'He was for his age a very good player and in his younger days must have been well up to county standard. He had a good, flat backhand and, as one would expect with a man of his energy, darted about the net and scored off anything less than a first-class shot. Naturally he slowed up considerably towards the end of his life. One summer, the summer before he died I think, I was playing in a four. The day was hot and for once we had all been invited to tea—I suspect by Lady Unwin. My partner, at the end of four sets, said, "I could just do with a cup of tea. Thank goodness Stanley is too old for five sets." At that moment, S.U. from the other end shouted, "Just time for another set before tea."

'Invitations to tea were not given freely by S.U. Perhaps because I came from south London, I was frequently invited to tea after the game, but the others were waved good-bye, with a reminder not to be late the following time. At tea Lady Unwin was a charming hostess and the conversation ranged over many and varied topics, on all of which S.U. was an authority. At the old house, a model of Kon-Tiki was in the middle of the table. S.U. was a great character and a special friend, and I for one miss him greatly.'

The designing and the building of his new house, and then the move to it, was another remarkable effort for a man in his seventies. S.U. was a substantial shareholder in the company which owned the estate where he lived, and before he would agree to its sale, for development, he managed to stipulate that the new owners should give him a free site and build him a house on it 'at cost', to his own design. The form of that house is not to everyone's taste, but it is full of ingenious gadgets which he thought out most carefully himself, and since it lies on a southern slope it has a pleasant, sunny aspect. The garden, inevitably, is dominated by the hard tennis court.

The comical feature, for those who had heard Stanley's critical account of his father's rebuilding of the great house at Bromley, was that the cost came out at about double what he expected and it all took twice as long as originally promised. Also, he and poor Auntie Mary had to survive in some discomfort for well over a year—far longer than planned—in their old home, while the rest of the houses on the original estate were torn down about them. However, such was the rise in property values that by the time the new house was finished, Stanley was assured that it was already worth more than he had paid for it (like most of his major purchases). All through the whole operation he never lost his zest for going thoroughly into every detail. Just before the move he took care to ensure that he secured the best price— was it 25s. or 30s.?—for the gas-cooker superannuated from the kitchen of his old house. It was a good bargain for the purchaser.

People are inclined to say, of men in his position who are excessively careful of their petty cash, that *that* is the reason why they always have plenty of money. I think this is largely an illusion. Not to throw one's money about is, of course, essential in one's early days, if one is to build up a business of one's own; but the grounds for Stanley's success lay essentially in his capacity to handle money boldly, to see immediately where the potentialities of profit lay. By comparison with this, the *pfennigs* saved in German tram-cars and the extra five bob obtained for the gas cooker represent no more than a habit of mind.

Since publishing and the international trade in books were his only real interest in life, retirement for S.U. was unthinkable. (Actually, the first Unwin ever to retire at 65 was my brother Rolf, formerly Managing Director of the family printers, Unwin Brothers, and I followed his example. Pleasant as it may be to ease off gradually into the seventies, there are very few men who can make a genuine contribution at the executive level after 65.) Our Chief was remarkable in finding ways to keep in touch with affairs. When he ceased to be a member of the Council of the Publishers Association himself, he saw to it that he lunched with one or two existing Council members at regular intervals, and so kept up with the latest subjects for discussion.

Elected as an Honorary Member of the Executive of the International Publishers Association in 1956—intended, I had always supposed, purely as a retirement honour—he promptly turned up at every meeting in whatever European city it might be held; and he could be depended upon for full value in every discussion. Similarly, he never missed any of the six International Congresses, held after the war, and at these he achieved the acme of his status as G.O.M.

Barely two months before the Barcelona Congress of 1962, in his seventy-eighth year, he underwent a prostate operation and he was then found to be diabetic. When I first saw him again, some weeks after, he looked a very frail little old man, but he was determined not to miss his Congress—and to Barcelona he went. The succession of late nights, crowds and a diet of doubtful suitability appeared to restore him completely. Those of us who thought the operation must mean a complete readjustment in his way of life were largely mistaken. It did in fact mark a turning point, to some extent a slowing down, and one could no longer rely upon his judgement as before, but he continued to drive himself relentlessly. The sacred rite of opening the post from 9 a.m. and seeing every incoming letter, followed by scrutiny of the outgoing ones from 4 p.m. onwards, continued. He handled less correspondence personally, and though the phrasing of his letters was as clear as ever, the speed of his dictation declined and pauses became much longer.

In spite of this, he still retained amazingly well his capacity to absorb and retain from the letters he skimmed through any significant fact bearing upon the potential profit or loss of a transaction, or anything which might conceivably be detrimental to A. & U. interests. He always spoke of memory as one of the most important requirements for a publisher, saying, rather oddly, that 'the value of his experience rests largely upon his recollection of the literature of any subject, and the record of success or failure that has attended not only his own, but other people's publications'. Such sales records can generally be ascertained without reliance upon memory, and I should have said that the value of Stanley's gifts in this respect lay far more in his remarkable capacity to recall the salient facts and circumstances of the negotiation and agreement for various books over many years. Very rarely did reference to our records of past transactions conflict with his recollection of them.

And he still played tennis, though I cannot think that it was not a factor in the heart trouble which developed towards the end. Late in 1962, six months after his operation, my Uncle went down with a bad attack of shingles, which left him very low. Yet, by the following February, he was insisting on another tropical journey with Charles, this time to East Africa. He looked so frail on the cold February evening when they set off that I wondered whether we should see him again (by now he had another favourite saying: 'If a man can't do what he likes when he's over seventy-five . . . !'). But, sure enough, the round of calls on booksellers, college principals and British Council officials did its work, and he returned looking fitter than he had done for over a year.

For one who for so long had enjoyed autocratic power he yielded gracefully in these last years to our pressure for certain major changes. First came the revolutionary idea of employing management consultants to reorganize the Museum Street warehouse and the whole system of handling the orders we received from booksellers all over the world. To pay out a couple of thousand pounds or more just for advice would have been anathema to Stanley at one time, but he agreed now and we had good value for money; the assignment was a complete success and led to a vast improvement in our speed of service to booksellers. We learned, amongst other things, by far the most efficient method of sending books all over the country was through a passenger-train contract, the cost of which was quite reasonable. Book parcels are comparatively small, clean, easily handled and have no smell, so they can conveniently travel in the guard's van.

The rapid growth of the firm around 1960 made it essential to plan for an altogether larger warehouse, and two or three of us were convinced that a move of that department out of London would be unavoidable. It was becoming uneconomic to store and pack comparatively slow-selling articles like books in the centre of London. The Chief was dead against it. 'You cannot run a publishing business efficiently in two different places', was his very understandable objection. It was analogous to his saying of some years before: 'There is a limit to the size to which a publishing business can grow and still remain efficient.' How I sympathize with his view!

Memory seems to tell many of us, however inaccurately, that our working situation was just about ideal when we were around fifty—but a business cannot stand still. At the very least, promising younger men and staff must be offered continual advancement in salary, which is only possible from larger gross profits.

My own situation was becoming a little embarrassing. I was dealing with most of the more important authors of our general books, and between us Charles Furth and I were responsible for about eighty per cent of all the firm's new books. As Stanley was naturally now handling fewer authors himself, it was vital for us to keep up our contribution. Rayner was still comparatively young in the firm, and he carried full departmental responsibility for sales, as well as the weight of all the Tolkien books and their ramifications. Fortunately, Charles Knight was now relieving us of time-consuming internal matters by assuming increasing responsibility for office reorganization, besides ensuring that our finances were still capably handled in rapidly changing conditions.

Yet it was just at this stage that I seemed to be offered a chance to take on some of those interesting extra-mural activities which can crop up in one's middle years—the Council of the Publishers' Association, the executive committee of the National Book Council, chairmanship of the Society of Bookmen—all rewarding and interesting, if time-consuming. One morning I received a hand-written letter from R. W. David of the Cambridge University Press, then reigning President of the Publishers' Association, to ask if I would accept nomination as his successor (at two removes). I would have been proud to serve my fellow publishers and the trade in this way, but when I recollected the burden which even Stanley had found it twenty-five years earlier, the fact that I would have been sixty by the time I succeeded to the Presidency, and that I was still without any personal assistant in A. & U., it seemed impracticable. I reckoned it to be more than a half-time job, and it would have been slavery unless I could have been relieved of about half my work within the firm, where I already put in much overtime.

A year or two later, feeling I had slightly 'let the Council down', I accepted chairmanship of the Committee which, with Industrial Presentation Ltd., organized the *World Book Fair* at Earls Court in 1964. The twelve months that led up to it were a time of more intense activity than I fancy the Presidency would have been, but it produced a more colourful and physically attractive exhibition of books than London had ever seen before. Besides the 140 British publishers showing, there were exhibitors from eighteen foreign countries. We were honoured by the presence of the Queen and the Duke of Edinburgh at the official opening, and with John Brown of the Oxford University Press, then President of the Publishers Association, I had the privilege of escorting Prince Philip in the royal tour of the exhibition.

We had a public attendance of 80,000 and could undoubtedly have worked this up to something far bigger after another year or two; but certain complexities of trade politics prevented another exhibition from being planned at once, and the idea was allowed to die.

After that, feeling it essential to concentrate wholly upon securing more authors for A. & U., I firmly retreated from Association affairs, where Rayner succeeded me and is now President.

One day in the early 1960s, when Stanley and I, with our customary frugality, were journeying up Shaftesbury Avenue on top of a bus, he suddenly said, at the very point where on a previous occasion the Nigerian trip had first been broached: 'If we have to move some part of the firm out of London, what departments have you in mind?' Whenever he began to discuss the technicalities of any idea he had hitherto opposed I knew that he was on the way to its acceptance. So it proved in this case. Charles Knight and I had already prospected Hemel Hempstead privately, when I went to visit an elderly relative in hospital there, and we had been shown what proved to be the ideal site. Rayner, too, was keen, and before long his father was enjoying the clash of argument over the terms of our lease with the New Town Corporation. Charles Knight and Rayner bore responsibility for the planning and supervision of the building, and with Geoffrey Cass, then a management consultant with Personnel Administration, most ably organized the move and the latter set up the new routines which enabled Allen & Unwin to give the fastest order service in the book trade.

It could be seen as a bowing to the inevitable on the part of S.U., but it was greatly to his credit that, nearing eighty, he faced and accepted with good grace a step to which he had been so strongly opposed. In the event we first moved warehouse, trade department and all the accounts department to Hemel in 1964. Four years later, to avoid the need for larger and inevitably much more expensive London offices, we transferred all other departments to Hemel, except for the editorial and certain others, including those directors whose presence in London was essential. The Chief quickly became thoroughly proud of the new premises and made a practice of visiting them regularly once a week.

Contrary to our fears, the Barcelona Congress was by no means his last. He managed two more, Washington in 1965 and Amsterdam within a few months of his death. Washington was an astonishing effort. For over forty years he had been a relentless critic of American copyright legislation, under which full protection can be obtained only if a book is printed in the U.S.A. It is an old, old story, familiar to all who have professional dealings with the sale of book rights to that country. My heart sank when I saw that S.U. had prepared a long paper for delivery at the Congress, outlining the American situation, with special reference to the villainies of their printers, who had consistently opposed reform. My feeling was 'Oh, not again!'—but I was wrong.

Sir Stanley Unwin, in his eighty-first year, white-bearded, clear-voiced, fearlessly outspoken, all but stopped the show. He was enthusiastically applauded, widely reported in the press and, all the way from Washington, got a prominent headline in the London *Times*. It was one more useful stone—his last—laid on the rough road towards fuller American participation in international copyright.

No description of my Uncle's international activities would be complate without reference to Frankfurt. Over a span of more than sixty years, save for the periods of war and Nazi domination, he attended the annual Fair of the German book trade. In 1904 he was probably the first and only representative of the English-speaking world at the Fair, then held in Leipzig. After the last war, he was invited to address the opening meeting as an honoured guest, when the Fair was held for the first time in the new buildings at Frankfurt. From then on he became about the best-known figure at this annual event.

He was tireless in his appearances on the firm's stand, spending most of the day there in the crowded stuffy atmosphere, jumping up at once to wring the hand of every German publisher who came along to click his heels and greet 'Sir Unwin'. Latterly, he always accepted the invitation to the delightful supper party ('to greet old friends') given by the firm of Brockhaus during the Fair, and his high spot there was to deliver, in German, a speech of thanks on behalf of the guests. It was a far, far cry from the hungry, lonely youth of sixty years before, who had been obliged to feed in his garret bedroom on bread and sausage 'bought by weight'.

In 1967, as he carried through his Frankfurt programme, bright-eyed and pink-cheeked, one feared he must be over-taxing his strength; and yet in the same breath thought what a wonderful way it would be for him to 'go' if he did have a sudden heart attack.

Already an insurance doctor had refused to pass him; his heart was no longer in the state of youthful perfection which S.U. supposed. 1967 was to be his last visit. Though he carried on manfully until September of the following year, presiding at every board meeting of A. & U., scarcely missing a day from the office, and playing tennis at the week-ends, he began to look increasingly frail and bent. One just hoped above all that he would be spared any long period of incapacity.

The end came with merciful swiftness. Faithful as ever to his beloved Switzerland, he went off with his eldest son David for a short holiday to a mountain resort. The height proved too much for his heart and a form of congestion of the lungs resulted. An immediate descent to a lower altitude, and some skilful Swiss doctoring, pulled him round, so that he was able to travel home after about a fortnight; but further rest was recommended. It was in a bed in University College Hospital that I saw him for the last time, looking better than before his holiday. As usual, he was completely on the spot, and we had a friendly little talk. It seemed that his oft-repeated claim that he would take up golf at ninety might yet be fulfilled, but two days later a coronary brought his long and vigorous life to its end.

14 My Time for Reflection

There is nothing like a memorial service to give one pause, and for me, never more than in the case of Stanley Unwin.

Having organized a dinner for his seventieth birthday and a buffet lunch for his eightieth, I had assumed that another would take charge for his ninetieth, since by then I should have retired. In the event—and I say it with no irreverence—I had the responsibility with Rayner for the greatest party which ever came together in his honour.

Doubts whether we were mistaken in deciding for so large a church as St. Martin-in-the-Fields were quickly dispelled as men and women poured in on that grey November morning. The decision to ask all the staff of Allen & Unwin to go up into the gallery was soon justified. By the time the service began more than one prominent publisher was obliged to squeeze into an upper window seat. We had been right in our belief that although S.U. had grown old and lost most of his contemporaries, his interest in everything to do with the world of books, his determination to keep going, and the respect for his achievement had left him with an amazingly wide circle. They were all there—his immediate family, of course, with his wife and his sister, both well into their eighties, and also distant cousins; then publishers, authors, editors, literary agents and booksellers—out of genuine respect for one who had probably irritated many of them at some time, caused surprise, annoyance and amusement, and provoked endless argument; but who had been above all, in the words of an American obituary, a 'consummate publisher', and in his own way, as Ivan Chambers, his bookseller neighbour in Museum Street, had said, 'quite a chap'.

To some, this service in a famous Anglican church might have seemed incongruous for a lifelong Nonconformist; but I am sure it was fitting. Few of the thousand and more present would not have felt reasonably at home there. The hymn

> 'Father, hear the prayer we offer
> Not for ease that prayer shall be
> But for strength that we may ever
> Live our lives courageously'

and Bunyan's immortal 'Valiant-for-Truth' seemed unusually appropriate.

Afterwards, in the portico of that great church, as the congregation streamed out, I found myself within seconds flashing through every sort of gathering of the past forty years—family parties, Council meetings of the Publishers' Association and the National Book League, a Booksellers' Conference, the International Publishers Congress, Society of Bookmen, the British Council, the Stationers' Company—familiar friends and faces from all of them seemed to appear; and as always at such times, one wished one could have it over in slow motion, with a chance to talk longer to everyone.

For a few brief moments one feels greatly moved and sustained by the mass of busy men and women, most of them working under pressure and bearing heavy responsibilities, who have taken time to attend this Service of Thanksgiving in the middle of the working day. Then, suddenly, all of them have gone; and except for a look into the buffet lunch served for all our staff in one restaurant, and a dash down to another, half a mile away, for relatives and friends, one's place is back at Museum Street—to get on with publishing.

The letters had been strangely affecting, as they poured in literally from all over the world. The phrase that stayed in my mind—used by one correspondent—was that Stanley had been 'a Gibraltar of publishing'. It summed up well so many sides of his endeavours: his unresting campaign against all forms of taxation or import duties on books (entitled rather oddly by *The Times*, 'Free Intercourse in Books', in connection with an article on the subject which he wrote for them). S.U.'s Gibraltar aspect was exemplified also by his continual opposition to book censorship. Victorian parental influence notwithstanding, he had appeared as a witness in support of Penguin's publication of *Lady Chatterley's Lover*.

Above all, I took that tribute also as an endorsement of his totally professional view of publishing. Whatever the book, whoever the author, all the technical details of the job must be carried through correctly and efficiently. A decent living for the publisher must be secured, but the extraction of *maximum* profit under all circumstances was never his object. He aimed, rather, at the creative building up of a sound, enduring business piece by piece, seldom bursting out into the grandiose and highly speculative, but always ploughing back a large proportion of the profit, always ready to keep on keeping on, and never doubting the intrinsic value or the good sense of his work.

This supreme self-confidence had been a quality which drew many of us to him initially, and the energy which he radiated gave an extra sense of purpose to those who worked with him.

Another whose letter I remember particularly was Dr. F. R. Cowell, who referred to S.U. as 'one of the props and stays of sanity in this cock-eyed world', thus putting his finger on another aspect of character which had served him so well.

Obituaries, especially in *The Times* and *Daily Telegraph*, emphasized

Stanley's work for books sold overseas; but unlike the Fisher Unwin obituaries of thirty years earlier—each in his time was designated the 'doyen of publishers'—there was little reference to the books he had published, apart from *The Truth About Publishing*, and in one paper, Russell's works, and in another *Kon-Tiki*. Yet, very fairly, David Holloway concluded in the *Telegraph*: 'Sir Stanley, with his drive, energy and dedication, was without a peer, and there is never likely to be anyone who will take his place.' Such a verdict on his life's work would, I think, have satisfied even S.U.

Inevitably I found myself comparing the achievements of my two publishing uncles. Fisher had lived quietly in the country for his last ten years, his circle had contracted and his name had largely disappeared, though many of his books continued to sell under Benn's imprint; yet on his death his considerable publishing achievement was recalled at some length. He had been the publishing pioneer in our family. With all his faults, he had provided the springboard for Stanley, the original lead into the book trade in Germany, the chance to learn the job in a well-run publishing office in England—S.U. adopted all the basic T.F.U. systems for A. & U.—and the open opportunity (as he did for me, in my time) to see the working of a publisher's mind at close quarters. As I suggested earlier, it is quite possible that without his step-Uncle Fisher, Stanley might never have been a publisher. His business energies might have run in quite different channels. As for me, I owe entirely first to Fisher, and then to Stanley, the chances I had to gain some place in the publishing world.

Nepotism has unfortunate connotations; but it can be said to have a legitimate, defensible side. Whatever the element of favouritism in my own start, at least it left in me a sense of obligation to go hard to justify myself. After all, even in a family business, uncles do not invite nephews to come in and 'have a go' unless it is thought they can eventually be of real use.

When the head of a personal business brings in a young man who is in many ways to act for him and relieve him of much of his detail work, there is always the risk that the younger man may become dissatisfied, revolt and go off elsewhere. Also, even when one's hair has gone thin or grey—as Charles Furth and I each discovered—to the Chief one still remains his 'young man'. Whether by luck or judgement, Stanley managed to pitch it about right in my case.

In my young days, I never saw myself seriously as attempting to establish a business of my own: S.U. was notably articulate on the difficulties and the exceptional combination of qualities needed for success. Carey Street indeed was full of failed publishers. I sought a decent living, but not a fortune, and essentially it was the dealings with authors and their books which attracted me. All this I had, and security besides, plus a chief who, even if he fussed, irritated, provoked argument, and could arouse all one's aggression ('makes you so mad sometimes, you want to go home and kick the cat!' as Malcolm Barnes, a devoted Siamese lover, once confessed to me), yet constantly infused life and energy into those around him and made the whole job more worthwhile.

Though I had two very full years ahead of me after Stanley's death, there was a sense in which I began to realize that my day of full-time office work was nearly done. I was sixty-three and had always intended, if not full retirement, at least a considerable easing off at sixty-five (embarrassing as it might have been to be seen off by a Chairman twenty-one years my senior!). The four of us—Charles Furth, Malcolm Barnes, Charles Knight and myself—who had borne the main day-to-day burdens for about twenty years were all due for retirement within the next five years, and our successors were already gathering. Rayner, who became the new Chairman, had made it clear that he did not intend to become so involved in management detail as his father had been, and Geoffrey Cass had been invited to join the board, subsequently becoming Managing Director. Shortly after the war I had promoted a book on industrial relations, when it was still a comparatively new subject, with the title *New Times, New Methods, New Men*—well, this was it!

Those two years passed in a flash. In spite of the considerable help of an excellent assistant, Peter Leek, who is now one of my successors, * I seemed as busy as ever. Rare was the evening when I did not carry off work from the office desk, and frequently there was a further dictating session in the evening (the tape-recorder, like most labour-saving devices, tends simply to make its user work that much more).

In my last full year I had sponsored seventy books, and it is difficult to cut down the number in a moment. I was proud, too, that as I went, among the many new books I left behind me in the year 1970 were Sir Julian Huxley's *Memories*, Anthony Smith's beautiful balloon book *The Dangerous Sort*, the first children's book by 'my' young poet Brian Patten, and Thor Heyerdahl's *The Ra Expeditions* to follow in 1971. We had secured Brian Patten by a great stroke of luck. About seven o'clock one morning, while dressing, I happened to turn on the 'Today' programme of Jack de Manio and heard Brian reciting one of his poems. Something in the quality of his sensitive northern voice and the direct simplicity of the poem caught my attention; then there was the announcement that he would be reading his poems at 8.45 that evening, a peak listening time. The B.B.C. put me in touch with him, we saw a good selection of the poems and learnt that Penguins had already decided to include some of them in their next anthology of Modern

* Augmented now by another good man Peter Evans

Poetry. Our gamble that here, for once, was a contemporary poet who would repay publication proved gloriously correct.

That we should have the great pleasure of doing Huxley's autobiography was largely due to another of those rapid decisions which Stanley and I had been able to take together—and upon a Saturday morning, as it happened! Though the story had begun earlier, the effect of it took place in my last year. Sir Julian suddenly rang me up to say that a leading publisher had quite unexpectedly refused to make an offer for the symposium of essays, by a distinguished group of biologists, which two of his former Oxford students had collected in honour of his seventieth birthday. It was to be entitled *Evolution as a Process*. Although it is a well-known fact that the *festschrift* seldom enjoys a large sale, we had done very well with Huxley's own book, *Evolution: the Modern Synthesis*, and were to publish the symposium *The Humanist Frame*, which he had himself edited. Even if we never made much money out of the book, we could scarcely lose and it must add lustre to our list. Stanley took the same view, and we were able to give Sir Julian an immediate 'yes' on the spot, which pleased him. Such can be one blessing of autocratic rule in a publishing business. Most satisfactorily, the book went into a second edition.

Curiously enough, we knew nothing of the *Memories* until the author telephoned my secretary, just before I returned from holiday, to say he would like to talk to me about it. Just on the quiet, he had written more than half of it without troubling to discuss a contract with any of his publishers. It was one of those manuscripts I read with delight all the way home in the train and aloud to my wife for most of the evening. Like any good autobiography, especially by someone known to the reader personally, one could 'hear the author talking'. Besides the enormous interest of the Huxley family itself, and the exciting career of the great biologist and zoologist, there was *for me* the attraction of Sir Julian's description of the special pleasures of boyhood bicycle rides and nature study in the countryside of west Surrey, into which my own father had led me half a century before. I had several delightful meetings, over tea and home-made scones, with the author and his enchanting wife in their Regency house in Hampstead, as we went through wonderful family photographs and talked over details of the book.

Having described one more successful, and particularly enjoyable piece of publishing, I hope I have left no reader with the impression that life with Uncle Stan was solely a procession of appreciative authors and profitable books. We had our spells, as must all publishers, when nothing seemed to go right—heavy corrections from authors, and disputed responsibility between author and printers, delayed publications, disappointing sales, loss for the publisher and a disgruntled author. There must be few businesses so susceptible to the biblical saying, 'To him that hath shall much be given, from him that hath not shall be taken even the little that he hath.' The general book that begins to sell can attract so many extras in serial rights, TV or broadcast treatments and sale of paperback, American, and translation rights; whereas the one that has failed to attract reviewers, and which booksellers have refused, gets none of these nice extras. In most cases the publisher has done his best, all his departments have gone through the proper motions, but this time to no apparent effect. It is the reading public ultimately who decides what books shall sell.

Retirement, like marriage, 'is not by any to be enterprised nor taken in hand unadvisedly, lightly or wantonly'—but it is almost as inevitable. Despite our publication of an excellent book on the subject, and all my advantages of adequate means and numerous interests, I still found the actual end of full-time employment as senior director of George Allen & Unwin Ltd. a strange experience. The rushed, high-pressure days, over-full with desk work, appointments, lunches, interruptions, phone calls and home work, suddenly run down. Many letters come in, some extraordinarily kind, from authors and others; it is like reading one's own obituary. Some say you will be missed; maybe you were a better publisher than you thought! Well, whatever you *were*, it is over now.

A full life in publishing is all-absorbing, and certainly in my case there was little time or energy left for extensive hobby activities. I was very fortunate in being able to continue some editorial work from home and retain contacts with a certain number of authors, but it is a mighty jolt to realize that the sunny book-lined room on the first floor, invisibly plastered with one's tears and sweat, cheers and curses over thirty years, the room about which authors and visiting publishers from all over the world sometimes made nice remarks, the battleground of a hundred well-fought arguments with the 'doyen of publishers'—this room is no longer one's own. No longer does one have executive authority or that guarantee of day after day filled with absorbing and usually stimulating tasks which must be got through somehow, and which automatically brings you to the evening, spent, and happy to relax.

Of course it happens to everyone in some measure, if he has enjoyed his work, and if he does not die on the job. I have been lucky, but my heart goes out to all those men, senior service officers for example, or executive victims of a take-over, who are retired at the 'height of their powers', perhaps around fifty. The pension may be all right, but it requires an effort of will not to mourn the loss of status or the almost total severance from associates and staff, for whom, in a civilized well-run office, one naturally develops respect and friendship.

I am, however, a great believer in the idea that as one door closes another opens, and I never forget a wise remark made by Professor W. A. Robson, formerly of the London School of Economics, who has been a most valued author and true friend to A. & U. for over forty years: 'The secret of happy retirement is serious work seriously undertaken.' So this book has been the first instalment of my new labours, and my home town of Haslemere, with a well-developed civic sense, is not short of jobs for those prepared for voluntary work. I have enjoyed the place for over thirty years without having made any such contribution.

My grandfather, George Unwin, had often expressed a wish to end his days in Haslemere, and in *his* retirement he took a lease, in 1903, of Town House, the fine specimen of William and Mary architecture which stands in the High Street, at the north end of the old town. With its superb panelled staircase, 'after' Inigo Jones, walled garden and empty stables, it was both beautiful and a perfect place for the visiting grandchildren, especially at Christmas. Domestically difficult to run, it was made comfortable by the efforts of an unfailing supply of maids, who in childish memory were always kind and cheerful in spite of the Christmas houseful. Altogether of another era are my memories of dropping off to sleep there, in a large top room, in company with four or five other grandchildren, the candle blown out (there was no gas supply above the first floor!), the glow of the dying coal fire in the grate, no sound but for the clip-clop of a solitary cab from the street below, and the wonderful knowledge that 'tomorrow would be Christmas'.

Grandfather's wish to die in Haslemere was granted all too quickly, in 1906, but my little grandmother, who had defied her dominating father, James Spicer, nearly half a century before, and had raised eleven children of her own, lived on for another twenty-one years, until 1927. The perfect embodiment of the Victorian little old lady, with her bonnet and cloak, she was still remembered by many people when I came to live in Haslemere in 1938, and the name of Unwin seemed good for unlimited credit. For much of the time grandmother was alone in that great house, except for her youngest daughter and the maids, but she kept it on for the sake of her family—who frequently arrived for a week-end—to say nothing of her twenty-four grandchildren, who loved to be invited to Town House winter or summer. Haslemere must have been as richly endowed with rainfall then as it is today, but in my memory the sun always shone in at breakfast time, the walks to Hindhead were in crisp, frosty air, and surely there was skating?

So, happily, I prepare to try to give something back to Haslemere. Strangely enough the Storr family used to occupy the house which is now the Georgian Hotel here, and that is where Mary (now Lady Unwin) lived for many years before she met her Stanley. There is, too, the odd coincidence that no more than ten miles away, at Heyshott near Midhurst, Fisher Unwin had his country home for over thirty years.

Each new generation tends, to some extent, to start where the previous generation left off. In a successful business the same applies. Retiring after forty-three years, with vivid memories of the low pay and Spartan conditions of one's youth, one may feel inclined to look askance at the salaries and lush fringe benefits which one's successors enjoy immediately ('Look how long we had to work before we had entertainment allowances, cars, first-class travel'—or whatever it may be); but then I recall that my father, until he was nearly thirty, worked until 2 p.m. on Saturdays and bought his first motor-car at the age of sixty. I have genuine respect for many of the new generation in publishing and begrudge them none of the material benefits which seem to come their way so quickly. On the contrary, I am proud to have had a hand in the building up of a firm which today can offer really attractive conditions to its young executives and I can stand back contentedly to watch the successful progress of my cousin Rayner, the fourth publishing Unwin.

As Charles Furth wrote to me so truly, just after my retirement, '. . . it is hard to think of any contemporary we need to envy'. We both started from scratch, fired to enthusiasm by the same exciting chief; we knew tough times, occasionally we rebelled jointly or severally, but we had the supreme satisfaction of seeing the little acorn firm grow to a sizeable oak. We knew originally the adventure and simplicity of S.U.'s 'one-man show'; thanks to him we always had reasonable security, but with the minimum of formality and organization. It was a full and interesting life with fair rewards, and if one is not a power-seeker what more can one ask? For the last word, I stand by what I wrote in the copy of my earlier work, *Book Publishing as a Career*, which I gave to S.U.: 'For Uncle Stan, who taught me most of it and gave me my chances to learn the rest.'

Bibliography

Unwins: A Century of Progress 1826–1926 (London: Unwin Brothers, 1926).

Albert Spicer: A Man of His Time 1847–1934 (Privately printed 1938).

Hilda Martindale. *From One Generation to Another* (London: George Allen & Unwin, 1944).

Carolyn Heilbrunn. *The Garnett Family* (London: George Allen & Unwin).

Edward Garnett. Introductory Essay to *Conrad's Prefaces to His Works* (London: J. M. Dent 1937).

Frank Swinnerton. *A Bookman's London* (London: John Baker. Revised edition 1969).

F. A. Mumby. *Publishing and Bookselling* (London: Jonathan Cape. Fourth edition 1956).

— and Frances Stallybrass. *From Swan Sonnenschein to George Allen and Unwin* (London: George Allen & Unwin, 1955).

Stanley Unwin. *The Truth About a Publisher* (London: George Allen & Unwin, 1960).

R. J. L. Kingsford. *The Publishers Association 1896–1946* (Cambridge at the University Press, 1970).

Index